Reasonable Doubt

CW00428704

Chapter One

The crack of the spine shattered the clinical silence of the room. I sat immobile and

contemplated whether I could place the damaged book on the shelf amongst my pristine

collection. I don't have OCD, you understand, I just like things to be…right.

The trill of an email arriving on my phone distracted me. Opening the email app I sighed

when I saw who the message was from. Over the past five weeks I'd lost count of the number

of messages from "victimavenger" at one of the generic mail servers, the anonymous persona

that I was sure, but couldn't prove, belonged to a relative with a connection to the last case

I'd worked on. I was tempted to forward the email on without even opening it but natural

curiosity wouldn't let me. "Find a new job, Bitch." Hardly original – about half the previous

messages had been the same. The others had ranged from veiled threats to outright promises

of violence. After the first half dozen I'd contacted the police and arranged to forward all

emails from that address to them.

I thought it strange they should contact me that particular day, though. The case had officially

been dropped and there was just a bit of paperwork to complete before I would move on to

my next investigation. The victim's family in the previous case would have been informed by

now that Nothing But Truth were no longer considering an appeal on behalf of the person

who had murdered their loved one. Perhaps the sender of the emails had just wanted to give a

parting shot at me. It was easy to make enemies in my job. Investigating miscarriages of

justice was the most rewarding job I'd ever had but my investigations could open up cans of worms that some people would rather stayed closed forever. It wasn't the first time I'd been

the recipient of hate mail and no doubt it wouldn't be the last.

As I tapped the screen to forward the email to my contact at the police station I wondered

whether DCI Mick Bannister would be at his desk when the message reached the team's

system. It was unlikely he'd even know about it as the tech officers worked on a different

floor. I hadn't seen Mick for over a month. Since he found out I was working on an

investigation into a high profile case where he'd been the arresting officer. I'd come home

that evening to find him sitting in this very kitchen, a packed suitcase beside him.

"Unless the first words out of your mouth are that you've stepped down from that case I'm

going," he said.

I honestly thought he knew me better than that. Even if I had given up the case, faced with

such an ultimatum every cell of my body would have screamed at me to let him go. And of

course I hadn't given up the case.

"Don't slam the door on your way out," I said, and turned on my heel, heading to the

bathroom. As I soaked in the bath for far too long I pondered why I'd treated Mick's

departure so glibly. Two years we'd been together. Two years with the most loving and

supportive partner I'd ever known. Now a crappy coincidence that had dragged our working

lives together looked like breaking us up. Why couldn't Mick see that it was just another case

to me? I don't know the meaning of the words "conflict of interest". I can always focus on

the facts and ignore personalities and relationships that could cloud the issue.

As soon as that case came up on the radar at Nothing But Truth I'd realised Mick was involved. I immediately sent an email to the CEO informing him of the connection and leaving the decision with him as to whether I could be the lead investigator. Everything by the book. Always. It was just a shame that Mick had heard through the grapevine what was going on before I had a chance to explain.

And the irony of it was, that case had now been dropped. After weeks of work no new evidence had been found to allow an application to appeal the conviction. It happened. It happened more often than not. All I wanted to do now was tell Mick the good news that no fault could be found with his investigation, and maybe talk about getting back together. When my phone had alerted me to the email just now, I'd been disappointed that it wasn't, instead, a message from Mick. The problem was we were both as stubborn as each other. They'd be figure skating over Hell before I would make the first move.

I would never have dreamed of admitting to anyone, least of all Mick himself, that I was missing him more than I would have thought possible. I wouldn't let myself think about the possibility that he might have gone for good. How would I ever find anyone else who would put up with my quirks, as Mick had called them when we first moved in together? Well, he put up with them but the thing that annoyed me most was that he seemed to see them as a challenge and he was forever coming up with "helpful" suggestions for getting rid of them. Can't stand having a creased book on your shelf? Get rid of the books and buy an e-reader. Sounds so simple. Try climbing inside my head and then ask yourself how simple.

But no matter how irritating Mick's suggestions were, I knew they were his way of showing me he cared. And that feeling of being cared for was still a novelty for me. If only I could bring myself to back down and text him. Or, unlikely though I knew it was, he might just be missing me too and decide to be the one to get in touch.

As if I'd wished it into being my phone beeped a text alert just as I'd replaced it on the kitchen work top. Grabbing for it, I swept it towards a sink full of water in my haste but just managed to save it from a watery grave. Once again I was disappointed. The text was from my PA, Susie, letting me know the files for a potential new case were now available on the system. I shouldn't still be thinking of Susie as "my" PA. Nothing But Truth had been undergoing a lot of cost cutting measures lately and one of the effects was Susie now being PA to a whole team, each of whom politely tried to gain more than their fair share of admin time. Susie assured me I was her favourite but I knew she said the same thing to everyone.

For a moment I considered ignoring the new case until the morning but why try to fight my true nature? Slamming a ding meal into the microwave I reached out my laptop from my work rucksack and switched it on. By the time I'd signed into the system my meal was ready and I settled at the table to read while I ate.

On 4th August 2012 police attended an address in South Manchester, having been called by John Mitchell, the owner of the property. The kitchen was immediately designated a crime scene due to an amount of what looked like blood on the floor and wall. John Mitchell's wife was missing. Mr Mitchell stated that he had gone to bed early the previous night due to a migraine and had found the bloody scene when he got up that morning. His wife had been downstairs watching television when he went to bed. He had no idea where she was now. At that point Mr Mitchell was cautioned and taken to the police station to make a statement.

I scrolled through several screens' worth of information. I would return to them later once I'd

read the summary of John Mitchell's trial. I could feel my enthusiasm already rising and, as

usual, had to remind myself that for someone's murder conviction to be questioned by my

organisation that meant there had to have been a murder victim. That victim was due all my

respect and consideration. But still I couldn't rein in my instinct to pull apart the case until I

came up with the truth. And if that truth turned out to contradict what had been decided by a

jury then so be it. In this case, though, there was an added ingredient. The body. Or rather the

lack of it. Because John Mitchell had been convicted of his wife's murder even though her

body had never been found.

This case didn't ring any bells but I'd been dealing with enough problems of my own back

then. I was aware of a few similar cases but this was the first time I'd had a chance to work

on one. At least I would be able to work on it provided the steering group allowed it. Nothing

But Truth was run by the CEO but in order to maintain a reputation for objectivity all cases

were put to the steering group before my investigative work could begin. The group consisted

of experts in various fields who volunteered their time and knowledge. I knew their motives

varied from a desire to put something back into society to the fact that working on behalf of a

charitable organisation might one day result in recognition and honours.

The next meeting of the steering group was scheduled for the following morning and I would

attend as usual. I wasn't senior enough to have a vote but it was useful to be aware of the

discussions that led to the group's decisions and to answer any questions regarding the

feasibility of investigating the potential cases. At any given steering group meeting there

might be between one and three cases up for discussion. There were a lot of self-professed wrongly convicted people sitting in prisons and a fair proportion of them were spending their time writing to Nothing But Truth asking for help.

The Mitchell case looked like being a strong candidate but there was one thing bothering me. I checked back over the notes a couple of times to make sure I hadn't imagined it. No, I was right. Although he'd pleaded not guilty at his trial it appeared that for the first month or so after he was convicted John Mitchell was silent. Only after that did he start writing letters and proclaiming his innocence. I had been doing this job for four years now and in every other case I'd worked on, the client had started writing to Nothing But Truth during the first few days of their prison sentence. I made a note to bring this up at the steering group meeting. Some of the group members were far more experienced than me. Maybe they'd come across this kind of delayed reaction before.

I made a cup of tea – as much to give myself a break from the screen as anything. As I waited for the kettle to boil I reflected on how lucky I was to be doing this work I loved. Okay, my personal life was a disaster but at least I spent my days doing something worthwhile.

After another hour or so concentrating I glanced at the clock on my laptop screen, yawned and decided it was time to call it a day. Living alone, hopefully only temporarily, it was sometimes easy to work on late into the night and end up regretting it the next day. As I settled into bed I realised with a jolt that I'd forgotten to check the children's bedroom. Well, that was a first. I always liked to make sure everything was tidy in there before I went to bed. Could I sleep if I simply stayed where I was and ignored the urge to go and check? No.

Chapter Two

I was up by six, sitting with a mug of tea in front of my latest box set binge. I never watched

the news first thing in the morning. My working days usually contained more than enough

encounters with the harsh realities of life and death. I wasn't sticking my head in the sand – it

was more about starting the day with a clean slate and a relaxed attitude. And on steering

group days that was even more important. I felt fully prepared for today's meeting and there

was no point dashing around at the last minute so this hour or so on the sofa in front of trashy

TV was exactly what I needed.

Not for the first time I thanked the lord that my office was a short drive away in a leafy

Cheshire town that called itself a village. The head offices of most charitable organisations

were based in London but when Nothing But Truth was set up in 2010 the decision had been

made to base it in the north. Technology advancements meant that many of the staff could

work from home or on the move anyway and the overheads were a lot lower. I thought of my

car as a mobile office, only travelling in for meetings such as today's, or for regular catch up

or supervision chats with my manager. The arrangement suited me perfectly. My habit of

working late into the evenings meant I never had to feel guilty for taking a few hours to

myself during the day. I was pretty much my own boss as long as the job got done in the end.

If I'd had any doubts about how well I was doing, my recent appraisal meeting with Jeremy

Parker, the CEO, had laid them to rest.

"There's only one area for improvement, Meredith," he'd said. "You need to stop being so hard on yourself. We're a team here at Nothing But Truth and when things go wrong, as they sometimes will, you shouldn't take on all the blame."

I knew he was referring to the recent case that had taken up so many resources and led to nothing in the end.

"I just felt as though there must have been something more I could do."

"It's the nature of what we do," Jeremy said. "Okay this was a particularly bad case – we'd usually have realised far sooner it was going nowhere. But you'll see. We'll have a case that makes up for it soon, we always do. And that's what keeps me, at least, going. There's someone sitting in a cell right now who's innocent and we're going to come along and right that wrong. Without us what would they do?"

"I know." Jeremy could see right through my pretence that I'd taken what he'd said on board.

"I was supposed to be making you feel better, not worse," he said. "My point is you're doing an excellent job. Keep doing exactly what you're doing."

I'd left the meeting glowing from his praise and fired up for the next case that came along. That's why this morning's steering group meeting was so important. Until they gave the go ahead I couldn't get my teeth into my next job.

The meeting was scheduled for 11 o'clock as usual so I timed my departure so I could listen to "Popmaster" on Radio 2. I had it down to a fine art that I could leave the parking garage at my apartment block just as the quiz was starting and arrive at Nothing But Truth's car park as it finished, though I occasionally lingered in the car for the last couple of questions if traffic had been particularly light. With a personal best score of thirty points out of a possible thirty-nine I hated missing the quiz and the chance to improve my score. I'd even phoned in a couple of times but chickened out at the last minute when it looked like I might have a chance of being chosen as a contestant.

I sometimes wondered if concentrating on the quiz questions was actually dangerous when driving. There had been all those studies into how distracting even a hands-free phone call could be. Might it be just as reckless to be giving all your attention to Ken Bruce instead of focussing on whether the traffic lights had changed? Today's performance was disappointing, with a score of fifteen in the first round and eighteen in the second. And that's why I'll never really make it on there as a contestant. That would be the day my mind went blank and I totally showed myself up.

At least the journey had been pleasant enough. The sun was gracing northwest England with its presence and I'd dug my sunglasses out of the glove box. As I drove past my former school, halfway between my apartment and the office, I felt the familiar pang in my chest. Whoever said they were the happiest days of your life hadn't shared schooldays with me.

Sitting in the queue at a red light, I wondered whether it was such a good thing after all to be living and working within a few miles of where I grew up. Maybe I should have moved away and made a fresh start. But I could move to the other side of the world and I'd still be me.

Shaking my head I forced myself to start getting into the right frame of mind for the meeting. Even after doing this job for so long I still found this one of the hardest parts. I knew why. I was giving up what control I had over my professional life to a group of people who each had their own agenda. And although I understood the need for the steering group it was still hard to sit there and listen to them decide how my next few weeks or months would be spent.

Parking behind the old Edwardian house that was now the headquarters of the organisation that employed me, I took a deep breath, muttered a vaguely motivational mantra and walked towards the building. Although I only came into the office once or twice a week I was familiar with the cars that belonged to my colleagues. But today one of the vehicles parked close to the space I'd taken stuck out like a sore thumb. It looked like one of Nothing But Truth's employees had treated themselves to a new car since I was last here. And what a car. A brand new white Mercedes convertible. In this Cheshire village which was populated with Premier League footballers and their wives cars like this were a common sight. But the people who worked here preferred a more understated mode of transport.

As usual there were a couple of people sneaking a quick cigarette on the fire escape outside the first floor window. Jeremy must already be inside – they wouldn't risk him seeing them as he arrived for work. I entered the building using the security passcode and started to climb the stairs to the main office. As I rounded the first flight of steps I glanced up to the landing above and caught sight of someone disappearing through the door that led to the office. Something about the woman's hair and the way she held herself ignited a spark of recognition that I immediately batted away as impossible. The person whose face had flashed up in my mind's eye had no connection to this place, no reason to be here. I tried to calm myself down but I couldn't prevent the burn of the flood of adrenaline that entered my system. Without really thinking what I was doing I diverted to the door at the other side of the landing that led to the ladies' toilets.

Leaning against a sink and staring at my reflection I tried deep breathing and a mindfulness exercise that soon had my heart rate slowing and within a few minutes I felt able to make my way to the office. On the way I stopped for a quick word with Susie who handed me half a dozen envelopes. Mail marked private or personal was never opened by the admin staff and Susie collected mine to hand over whenever I showed my face.

A quick stop at the coffee machine and I was ready to go through to the board room where the steering group meeting would take place. I was pleased to notice there were still five minutes to spare despite the episode on the way up the stairs. I was still congratulating myself on this as I sat down in my usual place at the far end of the table from the CEO who would chair the meeting.

"Hi," I said, looking along the oval table. Only then did it register that sitting next to the CEO was the very woman I had just convinced myself could not be there. It took a few seconds to process the thought and I felt ridiculous when I realised my mouth had opened into a perfect circle as if I was about to shout "Oh". The blood pounded in my ears so loudly I didn't realise at first that Jeremy was speaking.

"Good morning, Meredith," he said. "May I introduce Paula Reed? She's agreed to step in temporarily for Michelle."

"W-why?"

"Oh, didn't you know?" Jeremy said, shaking his head sadly. "Michelle's had to go away to deal with a family emergency. I know her mother's been ill for some time but she took a sudden turn for the worse, apparently. Michelle's going to be unavailable for some time."

"Right. No. Sorry, I had no idea." I knew I was babbling. Paula Reed was sitting impassively next to Jeremy for all the world as if she'd never met me before. An odd look had passed over her face when Jeremy was explaining about Michelle, but otherwise she might as well have been a statue. I needed to take the lead from her and act as if we were strangers before anyone noticed something amiss. Any further conversation was interrupted by the arrival of the other steering group members, noisily chatting as they sat themselves down. While Jeremy explained to everyone who Paula Reed was and why she was there, I surreptitiously studied the woman I had hoped with all my heart never to see again.

"Dr Reed is among the top psychiatrists in the UK," Jeremy was saying as he wound up his introduction. Preening. That was the only word to describe how Paula Reed was sitting there basking in the glow of Jeremy's words.

It took me about ten minutes to calm down enough to fully concentrate on the meeting. Fortunately Jeremy's next statement distracted me from my focus on Paula Reed.

"Before we begin discussing our next case there's something I need to let you all know," Jeremy said, knowing he had everyone's full attention. "As you're aware we've been experiencing some cuts to our funding and we've had to cut back budgets accordingly. I've been approached by someone who may be able to give us a much needed boost to our finances. But their proposal may not be to everyone's liking."

I resisted the temptation to roll my eyes. Jeremy was a brilliant CEO but his habit of beating around the bush when there was something important to say was infuriating. Luckily I wasn't the only one to feel that way and a few murmurs around the table encouraged Jeremy to get on with it.

"A TV production company has asked us to consider taking part in a series of documentaries again." Nothing But Truth had done this in the past and it hadn't always had positive consequences. The murmurs around the table turned into everyone talking over each other.

"It's not the BBC like the previous series, I'm afraid. These guys are more used to digging in with troops in a war zone than plodding along behind us in our enquiries. But they're keen. I haven't given them an answer yet, of course. We need to discuss this again when we have more time and I don't want to sacrifice today's agenda to it. What I have agreed to is that our investigator on our next case will film a series of video diaries until we decide whether to allow a film crew in."

I was taken aback that Jeremy hadn't bothered to discuss this with me before announcing it to everyone but there wasn't much I could do about it. And I wasn't against the idea at all. I'd always thought the TV documentaries were an ideal way to raise awareness of the organisation and the predicament of people who were in prison as a result of miscarriages of justice. I'd only taken part in two of them before the last series of documentaries had ended. Watching myself on TV had been a strange experience and I'd had to put up with some stick from my colleagues, asking for autographs and so on, but on the whole I thought the presence of the cameras was positive. One of those cases had ended in a conviction being overturned, with all its associated celebration and praise. The other had been one of those where Nothing But Truth ended up frustrated – sure their client was innocent but unable to find that vital piece of evidence needed.

While the concept of having a camera crew shadowing them sank in Jeremy asked each of the group members to introduce themselves for Paula's benefit. They went clockwise round the table.

"Jack Hill – legal. I'm a solicitor at Harlowe Martin, one of the largest firms in Manchester with a highly regarded criminal law department. They pay for my time working on cases here two days a month. I'm a relative newbie compared to the rest of the group. I've been here about eighteen months. My predecessor, also from Harlowe Martin, passed the baton to me when he retired and moved abroad."

I knew Jack was being modest. His firm might pay for his two days a month but he spent at least twice as long working on cases in his own time. He was enthusiastic – barely graduated when he started here – and his attitude was infectious. There had been many times when I'd been tempted to give up on chasing a lead on a case when Jack had restored my faith in the process. Given that barely one percent of cases that were reviewed by the appeal court ended up with a conviction being overturned, his optimism and energy were priceless. Alex Rogers was next in line around the table.

"I'm Alexandra Rogers and my field of expertise is forensic pathology. That basically means I translate post-mortem and other scientific reports into plain English for the group."

The typically brief speech from Alex didn't surprise me. Alex was never a keen conversationalist but whenever she did have something to say it was worth listening to. As she'd said she often translated things for the rest of the group and saved them having to do a lot of research into complicated subjects. In her main job she was a respected researcher.

"Richard Ferguson – another legal bod. I work closely with Jack, though he's usually on the criminal side whereas I've drifted towards the civil in recent years. Between us we try to understand why a client's defence team failed to get them off if they are indeed innocent. I spent too many years to recall working as a solicitor but I'm now retired and to tell you the truth the time I spend here is a wonderful excuse to get out from under my wife's feet."

Richard's bluff delivery of an introduction I'd heard him make many times made me smile. I wasn't about to spoil the comic effect by enlightening everyone to the fact that Mrs Ferguson was a lovely woman who had quite enough of her own interests. They had one of the most loving and devoted marriages I had ever come across. His years of legal experience were invaluable to the group and, if he could be kept on the subject without drifting off into irrelevant anecdotes, his opinion was usually spot on.

"Dave Harris – police sergeant based in Manchester City Centre. I'm seconded here by the force a couple of days a month and I see my role as providing a reality check. Let's face it most of the people asking for Nothing But Truth's help are guilty as sin. If Meredith can convince me she's onto something with a case you can bet there's something in it."

I nodded at Dave across the table. We had a healthy respect for each other's jobs but weren't exactly what I would call friendly. And of course there was the added factor that Dave worked at the same station as Mick Bannister. No doubt our separation, if that's what it was, had reached the police station gossip mill by now.

"Pam Philips – lay member of the group. Which basically means I'm not an expert in anything, apart maybe from common sense. Similar to Richard in that my husband took early retirement and expected us to spend every hour together. My day a week here is my safety valve otherwise you might end up looking into my conviction for murdering him one day. Joking aside I hope I make the odd valuable contribution."

Murmurs around the table assured Pam she was right. When the conversation had died down Jeremy returned to the meeting's agenda and gave the summary of the case that I had familiarised herself with the night before. Next I gave a brief rundown of my initial thoughts about the case, explaining that my main concern was that time lapse between John Mitchell's conviction and his first attempts to prove his innocence. As I'd expected, a couple of members of the group came up with reasonable explanations for it and after a brief discussion it was deemed to be irrelevant to whether or not Nothing But Truth took on the case.

The two legal representatives on the steering group argued that this might not be the best kind of case to take on in front of the cameras. Yes, there was the fascinating aspect of the conviction despite the lack of a body, but they both pointed to the CPS being certain of their chances for a conviction before they brought the case to court. It was no surprise that the two lawyers took this view – they did the same in most cases the group discussed. When it became clear they were in danger of going round in circles Jeremy suggested a short break before they voted.

This was a familiar pattern with the steering group meetings. I knew Jeremy would have a quick word with Jack and Richard over their coffees and that by the time they all returned to the table their views would have magically changed. No doubt on this occasion Jeremy would ask them both a rather obvious question – if we don't look into this case, which is the only one on the table this month, then what will we do?

In the end the group voted for the case to go ahead – though Paula Reed abstained because she hadn't yet been able to assess the client herself.

"Michelle's report is in the file," Jeremy said. "I assumed you would consider that sufficient."

"Never assume, Jeremy," Paula said. "Never ever assume."

Chapter Three

I parked in the multi-storey car park half a mile away from the prison. I'd been here several times before and learned that the hassle of applying for a visiting professional's pass for the prison car park wasn't worth it. Walking the short distance was preferable even with having to go through the same process as all the other visitors. I'd prepared well for today's first meeting with John Mitchell and felt confident and enthusiastic for the task ahead. The only slight niggle I felt was about Paula Reed's involvement. Although she'd been civil and professional to my face so far, I couldn't shake off the feeling that Paula had a hidden agenda. It just seemed too much of a coincidence that the person who had stepped in at the last moment to cover for Michelle was someone so closely linked to my life.

Whispering a thank you for the break in the heavy rain I made my way towards the entrance to the prison. There were half a dozen people in front of me, one of them a young mother struggling with a garishly patterned buggy. My heart sank as I realised the search process would be slowed down. But it wasn't as if John Mitchell was going anywhere or had anything better to do. Initial meetings with a client were usually taken up with trawling through the huge amounts of research they had done for themselves, using the prison computer and library. It was amazing how many people thought simply living in a prison could turn you into a legal expert. This was one of the most vital points in a Nothing But Truth investigation. The client – the convicted prisoner – had plenty of time on their hands to come up with compelling arguments to back up their case. But I had one golden rule that I worked by, sometimes known as my bullshit detector. Basically it meant that the first time I caught out the client in a lie, the case would be finished. The more reams of paperwork a client had collected by the time I met them, the more chance there was of uncovering a lie.

After the steering group meeting I'd been worried I might have to travel up to Cumbria with

Paula Reed. The psychiatrist had been adamant she needed to assess John Mitchell rather

than accepting Michelle Ashe's report. Thankfully Jeremy had managed to convince her that

he couldn't justify a second assessment to the prison authorities. Nothing But Truth as an

organisation depended heavily on the goodwill of people working on "the other side" so to

speak. I was surprised Jeremy hadn't defended Michelle's professional reputation rather than

claiming he didn't want to antagonise a prison governor. As far as I knew there had never

been any problems with assessments carried out by Michelle so why didn't Jeremy simply

point out that the assessment had been done and didn't need to be re-done?

The small queue of people shuffled through the door that had been opened by a security

guard. Although my fingerprints were already held on the prison's biometric system I had no

choice but to wait while some of those ahead of me were processed. Their fingerprints were

scanned and their identification matched against the documents they had brought with them

for their first visit. I glanced at my watch, relieved to see there was still half an hour to go

until my appointed visit. Susie had made the booking. Whenever I tried to do it myself I

always seemed to mess something up. It was embarrassing when you were refused admission

and in terms of wasted time it could be devastating to a case.

Next stop was the search by an unusually cheery female prison officer. I wondered if it was

her birthday, she seemed so pleased with herself, and she seemed a little distracted as I

succumbed to the necessary but unpleasant process. I always dressed in very plain outfits

with no pockets on visiting days – it speeded the process up somewhat. Then I glanced to my

left and noticed that another officer had been landed with the job of searching the baby, buggy and all. She'd also have to search the poor kid's nappy which must have been one of

the least popular tasks an officer could be faced with. No wonder her colleague was laughing.

There were no drugs dogs on duty today. Maybe that was a cost cutting measure or maybe

they just used them randomly so their noses didn't get worn out.

At last I made it to the visiting hall. It was a shame my visits weren't classed as legal

meetings. In that case I would have been able to book to see my client whenever I wanted and

talk to him in a private meeting room. Instead I had to fit in with any other general visitors. In

John Mitchell's case that wasn't too much of a problem. He had no friends or family who

came to see him. But in other cases it had been an issue when the client didn't want to

sacrifice their weekly visits. Sometimes I'd had to make do with the occasional phone call to

ask the client vital questions and update them on how the case was going. Not ideal.

I knew what John Mitchell looked like. I'd perused several photos and familiarised myself

with his dark good looks. But when I stood before him at the small table in the visiting hall I

had to make a conscious effort not to let my reaction show. He had a presence, an air about

him that set him apart, despite being dressed in the same faded blue sweatshirt and joggers as

the rest of the convicted prisoners in the room. A couple of men were dressed in jeans and

their own tops and this marked them out as remand prisoners still awaiting trial. All the

inmates wore a bright yellow bib over their tops. That first impression that made John

Mitchell appear not to fit in faded after a few moments but I filed away the feeling to

examine later. I prided myself on being professional with all my clients and I wasn't going to

change that just because the client happened to be drop dead gorgeous. Maybe not the best

choice of phrase in the circumstances.

I introduced myself and explained my role to Mitchell, deliberately taking my time. Although I had sat in this very room many times before I'd never been wrong-footed like I was now.

"I'm Meredith James, investigator with the Nothing But Truth organisation," I said, stating the obvious but determined to take the interview at my own pace. "We are often called in to help people where we can show there has been a potential miscarriage of justice. However I must warn you that in many cases we are unable to find compelling evidence to allow an appeal. I'm familiar with the background to your conviction but it would be helpful if you could summarise, in your own words, why you feel your case is suitable for our intervention."

John Mitchell's only reaction to my words was a raising of his left eyebrow. Then he let a silence stretch until I began to worry that he was wasting my time. Finally he spoke and his soft, measured tone surprised me once again.

"Thank you for coming Ms James," he said. "It's a pleasure to meet you. I don't have many visitors, as I'm sure you're already aware. In answer to your question I feel my case is suitable for Nothing But Truth because, quite simply, I did not kill my wife. I'm not even convinced she's dead."

"And yet at your trial the prosecution convinced the jury that not only was she dead but you had murdered her." I held Mitchell's stare, telling myself he couldn't hear my racing heartbeat that was making the blood pound in my ears. If he was going to turn out to be a game player I'd be disappointed but I wouldn't let him win. "You have about forty minutes left to convince me to take on your case. If you'd rather have a contest to see who's going to blink first, that's fine."

While Mitchell considered my words I thought about some of the other men – it was always men who were the time wasters – who I had visited once only to report back to my manager that the case was a waste of resources. Did they seriously think I would work my butt off to turn up a new piece of evidence once I'd seen through their charade? Perhaps it was just that they needed a diversion from the monotony of their lives serving a long sentence in a harsh environment. Whatever the reason, I didn't lose a minute's sleep over any of the cases I had brought to an abrupt end. I reserved my regrets for those occasions when, despite believing in the innocence of my client, I'd been unable to come up with the necessary evidence to take their case further. The insomnia brought on by those unhappy endings to cases had made me wish I'd chosen an easier path in my work life. Maybe I should have gone back to the paralegal work I enjoyed years ago. Or even revived my hopes of becoming a lawyer myself. But that dream had been well and truly dashed.

I glanced up at the large clock on the wall, noting that we were now down to thirty minutes left. Should I take the initiative and walk out? No, that would be unfair. Even if we had to sit in silence for the rest of the visit I owed it to John Mitchell to stay for the whole of this first meeting. If I ended up reporting back that the client had been uncooperative I was sure there'd be another new case to take this one's place soon enough. When Mitchell finally began to speak it took me a moment or two to gather my concentration and start to scribble down notes.

"The country was split in two," he said. "Either you loved sport and were glued to every minute of the London Olympics, or you didn't and you'd given up trying to talk about anything else to anyone. It was the first Friday in August and I'd had a pig of a day at work. I could feel a migraine coming on – I've suffered from them since my teens – so I decided to get an early night. Karen was meant to be going out for the evening but she was tired too so she said she'd watch TV for a while and then follow me upstairs."

"Sorry to interrupt," I said. "Your neighbour heard arguing – or raised voices at least – that evening at around nine. How do you explain that?"

"I was already in bed by then. I can only imagine Karen was watching something loud or that the noise came from outside. The old bat's always complaining about the noise, even when we're not in" After so many years it seemed odd that Mitchell was using the present tense when talking about his neighbour but I let it go.

"I slept like a log and didn't wake until about eight on the Saturday morning. Karen hadn't come to bed. You know how you can tell that their side of the bed hasn't been disturbed? I showered, dressed and went downstairs and that's when I knew something terrible had happened."

John Mitchell hadn't given evidence at his trial so this was the first opportunity I'd had to learn about his reaction to the scene in his home that morning, other than from transcripts of his police interviews. And of course he'd been advised by his solicitor to reply "no comment" to most of their questions. He had insisted, however, on re-stating his story about when he went to bed and what he found the next morning.

"Karen wasn't there. The TV was still on, talking away to itself about the day's events to come at the Olympics. I went towards the kitchen but I didn't enter the room because there was blood all over the floor and some on the wall. I can't remember exactly what I did, in what order because I was in shock but I know I phoned 999 and the police arrived pretty quickly. I told the officers exactly what I just told you and the next thing I knew I was in the back of the patrol car on the way to the police station."

It was a simple, straightforward account. There wasn't much for me to question and Mitchell's interviews at the police station had repeated the same story over and over. The frustrated interviewing officers' attempts to trip Mitchell up or make him contradict himself had failed. He stuck single-mindedly to the story that he had gone to bed before nine on the Friday night and found the bloody scene in his kitchen at shortly after eight the next morning. Of Karen Mitchell there was no sign whatsoever and her body had never been found.

For the first time John Mitchell showed a flicker of emotion as he said, "The only thing that was missing was Karen. Her handbag was on the chair where she always dumped it when she came home. I checked inside it and her mobile, her purse and other stuff like her driving licence were still in there. I didn't know every item of clothing she owned but it seemed to me nothing was missing from her wardrobe except the clothes she'd been wearing the previous evening."

"I know all this, Mr Mitchell..."

"Yes, but don't you see? If I'd killed her and was trying to make it look like she was just missing, I would've dumped her bag somewhere. And some of her clothes. And cleaned up the blood in the kitchen. It makes absolutely no sense that I would call the police with all that incriminating me, if I really had done it." He sat back in his chair arms stretched wide. It was so obvious to him that he couldn't understand why everyone else didn't see it.

It was something I had been thinking since I first read through the files on the case. But then I'd got myself tied up in knots wondering if it was some sort of double bluff by Mitchell. Had he expected everyone to think that way and decide that a guilty person wouldn't have called the police? If that was the case it had backfired dramatically.

"We'll be reviewing everything," I said calmly. "You can be sure we'll look at every single aspect of the prosecution's case." I was starting to feel a little unprepared despite the hours I'd spent getting ready for this meeting. Even to my own ears what I was saying sounded like platitudes.

The prison officer supervising the visiting room was making preparations for the end of visiting time. I began to gather my notebook and pen – the only belongings I hadn't left in a locker – then met John Mitchell's gaze again. I could tell from his expression there was something he hadn't told me yet. So far he'd given me no reason to doubt that his case was worthy of investigation. I hoped the next words out of his mouth didn't change that.

"There's something that didn't come up at my trial," he said, almost reluctant to let the words out. "It wasn't until later that it dawned on me. Believe me I've had plenty of time to think while I've been stuck in here. I said the only explanation for the neighbour saying she heard loud voices that night was the TV. But what if there was someone else there after I'd gone to bed?"

"I suppose that's possible, but wouldn't the police have investigated that possibility?"

"They had me charged and locked up – they weren't about to look for anyone else. And like I said, even I didn't start to think along those lines at first. But there's someone she could have been seeing. I think it could have been going on for a while."

This was another familiar pattern in the cases I worked on. The new theory dreamed up by the client to try and introduce some doubt about their conviction. A combination of having too much time on their hands and an active imagination. I'd heard all sorts of weird and wonderful stories in my time. But unless there was evidence to substantiate it, it was just a waste of time. And of course, most of the time, there was no evidence at all.

"I think she was having an affair with our financial advisor, Sam Raynor."

I jotted the name down on my pad. "What makes you think Karen was seeing him?"

Mitchell gave a wry laugh. "Her. Samantha Raynor," he said. The bell rang to signal the end of visiting time before we could discuss this any further. People at other tables were starting to say their goodbyes and shuffle towards the exit.

"Thanks, Mr Mitchell."

"John, please."

"Ok, John. I'll be discussing the case with my manager later and we'll plan a strategy for the investigation. I'll keep you updated as often as I can and I'll come and visit or arrange to speak to you by phone if I need to. I suggest you do your best to just let us get on with our jobs for now. And please keep in mind that we can't guarantee you'll be able to apply for an appeal. We investigate dozens of cases a year and only a couple go all the way."

"I understand. And thank you. You don't know what this means to me. It feels like the first time in years someone has really listened to me. I was beginning to think nobody would ever take me seriously. But about Sam Raynor..."

Before he could finish the officer in charge of the room tapped him on the shoulder and jerked his head towards the door.

John Mitchell was out of his seat and waiting at the door that led back into the prison wing before I realised he had gone. I briefly wondered what he had been about to say about Sam Raynor but whatever it was could wait until the next time I spoke to him. Now I thought about it, I recalled the name Samantha Raynor from the list of witnesses at the trial but I couldn't remember anything about her testimony. If she was the couple's financial advisor then she'd probably been called to give evidence about the state of their bank accounts and investments. The possibility that Karen Mitchell had been having an affair with Sam Raynor was the first new lead I had and I intended to follow it up straightaway.

****

2012

Karen Mitchell reached her mobile phone out of her large handbag. Her second mobile phone that is. The one with a single contact number programmed into it – the number of another prepay phone that couldn't be traced to its owner. She texted a brief message and sat back to wait for a reply. John going to bed early was an unexpected bonus. It would give them a couple of extra hours to carry out their plan. A reply soon beeped onto her phone and Karen smiled. Sam had understood her message and would be on her way soon.

Glancing round the room while she waited, Karen knew she wouldn't miss this place at all. She'd been nagging John for ages about moving but he refused to even consider it. He wouldn't consider anything she wanted. Now, after all the weeks of planning Karen could hardly believe this night had finally arrived. The night that was going to change everything forever. At first she'd been unsure about what they were doing. She knew she couldn't stay with John any longer. Their lives had become a nightmare round of arguing and avoiding each other. She couldn't remember the last time they'd shared their bed for a whole night. Karen had started drinking more than was good for her and more often than not she passed out on the sofa and woke in the early morning light cursing whichever bottle she'd emptied the night before. John had taken to going to bed earlier and earlier. His excuse of headaches would have been funny if she could have been bothered to react at all. Maybe she should have been worried about his constant headaches but there was no room in her thoughts for concern about her husband's health.

Karen couldn't pinpoint when she'd started to think her life would be much easier if John did have something seriously wrong with him. Something terminal that wouldn't take too long to finish him off. She knew that made her a terrible person but she couldn't help it. On good days she fantasised about leaving him rather than him dying. What was stopping her? She was the one with the money after all. She'd never had a day's worry about finances before – Daddy had seen to that with his generous allowance while he was alive and the trust fund provisions after he died. But John seemed to have taken it as a challenge to spend as much of Karen's money as he could as quickly as possible. Last time they'd met with their financial advisor, Sam had told them straight. The spending had to be controlled or they'd have problems further down the line. It had hit Karen like a bolt from the blue and without telling John she'd met with Sam Raynor separately the following week.

"I want you to represent me from now on, Sam, not both of us. Is that possible?" Karen said.

Sam had waited a moment before answering. "It's possible, yes. I can recommend a colleague to John and we can look at unpicking all the accounts and separating them if that's what you really want."

It had meant a lot of work and a lot of late meetings for Karen and Sam. There was a prenup in place that would have meant Karen had to split everything fifty-fifty with John if she left him. Sam told Karen not to worry about that – she had a way of getting round it. Perhaps it was inevitable, working so closely together, that they would become closer on a personal level too. And when Sam started to talk about a way to get rid of John without him actually dying, Karen was a keen audience. It wasn't like Karen to get carried away with such surreal ideas but she was under Sam's spell.

Now Karen answered the light knock on the back door and fell into Sam's embrace as she entered the kitchen. The light in Sam's eyes matched Karen's – half excitement, half fear. The two women worked quickly. They had prepared for this night for weeks. Karen had suggested storing phials of her own blood at the back of the freezer. She'd learnt how to extract small amounts at a time from the crook of her elbow by watching YouTube videos and wanted to save enough to make a generous puddle on the floor tiles. But further research had suggested that forensic testing could show that the blood had been stored for some time and that didn't fit the plan. So now Karen gritted her teeth and, using one of the knives from the block on the kitchen worktop, she made a slice in the top of her forearm. It was enough to bleed a lot but not such a deep cut that it would need medical attention. When Karen had dripped some of the blood on the floor, Sam splashed a little on the wall near the door, then bandaged Karen's arm. They'd decided not to try and make any tracks or drag marks – the CSIs would be sure to find something that didn't fit with a murder. Faced with just a small puddle of blood and a couple of splash marks they'd find it hard to explain what had happened to the body. And that was exactly what the two women wanted.

Now it was time to leave. Karen hadn't packed because the whole idea was meant to be that she had disappeared without a trace and had taken nothing with her. Everything was meant to point to John having killed her and somehow disposed of her body. After that Karen would lie low in a cottage they'd bought (cash sale, fake documents to disguise any paper trail). If the plan worked and John was convicted of murder and sentenced to life in prison, phase two of the plan would begin. Having rescued Karen's finances, Sam had put in place plans to create new identities for them both. They hadn't yet decided where in the world they would begin their new lives. Karen planned to spend the next few months doing exactly that. She had no regrets or fears about leaving her current life behind. Her only living relative was her

sister and they hadn't seen each other since Dad's funeral. What few friends Karen had were

really just acquaintances. There was nobody she would miss if she transformed herself into

someone else in another part of the world. The only person she cared about was Sam and she

would be with her as they set out on their adventure. Life as Karen Mitchell had become so

miserable she would have done anything to escape it.

They travelled to the cottage in Lancashire using minor roads so they could avoid any

cameras. Karen's prepay mobile was ditched in the first waste bin they passed. Sam had

taken care of decorating and furnishing the cottage and until now Karen hadn't even seen it.

There had to be no way of linking her with the place. Sam parked her car a short distance

away – she'd always been careful to do so in case anyone took notice of it parked by the

cottage. Karen's new temporary home was accessed via a lane tucked away on the edge of a

village on the outskirts of Blackburn. There were twenty cottages built around three sides of a

square, all dark stone and small windows. They used to belong to the now ruined mill on the

edge of the village. As you looked around the square the cottages grew slightly bigger. When

a mill worker was promoted they would move into the next bigger cottage in a kind of

musical chairs. The one that Sam had bought was halfway round and easily big enough. It

would have housed a large family in the mill's day. Now it just needed to keep Karen

comfortable for a few months while they waited for their plan to evolve.

"Won't the neighbours think it's odd that I never go out?" Karen asked as she wandered

around getting her bearings. She was beyond pleased with the cottage and couldn't wait to

settle in.

"I'll be coming and going," Sam said. "They'll think I live here alone as long as you're careful not to be seen. I'll bring food shops and stuff. Don't worry about a thing."

The place certainly had character – that's what the estate agents blurb kept repeating. The only way upstairs was by a wrought iron spiral staircase from the kitchen. It took up a fair amount of the floor space and Karen was concerned about the lack of room.

"Why do we need that huge chest freezer?" she asked. "The kitchen would be far better without that. Did it come with the house? It looks brand new."

"Oh, I thought I could stock it up with ready meals and pizzas and stuff for you but I haven't got round to it yet."

"But you just said you'll be coming every few days and bringing shopping."

"You can never tell with the weather up here in the winter," Sam said. She'd had enough of this conversation. She gently pushed Karen ahead of her up the staircase.

They reached the master bedroom and Sam flung open the wardrobe to show Karen all the clothes she'd bought for her. Then they both glanced at the bed and collapsed in laughter together, rolling on the luxurious quilt.

"Let's christen this thing," Sam said hoarsely. She'd enjoyed using some of the funds she'd squirreled away over the past few weeks to furnish the cottage. But now it was time to enjoy the fruits of her labour – and take Karen's mind off any problems with the kitchen.

******

Next morning Sam left the cottage early and returned to her apartment in Manchester city centre. Well, it wasn't really hers – she was sort of house sitting for the owner. Her own place was a depressing flat in Salford and she hated it. She just used it to store her things now and spent most of her nights at the luxury Manchester apartment.

Before she'd left Lancashire she'd repeated to Karen how important it was that she shouldn't be seen at the cottage and promised to return later that day. And she'd already made up her own mind that she wouldn't stay overnight at the cottage again. They'd set in motion their plan to implicate John Mitchell in the murder, or at least disappearance, of his wife. Now Sam wondered how long it would be before the story hit the local news. She didn't have long to wait. BBC Radio Manchester gave it a brief mention halfway through the afternoon, saying police had been called to an address in South Manchester that morning and a man in his forties had been arrested.

Here we go, Sam thought. Hold on tight, folks, it might be a bumpy ride.

Sam knew that Karen would be listening to the news bulletins too and she gave a small sigh of relief that she'd convinced Karen not to have a mobile phone at the cottage. Sam knew Karen would have been on the phone to her by now having heard the radio news and that could have potentially ruined their plan further down the line. It had to look as if Karen Mitchell had disappeared off the face of the earth. There had to be nothing to tie her to the cottage or to Sam. That was vital.

Karen's ability to handle the stress of the situation was the only thing bothering Sam now. She had surprised herself by how calm she was being, considering what they had got themselves into. But she knew Karen would find it difficult being isolated at the cottage even though it was only for a few weeks – maybe a few months. They weren't in control of how long it would take to investigate Karen's disappearance or whether the police would decide a crime had been committed and that John Mitchell had committed it. Their best case scenario was that John would end up sentenced to life for Karen's murder. Worst case scenario was that the investigation would be classed as a missing person case and John would get away scot free. That last thought should have made Sam at least slightly anxious but she considered it as calmly as the rest of the situation she'd created. Whichever way things went, Sam had an exit plan to match. And not all the exit plans included Karen. It had been fun getting to know Karen Mitchell better and the sex was great. But Sam had realised long ago that there was only room in her heart for one person.

Chapter Four

On the drive back to Cheshire I thought through my discussion with John Mitchell. I would

need to send a brief report through to Jeremy, confirming that, in my opinion, this case

should be looked at in detail. A factor as important as a relationship the dead person had been

having, that was not known to the police at the time of the investigation, was a possible lead

in searching for new evidence. It would be my top priority to track down Samantha Raynor

and interview her if possible. Of course, if Ms Raynor was involved in any way then she

might understandably be a hostile witness.

The other thing that was nagging at me was the strong physical reaction I'd experienced

when I met John Mitchell. It had been a long time since I'd felt such a jolt of attraction and it

had certainly never happened to me in a work context. I didn't think he'd noticed anything

strange but I knew I must deal with it before I saw him again. I had to be sure it wouldn't

affect my professionalism and I made a mental note to share it with Susie as soon as I had

chance. I hoped her down to earth attitude to such things would bring me back to reality.

There was no real reason to go back to the office, though, so I drove home and spent the

afternoon doing a few dull but necessary household chores. At the same time I sorted my

impressions from the visit to John Mitchell in my head and came up with a basic draft report.

I'd type it into the system later – I always concentrated better in the evening and the few

hours in between would allow me to consider the case properly rather than rushing to share

my thoughts with the rest of the team. I sent a quick email to Jeremy to let him know that's

what I planned to do and he replied almost immediately – just a thumbs up symbol to let me

know he understood. One thing I was sure of though – my report wouldn't include my extraordinary reaction to meeting John Mitchell. Jeremy wouldn't be impressed to hear

there'd been a spark of attraction between his lead investigator and their latest client. That

was a complication we could definitely do without.

I noticed a few emails that had arrived when I'd been distracted by what I was doing. The

loud music I always played when I was sorting the place out must have drowned out the

email alerts. I cleared out junk emails first then noticed one had arrived from victimavenger.

Why hadn't they stopped? It was days now since that case had ended. Sighing with

frustration I opened up the message. If anything, rather than stopping, my email stalker was

intensifying their attack: "I know where you live. Now back off bitch." It went on to detail

exactly what would happen if I didn't heed the warning. With each email the threats seemed

to be getting more brutal.

This was getting personal. I wasn't easily spooked but as I forwarded the message to my

contact at the police I felt uneasy. What if this wasn't directly connected to the previous case?

What if it was directed personally at me?

****

I decided it was time to try and get an update on the police investigation into the threatening

messages. It was also time to stop assuming they were a harmless method of letting off steam

by someone connected to the victims in the previous case. I phoned my contact at the police

station and arranged to go in for a chat, though the officer didn't exactly sound enthusiastic.

"I'm not sure how much I can tell you, Meredith. But if it'll make you feel better come over for a cuppa and I'll talk you through where we're up to."

On the drive over to the police station I faced up to my real motives. I wanted to check how far the police had got with the messages, of course I did. But there was another reason I'd been keen to visit the station rather than discussing things over the phone. It was the station where Mick was based and there was every chance he would be there. If I happened to be at his work place discussing an ongoing investigation and if we happened to bump into each other – well, I couldn't be accused of making the first move, could I?

As it turned out it looked like I was to be disappointed on that score. Apparently Mick and most of the other senior officers were over at the central Manchester headquarters for a meeting about budgets and manpower. My contact had told me all this, without even being asked, while the kettle was boiling. Apparently my motives were as transparent to everyone else as they were to me. But I was nothing if not professional and I shrugged off the situation with Mick and concentrated on my other reason for being there.

"I think we can forget the messages being connected to my last case," I said. "They've carried on even though that case was closed and, if anything, they're more frequent now than ever. Did you get the one I forwarded earlier?"

"Yep. And it could be our best lead yet. You know we've been tracking the source of the emails. The actual computers they were sent from?"

"Yes." I knew most of the emails had been sent from computers in various locations such as community centres and libraries dotted around the Manchester and Cheshire area. The police had visited each venue and looked at CCTV footage but nothing had come of it. Either the person using the computer wasn't in the line of the camera or they were wearing a hoody that obscured their face. The best they'd come up with, from the size and body shape, was that it was probably a woman. It was disappointing but I counted my blessings. If it wasn't for my relationship with Mick Bannister I knew I wouldn't be getting this level of attention.

"Well, this morning's is different. It was sent from a smart phone instead of a computer. That means a couple of things. One is that the sender has changed their pattern of behaviour for some reason. The other is we can't tell exactly where it was sent from but we can identify the unique device – the phone – that was used." This sounded promising! "Sorry," the police officer said. "I should have warned you there was some bad news. It's a prepay phone and though we can track where it was bought, it was paid for in cash and the buyer gave a false name and details."

It was like one step forward, two steps back. I wasn't sure how to react. "Can I block the sender or something?"

"You could, but if they're determined to keep harassing you I'd be surprised if they didn't start using a different email address if you do. They could carry on doing that indefinitely. I think you'd be best, if you can put up with it, carrying on as you have been. Forward them to me and eventually they'll make a mistake and we'll have them."

I said goodbye and thank you, making sure to promise celebratory drinks once they'd cracked the case. It might only seem trivial to some people but it was starting to be a real pain for me. Every time I opened my emails I had to prepare to be abused and I'd done nothing to deserve it, had I?

As I signed out of the building and searched for my car keys in my rucksack, I heard a familiar voice that drew my attention to the door. Mick Bannister was walking through while talking intently into his mobile phone. He didn't notice me until he was a few feet away.

"Meredith, hi," he said. Then into his phone, "Can I call you back, mate?"

I was busy trying to regulate my heart beat but not too busy to notice the implied compliment. Hanging up a work call to speak to me – had to be a good sign, right?

"Hi, Mick. I was just here to catch up on what's being done about those email threats I've been getting."

"Oh, right. Hope the tech guys are getting somewhere."

A silence fell between us and I started to panic. Surely after all we'd been through we could find something to talk about other than some crackpot's threats. Just as it was starting to become embarrassing we both spoke at once.

"How've you been?"

"How's things?"

The laughter broke the ice at last. But then Mick glanced at his watch. "Look, I have to be somewhere, like, half an hour ago. But can we meet? Talk?"

"I'd like that." Relief flooded through me until I realised I had no idea what Mick wanted to talk about. For all I knew he just wanted to arrange picking up the rest of his things from the apartment. Where had he even been staying all this time? And who with? As usual my thoughts galloped off unchecked while Mick stood there just a moment longer before giving me a light kiss on the cheek and disappearing towards his office.

It was only as I drove away that I realised we hadn't arranged when or where to meet. I was back to square one. If I texted him to ask, was that me making the first move after all? And would that really be so terrible? I couldn't answer my own questions but I recognised another example of trying to relax the tight rules I lived by. The rules that made it possible to function and to be great at my job. But the rules that also stopped me enjoying normal relationships. Whatever they were.

****

Jeremy Parker was looking forward to telling his staff that the TV documentary would be going ahead. As he thought about how to announce the news he looked around the office where he spent more hours than he did in his own home. Despite being in talks with the TV company for several weeks he'd only shaken hands on the deal half an hour earlier and the relief he'd felt was still flooding his system. He was relieved, too, by Meredith James' attitude to the cameras. Not for the first time Jeremy congratulated himself on his decision to

employ her. She'd certainly never given him any reason to regret it, despite his initial doubts.

Jeremy hadn't told anyone just how dependant Nothing But Truth was on the funding the

documentary would attract. There had been a very real chance that the organisation would go

under without it. His biggest fear now was that Meredith would report back that the Mitchell

case was not worth pursuing. Gone were the days when he could write off the costs of an

abandoned case easily. And no Mitchell case would mean no TV documentary.

Jeremy ran his hands through his thinning hair and tried to force himself to think positively.

Meredith would find evidence for an appeal. She just had to.

Chapter Five

2013

The trial. It had come around more quickly than John Mitchell expected. He'd been on bail for a few months despite the charge being murder. A combination of the fact Karen's body hadn't been found, his previous good character and the overflowing remand cells at the country's prisons according to his solicitor, Simon.

John thanked his lucky stars that Simon Johnson had been the solicitor on call that Saturday back in August. The only lawyers John had known were corporate types and although they might have been able to recommend a defence lawyer there would have been a delay while the police waited for his chosen lawyer to turn up.

He and Simon had hit it off straightaway. The solicitor was a no nonsense guy who had grasped the situation immediately. The police had given him a summary of the evidence they had against John – basically the blood in the kitchen and the absence of any sign of anyone else being in the house. A five minute chat had been all it had taken for Simon to write a brief statement on John's behalf, then they'd been taken to an interview room. John hadn't yet been charged – he was supposedly helping with enquiries. But Simon warned him the police might want to hold him for as long as they were allowed before either charging him or letting him go. As far as the interview was concerned, Simon read out the prepared statement and told the officers his client would be answering "no comment" to any other questions. John had watched scenes like this dozens of times on TV but he hadn't realised how disempowering it would be to be faced with a barrage of questions from two detectives.

Simon's presence was incredibly helpful and the only thing that stopped John going to pieces. Why didn't the police understand how traumatised he was? His wife was missing, presumed murdered and instead of being able to look for her he was here in this soulless room.

At the end of that first interview it was decided to hold John for further questioning, as Simon had predicted. Their enquiries obviously hadn't progressed any further by the next day, though, because the same officers snapped the same questions at him in another interview. His "no comments" must have been starting to irritate because one of them started making comments rather than questions. Saying he didn't believe John's statement. Simon soon clamped down on that though, reminding the officer that the purpose of the interview was to provide evidence and that calling his client a liar was unacceptable.

It wasn't long afterwards that the police officers left the room for a short while and then John was taken to be formally charged with Karen's murder. As he listened to the charge being read John had the strangest feeling, as if he was watching the scene on TV. The suspect being formally charged while inwardly pleading for this to be a nightmare and for his alarm clock to go off and bring an end to it. Then he was taken back to a holding cell while Simon went off to prepare for a bail hearing. The hours before Simon returned gave John plenty of time to contemplate his immediate future. For the first time he understood why people who are locked up in prison sometimes take their own lives. The relief he felt when his application for bail was granted was mixed with guilt. The police believed he'd killed his wife. He hadn't but if they were right and Karen was dead he should be grieving, not celebrating his freedom.

Although he'd technically been free to carry on his life as normal, as long as he didn't break his bail conditions, John had become a virtual recluse because he was convinced his every move would be watched by the police.

"They don't have the resources to keep tabs on everyone who's awaiting trial, you know," Simon said one night when he'd tried to convince John to go out for a drink and relax for a few hours.

"I know. But because Karen's still missing they might think I'll lead them to her." John couldn't bring himself to say what he really meant. That Karen's body was still missing and the police wanted him to lead them to it. He was adamant about laying low and Simon gave up trying to change his mind. Privately the lawyer thought John should be making the most of what might be his last months of freedom for a very long time. Although he took a pride in being a great defence lawyer Simon knew how unpredictable juries could be.

Even if John had wanted to return to his normal everyday life while awaiting trial he soon found out that normal life had other ideas. He was suspended from his job pending the result of his trial. Simon told him he could fight that decision but John didn't have the energy or the inclination. He preferred staying locked in the house. As soon as he'd been given permission by the police he called in professional cleaners to scour the kitchen but he still couldn't bring himself to use the room. Thank heaven for takeaway deliveries and online food shops. He moved the kettle and microwave into the dining room and lived on a diet of microwave meals for lunch and takeaways in the evenings. The only person he allowed in was Simon, whose visits increased as the trial date loomed.

On the first day of the trial Simon picked John up and they travelled to Manchester Crown

Court together. There were some local reporters and a camera crew from BBC Northwest

Tonight – the murder without a body angle had captured people's imaginations. John had

watched scenes like this on TV himself and always wondered whether the reporters really

expected someone to stop and answer questions on the way into a building where the course

of the rest of their lives was to be decided.

Once they made it inside Simon hurried off to find the barrister he'd instructed. John had

only met the barrister a couple of times. Her services were in demand and she was juggling a

large caseload. Simon had deliberately chosen a female barrister, claiming the jury would see

having a woman on John's side as a point in his favour. John waited in the corridor

surrounded by the overpowering scent of furniture polish. When Simon returned with the

barrister there was barely time for a quick "hello" before they had to go into the courtroom.

Although his future depended on this woman, John realised he was just another in a long line

of clients to her.

The trial was expected to be relatively short for a murder case. The forensic evidence related

to the murder victim was limited to the blood that had been found at the Mitchell home. The

police and CPS had a case based mainly on that blood evidence and their investigations into

the state of the Mitchell marriage. And there can't have been many witnesses to that. Sam

Raynor probably and that old battleaxe from next door. If she'd been called as a witness it

would be the most exciting thing that had happened to her in, well, forever.

The first part of the prosecution case was taken up with presenting reams and reams of print

outs of text messages exchanged between the couple. John wondered if people realised that every single message they sent could be served up to the police by their mobile phone provider. He certainly hadn't. And some of them didn't exactly show him in a good light. But the court procedure was so tedious he found himself wondering about the poor sod whose job it had been to trawl through literally thousands of messages about what time either one of them would be home, or reminders to pick up the dry cleaning, in order to pick out the pearls here and there that betrayed the bitterness that was creeping into the Mitchell marriage.

Despite the unpleasant text messages John still thought it could go either way. He'd never understood how someone could be convicted of murder without there being a dead body. Could he hope for a jury of people who thought the same?

****

Sam Raynor had known this day had been coming for months but that didn't stop her waking up with a feeling of dread in the pit of her stomach. She tried to play a psychological trick on herself. After all, a day off work in the middle of the week was a rare treat. Her employers hadn't been able to refuse her request when she told them the reason. Giving evidence in the murder trial of one of your clients wasn't exactly run of the mill. Especially given that the murder victim was another client. Sam jumped into the shower and tried to convince her racing brain that today was just an extra holiday. All she had to do was show up at court and answer a few questions and the rest of the day was her own.

At least that had been the theory. She'd been warned that she'd be called to court when the prosecution lawyers thought she'd be required, but there was every chance that if the witness before her overran she might have to return the following day. It was already lunchtime and

Sam was sick of the sight of the four walls in the witness waiting room. She went out for some fresh air and to find a sandwich shop but once she'd bought herself lunch she realised she had no appetite. Half an hour after returning to the stuffy waiting room a court usher came to fetch her.

"Samantha Raynor?"

"Yes." Sam followed the usher along the corridor to the courtroom. Her breathing was becoming rapid and shallow and she was worried for a moment that she might have a panic attack. But some deep breaths on the way to the witness stand helped to calm her down. The moment she'd been picturing for weeks was here. John Mitchell was sitting in the same room as her, watching her from the perspex cubicle that formed the dock. It was time to put on a performance that would pass an audition for RADA.

After taking the oath Sam glanced around the room, taking in the prosecution and defence tables and the crowded public gallery. She caught sight of a familiar face – was that Karen's sister? Couldn't be bothered to keep in touch but able to spare the time to be here. Typical. And now, quickly, before the questions started, Sam allowed herself one look at John Mitchell. He was staring straight ahead. Seemed to have lost a bit of weight from his face. Hair could do with a trim. Whoever had advised him what to wear had got it spot on with the dark grey suit. Sam's attention snapped across to the prosecution barrister.

"Ms Raynor, please state your relationship to Karen Mitchell and John Mitchell."

Sam cleared her throat. "I'm a financial advisor. The Mitchells were my clients. Since 2008.

Then last year Karen asked me to work for her alone."

"Is that an unusual request, in your experience?"

"No, I've had other clients, couples, who were considering divorce and one or other of them

would ask me to keep them on as a client."

"So the Mitchells were considering divorce?"

"No. I don't know. That's just one reason a wife or husband might ask me to separate their

affairs from their spouse."

"I see. But in this case. Are you aware of another reason?"

"Well, I'd had to bring it to their attention that their expenditure was out of control. Mrs

Mitchell's money from her trust fund was being run down rapidly."

"By Mrs Mitchell?"

"I don't know. I just saw the figures. The bottom line of what was left in the accounts. I'm

not aware of how it was being spent. But after that meeting when I advised them to keep their

spending under control, that's when Mrs Mitchell asked me to represent her and recommend

a colleague for her husband."

"Thank you. Now, between that meeting and 4th August 2012 did you meet with the Mitchells again?"

"I met with Mrs Mitchell several times. I didn't meet with Mr Mitchell."

"And what was the purpose of the several meetings with Mrs Mitchell?"

"As I've already said I needed to separate her accounts and investments from her husband's. With the trust and so on it was quite complicated and took several meetings to discuss and sign documents."

"Did any of these meetings take place at Mrs Mitchell's home?"

"Yes. Most of my meetings are at clients' homes. I checked my diary this morning so I can be sure of the details. The last time I met with her was on Friday 3rd August, in her home."

"And what was the purpose of that meeting."

"I had expected to go through some more of the paperwork required to separate the Mitchells' finances. But when I arrived it was clear Karen was upset and she just wanted someone to talk to."

"Please tell the court what you discussed with Mrs Mitchell that day. The day before her disappearance."

Sam paused and rubbed her hand across her mouth. "She said John wasn't happy about what we were doing regarding the accounts and investments. She said he'd threatened her that if we didn't put everything back as it was she'd be sorry."

"What did you take that to mean?" Sam didn't get to answer that question because the defence barrister jumped up from her seat to object. Of course, by then the damage was done in the eyes of the jury. Sam had achieved what she'd set out to do. Maybe she should've had a pang of conscience about lying under oath but she didn't. She was too busy trying to stop herself smiling.

****

Sam Raynor wasn't sure how long she could go on living like this. Ever since the night of Karen's "murder" she had been juggling work commitments with trying to keep Karen happy by visiting the cottage as often as possible. She always managed somehow to convince Karen that her voluntary imprisonment at the cottage would be worth it once John was in prison for life.

"But what if he isn't found guilty?" was Karen's favourite downer. Of course, that had been a risk all along and Sam had a contingency plan up her sleeve. But she hadn't expected Karen to be so, well, annoying. At least tonight she had good news for Karen – if she hadn't already heard it on the radio or TV news by now. The jury had been sent out to consider their verdict. A shot of adrenaline had coursed through Sam when she'd heard and it had left her feeling tired and twitchy. She'd share the bottle of wine she'd brought with Karen and that would calm her down. But as always she'd only have a couple of glasses – couldn't risk being stopped for drink driving at this stage.

"Honey, I'm home," she called once she'd closed the front door behind her. Karen never seemed to tire of that joke and she came out of the kitchen to greet Sam with a hug.

"The jury's out," Karen said with a wide grin. She seemed more like the old Karen that Sam knew so well. "I've cooked. Come on we can talk about it while we eat." Karen took the wine bottle, opened it and poured two generous glasses. Sam raised an eyebrow.

"Easy, just the one glass for me if you're filling them to the brim. I have to drive later."

Karen's face fell. "I thought you might stay tonight, considering the news."

"No, sorry. We have to keep to the routine. It's more important than ever now we're so close."

Karen got over her sulk more quickly than usual and the two women spent the evening trying to second guess the jury in their deliberations. By the time Sam checked her watch it was nearly midnight. Shit, she thought. I'm going to be fit for nothing at work tomorrow.

During the tedious drive home, always on the minor roads to avoid cameras, Sam thought through what she had to do over the next few days. Although juries could take days or even weeks to come up with a verdict, the likelihood was they would come back in the next few days. Sam found it frustrating that she wasn't in control of the timing of this next part of the plan but she had to get used to it. With luck, though, this would be one of the last times she had to do this god awful drive. As soon as the verdict was in, Sam could move her life on to the next phase. She told herself off with a smile as she realised she shouldn't just be thinking of her own life moving on, but that of the person who was the love of her life.

Chapter Six

I had hoped to be in and out of the office building before any of the steering group members arrived. This morning had been set aside for the film crew to do some brief interviews to camera, explaining everyone's role in the organisation. Jeremy had done his usual trick of chatting to each of the steering group separately until he knew he had the backing of the whole group for having the documentary makers involved. I'd often wondered why he didn't go into politics as he obviously had a talent for it.

I wasn't included in the "introduction to the cameras" exercise – they would be seeing enough of me in the next few weeks as I went about my job. But I'd needed to pop in and check my post. Of course, once Susie collared me for a gossip the pop in turned into half an hour over a cuppa. As often happens, the person I was most hoping to avoid appeared just as I was going out of the main door.

"Meredith, hello," Paula Reed said. She'd plastered on make up for the benefit of the cameras and looked like she'd had one of those makeovers done in a department store beauty department.

"Hi," I muttered, trying to leave it at that. But Paula had other plans.

"I was hoping to bump into you at some point. We need to talk."

"We really don't." I knew I was coming across as unfriendly and impolite but I couldn't cope with chatting to this woman.

"Look, can we meet for a drink sometime? Or coffee maybe?" Paula did genuinely seem to

be trying to be friendly but all my defences were on alert. "We really do need to talk. And if

you're reluctance is because you think I want to rake up the past – well, I don't. We need to

work out a way forward for the future. This evening?"

In the end I couldn't refuse. "Okay, look, I have a few things to do and you have your

interview with the TV crew. How about we meet at the Starbucks on the bypass at about

six?" I could hardly believe I was hearing myself say the words. Before I met Paula Reed I'd

never hated another person in my life but now I knew it was possible for one person to take

your personality and flip it into something you yourself couldn't recognise.

Paula gave me a small smile, as if she was trying not to crack her caked on foundation.

"Great, see you then."

The prospect of the six o'clock meeting loomed over me all day but I managed to divert my

concentration towards details that needed chasing up on the Mitchell case. My first priority,

of course, was to locate Samantha Raynor and if possible speak to her about her relationship

with Karen Mitchell. It wasn't too difficult to track down the firm of financial advisors Sam

Raynor worked for and, as I had a couple of other errands to do in Manchester, I decided to

pay a visit to their offices. If I was really lucky Ms Raynor might even be there, but I laughed

at my own optimism – I was never that lucky.

I rarely drove into Manchester city centre. Traffic was always a nightmare and parking

expensive and hard to find. I preferred to park near a tram station on the outskirts and complete the journey on one of the regular trams. As I waited at Sale Metrolink station I

drifted back in time to when I lived in one of the streets nearby as a student. As one of a

generation of guinea pigs for the new student loans and tuition fees, it had been touch and go

whether I'd go to university at all. I certainly didn't expect any financial help from my

parents. But I was glad I'd been brave enough to go ahead regardless. In fact I'd probably

been as well off financially then as at any other time in my life, mainly due to a temporary

job I had as part of my business course. One of the largest computer companies in the world

had a base nearby and my friend Hannah and I had been taken on for a year as trainees before

returning to complete our studies. The company's policy of paying such interns the same rate

as their graduate trainees meant we found ourselves with more money than we knew what to

do with. Sharing a flat and working together we had the time of our lives for a year and even

managed to put aside a small amount of money to cushion the blow of returning to student

life the following year.

The tram arrived, breaking into my thoughts and dragging me back to the present day. I knew

the offices I was looking for were close to a tram stop near Piccadilly gardens. On the short

journey I checked I had my notebook and pen and my iphone in case I decided to record the

interview. It was only then that it dawned on me that this meeting with Sam Raynor was

exactly the sort of thing the camera crew would have wanted to accompany me on. Too bad.

Jeremy was always telling me not to blame myself when things went wrong and in this case I

couldn't help it if the camera crew were busy doing other stuff on a day when I was doing

something interesting. If anything came of it I'd have to ask Sam Raynor to speak to me

again at a later date for the benefit of the camera. I didn't like fitting an investigation together

like a jigsaw for the TV company's benefit but I had to bear in mind what Jeremy had said

about Nothing But Truth needing the income.

Checking my watch as I got off the tram, I wondered whether to grab a quick early lunch but

decided against it. I headed towards Sam Raynor's office, rehearsing in my head how I would

open the conversation. Perhaps I should have phoned ahead after all. But it was funny how

often I gained the best information from someone by turning up unannounced. A receptionist

glanced up as I walked through the door into the building that was sandwiched between a

take away and an off-licence. Not exactly an upmarket neighbourhood which was surprising

considering the amounts of money Sam Raynor would have been dealing with for the

Mitchells.

"I'm Meredith James from an organisation called Nothing But Truth. If possible I'd like to

speak to one of the advisors – Samantha Raynor."

The receptionist looked all of about eighteen years old. She frowned and answered, "I'm

sorry I don't know anyone of that name. But I've only been here a few weeks. Maybe it's

someone I haven't met yet. Just give me a second." She grabbed the phone receiver and asked

one of her colleagues to come down from the main office. Flashing me a glossy smile she

asked me to take a seat in the reception area.

I did as she asked, feeling puzzled as to why even a new receptionist wouldn't know someone

who'd worked there for several years. You'd think it would be a pretty basic requirement of

the job for the receptionist to familiarise herself with all the staff. A couple of minutes later

an older woman appeared from the lift.

"You were asking about Sam Raynor?" she said, her eyebrows puckered into a determinedly serious expression. "I'm one of the managing partners here. May I ask the nature of your enquiry?"

The overly polite language put me on alert. There was something odd going on here – something this woman knew and I didn't. "It's part of an investigation my organisation is undertaking. It would be extremely helpful if I could speak to Ms Raynor." I could do polite when I had to.

The managing partner sighed as if she'd just given up an internal battle. "If there's something I or one of my colleagues can help you with, we'd be happy to. But I'm very sorry to have to tell you that Samantha Raynor died in 2013."

Chapter Seven

2013

Sam Raynor tidied her desk before leaving. It was part of her daily routine to leave everything as she would like to find it the next morning. There had been some discussion about having a clean desk policy whereby everyone left their work space completely clear. Sam thought this was just a way of preparing the staff for a future where they might end up hot desking. She was glad she'd be out of the way before anything like that was brought in. No, she preferred to leave whatever she'd be working on next day out and ready for her on the desk. Obviously she wouldn't leave anything confidential lying around but she rarely worked on anything more complex than a client's investments or retirement plans.

Although she did this preparation every day Sam was aware that today she was also procrastinating. Once she left the office she had a set list of tasks she needed to complete and one of them in particular was preying on her mind. The only way she'd be able to cope was to take things one at a time without thinking ahead to the main event. But that was far easier said than done.

"Doing anything nice this evening?" One of her colleagues asked the inane question as she watched Sam laying out files and pens on her desk.

"What?" Sam had heard perfectly well but she couldn't come up with the required stock answer for a moment. Then it was there. "No, just a quiet night in with the TV. You?"

Sam tuned out the response about her colleague's plans to go to her Slimming World weigh in, followed by a take-away and a bottle of wine. Sam had always opted out of the girly chats that took up a large part of some of her colleagues' working days. But tonight this particular person had obviously latched onto her because everyone else had already left. At last Sam's desk was how she wanted it and she could make her escape.

First stop was the apartment just a short walk from her office. Peeling off her business suit persona, she showered and changed into the casual clothes that she loved. For a moment she thought how wonderful it would be if she could just lounge on the sofa all evening watching the TV. But there would be plenty of time for lounging around in the future. She hugged the thought of those future times to herself for a moment, then shook her head. For now she had to stay focused for just a little while longer.

Sam wondered whether to grab a bite to eat but then realised her shopping list would be more authentic if it contained a few more items. She'd buy some cooked chicken and salad and share it with Karen at the cottage. Karen had been less and less motivated to cook or look after herself this last couple of weeks. The stress was really getting to her. It was getting to them both but Sam was better at just getting on with things. She was starting to worry a little about her ability to keep a poker face and regulate her mood to order. Her reaction to the news she'd heard just a couple of hours ago was a good example. She'd been waiting to hear this news for such a long time and yet she'd been able to meet with a client and complete her day's work as if nothing at all had happened.

Sam wore the hoodie she'd been saving for this occasion. It was exactly the same as one Karen owned and had been wearing on the night they left Karen's home for the last time. She tucked her hair into the hood and set off to the first large supermarket on the route from

central Manchester to the M60 motorway. Chicken, salad and two bottles of champagne. It

always surprised Sam how heavy a champagne bottle was and two of them made her basket

almost impossible to hold comfortably. She paid cash, going through one of the normal

check-outs, not wanting to draw attention by an alarm going off at the self-serve tills because

of the alcohol. That almost backfired when the woman on the checkout tried to engage her in

conversation, remarking on the champagne. Sam forced herself to give a polite reply,

something about a special birthday. Minutes later she was back in her car and heading

towards the motorway.

At last she could let the effects of this afternoon's news start to filter through. Shrugging off

the cover of calm and control she'd had to wear since she heard, Sam shouted at the top of

her voice, "Woo hoo!" then laughed hysterically until she thought she'd have to pull up on

the hard shoulder if she didn't settle down and concentrate on her driving. That's when she

realised she was using the wrong route. All these weeks and she thought it had become so

familiar she could drive there on autopilot, but here she was stupidly using a motorway where

dozens of cameras would capture her car's image. Sam left the motorway at the next junction

and worked her way back to the minor roads she should have been using.

"Honey, I'm home," Sam called as she closed the front door behind her. Karen was in the

sitting room, slumped in front of the TV. She was halfway down the bottle of wine Sam had

brought round the previous evening. For an instant Sam was furious. Karen was lounging

around while she was having to drive from Manchester and back after doing a full day's

work. She'd been visiting daily since the jury retired to consider their verdict and it was now

day four. It was costing Sam a fortune in petrol going backwards and forwards. Batting that irrelevant thought away, Sam noticed Karen was watching a box set episode – Grey's

Anatomy by the look of it.

"Haven't you seen the news?" she asked.

"No. I got sick of constantly checking it. What's happened?"

Sam pulled Karen to her feet and hugged her hard, then held her at arm's length looking into

her eyes. "It's over, Karen. They've found him guilty."

Karen collapsed onto the sofa. It took her a few seconds to digest the words and Sam left her

to it for a moment while she switched the TV to Sky News. Just a few minutes later their

news on a loop came round to the John Mitchell trial verdict. John had been found guilty by a

majority verdict – presumably that's why it had taken a while for the jury to come back. A

murder conviction meant a mandatory life sentence but they wouldn't know for a while what

his minimum term would be.

The reporter looked as though she was relieved that this would be the last time, for this trial

at least, she had to stand outside Manchester Crown Court in the freezing rain. The presenter

in the studio, warm, dry and smug, seemed to be drawing out the sequence on purpose, asking

about the defendant's demeanour when the verdict was given.

"Completely impassive," was the reply. "No reaction at all to the guilty verdict and he

rejected the opportunity to say anything."

If Karen or Sam found that surprising they didn't say so. They rewound the TV and watched the report several times because Karen was finding it hard to take in. This was everything they'd hoped for but she wasn't sure how to react.

"I know it's a shock," Sam said. "And it must feel a bit weird hearing that your husband's been found guilty of your murder. But we should eat something. Keep our strength up for what's to come in the next few weeks."

"Few weeks?" Karen said. "What are we waiting for? I want to get out of here tomorrow. Everything's ready after all."

Sam hadn't expected this. Although Karen had been moaning about being cooped up in the cottage for so long, she had always bowed to Sam's reasoning and done as she was told. The plan had been working perfectly but had Karen now reached the end of her tether? Sam couldn't risk Karen spoiling everything at this stage. Perhaps it was time for her next task after all, rather than sharing a nice meal first.

"I've brought food and some champagne. Thought we should mark the occasion. But then, okay, I'll try and bring things forward to the next few days rather than weeks."

Karen seemed to accept this and went to look in the shopping bag. "You're right. Looks delicious. And two bottles?" Her eyes widened. "Are you staying?" Karen had never come to terms with Sam's reasons for refusing to stay overnight at the cottage. Why couldn't she understand that everything Sam had done up to this point had been meant to ensure their plan worked?

Sam groaned inwardly. "We'll see," she said.

****

They hadn't eaten the chicken salad after all. Or opened the champagne. Sam had packed it

all into the shopping bag and gone back to her car. As she drove back down to Manchester

she listened to the loudest rock music she could find, trying to flood her brain with sound to

remove the memory of what she had done. It hadn't worked. Over the thud of the bass she

could still hear herself inwardly repeating "Oh my God. Oh my God."

In a way Sam found it comforting that she was feeling so bad. She'd always thought she'd

been born without a conscience. That she could do anything without a twinge of regret or

guilt. She could think of plenty of examples of times when she'd done shameful things

without giving it a second thought. But this? This was different. Maybe there was hope for

her as a human being after all. But if this was what it felt like she'd give it a miss. She spent

the rest of the journey thinking about the weeks ahead and putting what was done firmly in

the past.

****

Samantha Raynor's manager was very pleased with her. These past few weeks Sam had been

working harder than ever before and clients were singing her praises. She called Sam in for a

chat, to pass on the good reports and, for her own benefit, to make sure Sam didn't have any

plans to leave and go to work for one of their competitors. The strain of keeping up appearances all these months was starting to show on Sam's face and her manager was concerned.

"Is it the Mitchell situation that's worrying you, Sam? Feel free to take some leave if you think it would help. But I must say it doesn't seem to have been affecting your work."

"Everything's fine," Sam said. She couldn't let her manager suspect that she'd soon be "taking leave" permanently. Everything in her life had to appear normal until she'd gone for good. She knew she was looking tired because she hadn't slept at all last night. And it wasn't to do with guilt or stress – it was excitement.

There was one piece of the puzzle to fit and she'd be doing that later tonight. Just one phone call. Then all she had to do was sit back and wait for justice to take its course. It was so close she could almost taste it. The future she'd been dreaming of since this whole crazy plan started.

"Maybe I'll just leave early today," she said to satisfy her manager. That would give her a chance to check that she hadn't missed any tiny details. But then she remembered an appointment she'd made earlier with one of the firm's most important clients. "Forget that. But I will take some time off soon, I promise."

Leaving the manager's office Sam grabbed the client's file and set off to the meeting she'd arranged at their home. It would mean driving out of the city and back again before she could get on with what she needed to do, but at least she'd be going against the worst of the traffic.

****

There had been something nagging at Sam's brain ever since her last trip to the cottage three weeks ago. It was only when she stood in her apartment kitchen, unloading the contents of the small bag of shopping she'd picked up on her way home, that she realised the mistake she'd made.

It hit her like a physical blow. She thought back to that other shopping bag. The one she'd taken with her to the cottage last time. This changed everything. For weeks she'd been consoling herself with the thought that she never had to visit the cottage again. But the whole point of what she had done was wasted. Unless she did that bloody awful drive yet again. She was physically tired and emotionally drained. The meeting with the important client should have been straightforward but she'd walked into a battleground between husband and wife. It was so like the situation with the Mitchells it was uncanny and it had taken her far longer to deal with than she'd expected. Then the main road back into the city had been closed by a burst water main and it had taken over an hour to navigate the diversion.

Driving up to Lancashire now was the last thing she wanted to do and yet she knew she had to. But first she had to find that vital item to take with her. She tried to calm down enough to visualise what she had done when she came back from the cottage that previous time. She'd put the bottles of champagne and the food in the fridge – she'd eaten the chicken the next day but the champagne bottles were still there awaiting a future celebration. Over and over it she went in her mind until at last, like someone switching on a light, she knew. Relief flooded her as she retrieved the item, stuffed it in her pocket and left the apartment.

It was raining heavily now which made the winding roads she used hazardous. The car's wipers could hardly keep up with the deluge even on their fastest setting. Sam had a couple of near misses driving through a village a short way from her destination and by the time she reached the cottage she was shaking.

It took a couple of attempts to fit the key into the front door lock and when Sam finally made it inside out of the pouring rain she slumped with her back against the door.

"Honey, I'm home," she whispered, tears mingling with the drips of rain down her face.

****

Driving back down the lane Sam realised she'd done something she'd never done before – parked directly outside the cottage. The combination of the rain and her exhaustion had caused her to be careless. The prospect of retracing her route in this weather and so tired didn't appeal to her at all. It would be just her luck to end up in an accident at the very moment when the plan was coming together. She made the decision to head for the M61 motorway, the most direct and quickest route home. Driving along the middle lane to overtake a huge articulated lorry, Sam put her foot down but the car didn't respond with the power she needed. At the same time, and for the second time that evening, Sam realised she'd forgotten to do something that was vital to the plan. She couldn't wait until she got home in case the location of the call could be traced. She reached for her pay and go phone from her bag on the passenger seat. She was about a third of the way along the length of the lorry when its driver pulled out to avoid a slow vehicle. He couldn't see Sam's car because he was in a left hand drive European vehicle. The heavy truck side-swiped Sam's car, a massive blow that sent the car crashing through the central reservation and into the third lane of the

opposite carriageway, into the path of a van. Sam was dead before the emergency services

arrived.

Chapter Eight

I was still reeling from the news of Samantha Raynor's death when I boarded the tram on the way back to my car. Was it simply coincidence that the financial advisor had died such a short time after one of her former clients had been convicted of the murder of another client, his wife? And not only that. John Mitchell's theory that Karen was having an affair with Sam Raynor might implicate Sam in Karen's murder. I tried to make sense of it all as I watched the city centre give way to its built up suburbs.

The tram was quiet at this time of day and I enjoyed the chance to sit quietly for a while without feeling as if I should be doing something. Glancing at the few other passengers nearby I wondered what they were travelling to and from. The young student plugged into her favourite music while flicking through a magazine. The older woman clinging on to her shopping trolley for dear life as if I might suddenly grab it and make a run for it. The young couple sitting as close to each other as they decently could in public and holding hands to make sure everyone knew they were taken. The story of Sam Raynor's death had focussed my mind on how short life could be. It was the sort of thing I could find myself obsessing about for hours. Did any of these other people ever wonder if their story might end with this journey?

Probably not, because it wouldn't be normal, would it?

Then again, sometimes I noticed how my tendency to dwell on a problem could help in my work. Where someone else might give up on a lead that was going nowhere, I would worry at it constantly until I solved the puzzle. I might get on with everyday tasks at the same time but the puzzle would always be on a back burner and I couldn't switch off until I'd either worked

it out or the case had been closed. There had been several cases where I had argued with

Jeremy until I was blue in the face that I should be allowed to carry on but luckily for my

peace of mind he always had the final say. Then I would back off and lick my wounds, sulk

for a while, and bounce back fired up for the next case.

The Mitchell case looked like becoming one of those that would occupy my brain full time.

After the manager at Sam Raynor's office had broken the news of Sam's death she'd invited

me up to her office for a cup of tea and a chat. My shock at the news must have shown on my

face and the older woman didn't want to simply show me the door.

"Thanks for this," I said, accepting a mug of insipid looking tea. I like my tea strong with

barely any milk. This looked more like a milk shake but I told myself to be polite and forced

myself to drink it. "I didn't know Ms Raynor personally but I must admit finding out she's

passed away will have an impact on my investigation."

"Passed away sounds so peaceful, doesn't it? I'm afraid Sam's death was anything but. It was

a terrible accident on the motorway. But the sad thing was there wasn't really anyone to

mourn her, apart from her colleagues and clients here."

"No family? Or partner?" I was hoping for a snippet, anything that would give me another

lead to follow.

"No. I don't even know who organised or paid for her funeral. I went, of course, to represent

the firm. But there were no more than a handful of others there. So sad. Especially for a young person's funeral. Just a quick service at the crematorium. No wake or anything

afterwards." The woman seemed to be feeling guilty because she hadn't given Sam Raynor a

thought for a long time.

I realised there was nothing to be gained by any further questions so I made my excuses and

left. The young receptionist was sitting at her desk staring into space and barely

acknowledged me leaving. I wondered what it would be like to have a job like that. One

where you turned up at your desk each morning and left each night having done exactly the

same thing you'd done the day before. Hell for me, I was sure.

Having lost my most promising lead on the case I didn't know where to look next. I'd have to

see if Jeremy had time for a quick brainstorming session because otherwise I was stumped. It

was amazing how many times half an hour with him could produce a number of possible

lines of enquiry I hadn't thought of before.

Once I reached Sale and found my car I sat for a while contemplating what lay ahead in the

next few hours. Why had I agreed to meet with Paula Reed? Every instinct should have

screamed at me to refuse to talk to the woman and yet I'd heard myself suggesting a time and

place. Sometimes I was just too polite for my own good, even when I was dealing with

someone I would have done almost anything to avoid. I knew that partly it was due to my

chronic inferiority complex that always made me think other people were in the right, no

matter how often experience showed me otherwise.

It was a battle I faced every day. My rational mind knew I was good at my job and worth just

as much as anyone else. But it only took the slightest criticism for me to draw into myself and this had made me miss out on so many opportunities over the years. The flip side was that I also found it impossible to say no to anyone I perceived as superior, in other words everyone. The dilemma I was dealing with now – the dreaded meeting with Paula Reed – was a case in point.

It crossed my mind to send a text cancelling, giving the excuse of developments on the case that I needed to chase up. But that really wasn't an option because I didn't have Paula's mobile number and I couldn't face asking the receptionist at the office for it. Best to get it over with. At least I didn't have the camera crew with me yet. Imagine trying to explain to them why they couldn't be in on a meeting between me and one of the steering group members. That reminded me. I reached my iPad out of my bag and spent a few minutes recording a video piece about my trip to Manchester. Playing it back to make sure it looked okay, I was struck again by the odd coincidence. I'd asked Sam Raynor's colleague to tell me as much as she could about Sam's accident and it was the date it occurred that stuck in my head and wouldn't budge. I'd checked my notes twice and knew that it was within a few weeks of the date John Mitchell had started his prison sentence.

Of course, it could simply have been just that – an odd coincidence. I had come across stranger things in my job. But I had also developed a kind of sixth sense to help weed out the things that were irrelevant in an investigation. Sam Raynor's death felt far from irrelevant. I had the feeling it was connected to something else that had struck me as strange but for now I couldn't make the connection.

My pondering about how short life can be had given me a renewed motivation to get on with my job. If I'd known how much trouble I was heading into with this investigation I might have thought twice about my enthusiasm for chasing up leads.

Chapter Nine

2012

Extracts from ward round notes, Pennine View Clinic:

6 August

Patient was admitted via A&E at the Royal on Saturday 4 August. On call psych assessment

identified risk of harm to self or others. In house assessment scheduled for 8 August

following observation period.

13 August

Patient became agitated two days after admission and was prescribed combination meds (see

medication sheet attached). Assessed by senior nurse on 8 August. Complains of inability to

sleep. Short term medication prescribed. (see meds sheet). Physically fit and well. Suicidal

ideations continue. No further risk to others identified. Admitted to main ward.

Note: Consultant requests this patient be included in latest batch of case studies.

20 August

Medication adjusted due to overly elevated mood. Anti-psychotic meds added (see meds

sheet). Patient expressed wish to go home. Named nurse will explain that patient is likely to

need to stay at Pennine View for several months rather than weeks. Staff have expressed

concerns about patient's manner on ward.

Note: Schedule this patient for extra sessions with consultant regarding case studies project.

27 August

Staff have registered further complaints regarding patient's behaviour on the ward. Patient

refuses to acknowledge unacceptable behaviour. Patient expressed intention to leave ward

(currently voluntary patient). Explained to patient that our observations indicate that if the

patient attempts to leave we may need to detain under Mental Health Act.

3 September

Patient has continued to disrupt ward. Attempted to leave ward when a visitor was entering.

Informed patient of change in status – now detained. Patient reacted violently and was

restrained by staff (included administering sedative injection) and transferred to psychiatric

intensive care ward on 1 September. Staff observations indicate calm mood since then.

10 September

Patient transferred back to main ward following a week of calm, level mood. Re-assessment

indicates diagnosis of bipolar affective disorder. Medication adjusted accordingly. Note:

patient has requested a tribunal to appeal detained status.

17 September

Mental health tribunal ruled in patient's favour. Status now voluntary. Patient has requested

home visit, stating that she wishes to see her children. However family member has contacted

the ward and raised concerns about this. Consultant liaising with family and will arrange one-

to-one counselling with patient to discuss issues regarding children.

Discharge Summary of ward rounds since 24 September 2012

Staff report patient is passive and no longer disruptive on main ward. Complying with medication and therapies without complaint or comment. Multi-disciplinary meeting arranged to finalise treatment plan. Patient will be discharged as soon as community mental health team confirm accommodation and follow up support is in place. Consultant reports issues regarding children dealt with satisfactorily.

Note: Case study completed.

****

I remember sitting in a cubicle at A&E. I was screaming because I thought the cubicle was full of spiders and beetles and flying insects that were swooping round my head. I heard a man asking the staff if they'd like him to sit with me because they were so busy and he was experienced working with distressed people. I don't remember his name but he sat with me for hours and he was so kind. His gentle voice calmed me down and I stopped the screaming. I sometimes think about that man and wonder who he was. It would be nice to be able to find him and thank him. But I was a different person then and maybe it's better to keep my "before and after" separate.

I don't remember getting to the hospital but Daniel must have taken me. I wonder where he left the children? We had no friends, no family nearby. Anyway he left me there so he must have had to get back to them. I didn't think about them at the time, of course. My mind was a complete blank. A doctor came eventually. Asked me a lot of questions but I only answered one. When he asked how I felt I told him I felt nothing. Hours passed and another doctor came. I didn't want to be there anymore. I didn't want to be anywhere. But most of all I didn't want to be at home with Daniel. So I answered all the questions this time. Told them what I thought they wanted to hear. Whatever I could say that would mean I didn't have to go home. I had no idea how soon I would want exactly the opposite.

The next thing I remember is standing in a bedroom. It was at a place called Pennine View Clinic. I'd never heard of it but I know now that it's somewhere the NHS use as an overspill for their psychiatric wards. I was surprised the room they'd put me in was a bit like a room in a budget hotel. I suppose if I'd ever thought about it I would've expected this sort of place to be full of large wards with about eight people in. Instead I had my own small bathroom with a shower, sink and toilet. No shower curtain though, and no rail for one. The bedroom had a single bed, a desk/dressing table and a chair. There were shelves for my clothes but no wardrobe. The window looked out onto a courtyard two floors below and the window itself couldn't be opened.

I felt quite calm by now which surprised me. I was asked if I wanted some tea and I followed the nurse to the kitchen where a dozen other patients were eating. That new kid at school feeling hit me and I tried to make myself invisible but I soon realised nobody cared. Everyone was tied up in their own little world. It took a couple of days to register with me where I'd ended up. The relief of not being at home lasted that long but then reality threatened to kick in. The next few days are a bit of a blur. I think they drugged me to the eyeballs to combat my anxiety. The trouble is a side effect seemed to be insomnia and after a few days I was exhausted. Then a nurse handed me a sleeping pill with my other meds one night. Handed it over like a precious treat. After that sleep wasn't a problem, but waking up was. About the same time I was moved to a bigger ward with more patients. I spent most of my time in my room, which was exactly the same as my room on the other ward.

After a week or so on that ward I started to feel better. So much better. Better than I've ever felt before. I could do anything – if only they'd let me out of there. One of the nurses explained that wasn't going to happen any time soon and that I needed yet more drugs. Anti-psychotics. That sent me searching for a dictionary and freaking out because psychotic and psychopath were next to each other on the page.

Whatever the anti-psychotics were meant to do, I'm not sure they worked. I only have flashes of memories of that time but what I can remember makes me cringe. I remember smashing all the coffee mugs in the kitchen because I couldn't get the attention of one of the staff (they were in a meeting and all the mugs were wrecked by the time one of them came out). I hounded a patient who had issues with personal boundaries, constantly trying to touch her hand or go into her room. An old lady who'd been there for years spoke to me one day, saying "Your children are going to die" and I completely lost it, screaming at her. I realised long afterwards that she said the same thing to everyone. It was her "thing". I remembered Daniel saying to me when we went to the hospital that he was going to find a safe place for me. So I set out to prove him wrong. I smashed a plastic water jug in my room and used the shards of hard plastic to cut my forearms to shreds. I went to show a nurse who shook her head and waved me away, muttering something about being too busy to deal with self harmers. It wasn't until a few days later that another nurse cleaned and dressed the wounds that were now infected.

I was warned a few times what would happen if I carried on behaving badly. But to me it felt as though I was behaving completely normally. I asked permission to leave the ward for a short while but it was refused. So next day when a visitor arrived I sneaked out of the door before it closed behind them. I sat on the wall outside the building, basking in the sunshine.

When my consultant walked by I waved and shouted a greeting. When I went back inside, before I could try and explain that I'd needed some fresh air and a small taste of freedom, I was informed that I was being sectioned. Next thing I knew I was stabbed with a syringe and two nurses were dragging me down some stairs, semi-conscious. When I remember that episode I hope I've made some of it up. I hope there isn't a nurse, maybe still working on that ward, who would drag a patient from the ward while hissing in their ear "This'll teach you, you time-wasting, attention-seeking bitch". I was shoved into a room, the door locked behind me. When I looked around I saw I was in a bare-walled, bare-floored room. The only furnishing, if you could call it that, was a few plastic-covered shapes like you would find in a children's play area. It took a while to dawn on me that this was the equivalent of the classic "padded cell" that people speak of. Except that it wasn't padded at all. The concrete walls bore the evidence of previous patients who had bled against them. I was being watched through a porthole in the door so I stayed perfectly still and eventually I was led out and taken to my bedroom. My belongings had been brought from the main ward – a few clothes and photographs mainly. But they'd obviously been searched and anything sharp removed. A picture frame no longer had its glass cover. I wasn't to be trusted.

It was about this time that it dawned on me that I hadn't had any visitors. I thought Daniel would've made the effort at least a couple of times a week but no. Just when I was starting to think about wanting to be at home my husband seemed to have abandoned me. Okay, he was having to juggle work and child care but surely he could fit in an hour or so to see his wife. As the possible implications of his absence started to sink in my fear of going home crept back.

The week I spent on the psychiatric intensive care unit was like a holiday. Caring staff,

relaxed atmosphere. Being allowed outside into the courtyard that the clinic was built around.

Chatting to other patients about nothing but feeling better for just having connected with

someone. I felt myself slowly coming back. But of course all good things must come to an

end and I soon found myself back on the main ward. Next thing I knew I was being told I'd

been diagnosed as bipolar. Wow – I had something fashionable for once - lots of celebrities

had that didn't they? I didn't have a clue what it meant and nobody was about to educate me.

There was a patients' resource room with lots of leaflets and information and from those I

slowly began to learn about my diagnosis and what it would be like to live with it. Some of it

freaked me out and I desperately needed to talk to someone about it but the staff didn't want

to know.

I'd seen a poster on the ward notice board about mental health advocates. Someone to be

there for you if you had nobody else. Well, people weren't exactly queuing up to be on my

side so I asked to meet one of their volunteers. They helped me fight my sectioned status and

I requested a home visit – the first step to being allowed out of the clinic for good. Now that I

was feeling more myself I realised I had to face up to Daniel and to going home some time.

As the weeks had passed I'd had to try and come to terms with him not wanting me anymore.

But whether he wanted me there or not I had a right to be there. A right to be with my

children. Didn't I? If I was going to have to fight for that right it may as well start now. I

went to my next ward round meeting eager to hear the arrangements for me to spend a

weekend at home. Each staff member gave their opinions of how well I was doing, how much

good a home visit would do me etc. Then the bombshell. A phone call had been received from a family member expressing concern. Something to do with the children I think, but I

can't be sure exactly what it was.

You know when someone says they wished the floor would open and swallow them up? Well

at that moment I didn't wish it, it just happened. Each week when I'd entered that room for

the meeting that would decide my immediate future, I'd hesitated on the threshold. There

might be as many as ten people in there. Some I knew as the staff who worked on the ward.

And in charge of it all, of course, was my consultant. But others would come and go – no

introductions, no asking me if was okay for them to be there. I suppose they were students

but nobody ever explained. It was daunting but I made myself step through that door each

time in the hope that today was the day I would hear what I wanted. My hopes were so high

that day. I just knew I'd be preparing to go home after that meeting. Instead I was shoved

back into the depths of despair. And even worse than before, my hope had been taken away.

Was it Daniel who had vetoed my home visit? More likely it was his bitch of a mother. I

know it's a cliché but our mother/daughter-in-law relationship had never been good. But

would she really kick me when I was down like this? Of course she would.

I've tried many times to describe how I felt at that moment. The moment when hope was

snatched away from me and I started to realise for the first time that my life would never be

the same again. The best I can come up with is a combination of shock, disbelief and

emptiness. My advocate was there – I hadn't noticed him before in my eagerness to hear what

I wanted. But he spoke up now. Asked for the meeting to be brought to an end. My distress

was obvious to everyone and the consultant was unable to ignore his request. I ran to my

room and hid myself away, refusing meals and any attempts to extract me from my solitary misery. The only thing I couldn't avoid was medication time when I dutifully queued up with the rest of the patients for my cocktail of drugs.

It felt like weeks later, but was probably only a couple of days, when the next heat-seeking missile struck the ruins of my life. An official looking letter. Strictly private and confidential but it had obviously already been screened by the staff. My sedated brain could barely understand the legal vocabulary but the gist of it was clear. Daniel was preparing to divorce me. It's a measure of my feelings for him that all I cared about was whether he planned to take away my children.

The next week or so (I only estimate that time after trying to piece together what happened) is a blank apart from a few snapshot moments I'd rather forget. Standing in my room looking around the floor at dozens of mangled playing cards. I'd been enjoying playing solitaire with my pack of cards – found it soothing and therapeutic. I don't know if I trashed the cards myself or if someone else found their way into my room and destroyed my only pastime.

At one point I got it into my head that if I wasn't allowed to go home, that must mean I was staying at the clinic forever. The concept of staying there until I was well and then being allowed home, as was probably the plan at that time, didn't make sense to me. So I set about changing my address on all the official things like bank accounts and so on. The staff weren't happy when I started receiving correspondence via their office. I'd also started ordering all sorts of things for my room, using Daniel's credit card details – did I mention I have an amazing memory for numbers? Dozens of parcels arrived and had to be sent straight back.

I remember sneaking out of the ward again but knowing, even in my dazed state, that I shouldn't just sit on the wall this time. Walking into the town centre – a good five miles away – and trying to buy a laptop on credit. When the salesman asked me my income I was completely honest and told him zero. The look that passed between him and his colleague penetrated my trance and I ran out of there before they could throw me out. Knowing I needed to get back to the clinic but instead diverting to the Royal Infirmary and booking in at A&E claiming to have the symptoms of appendicitis. When they asked if they could contact my next of kin I realised this could be my chance to see Daniel at last. Force him to see me and talk to me. Surely he wouldn't refuse to come if the hospital staff rang him. But he did. Refuse that is. The nurses were sympathetic until I jumped off the trolley and left. Walking back to the clinic, exhausted, and pressing the buzzer to be admitted to the ward. No response. I know now that they could see me in the office on the video monitor but none of the staff came to let me in. Banging on the door until my knuckles bled then pounding with the palms of my hands until they were at risk of shredding too.

At last the door opened and I fell forwards into the entrance hall. My consultant stood there shaking her head and muttering to the burly security guard who accompanied her. He left us alone and she hissed at me to get up off the floor and follow her. Instead of going into the ward we went downstairs to the treatment rooms. I'd previously only been into the general room where blood tests were done but this time I was led further in until we reached another door. The sign said it was the ECT suite. ECT – Electroconvulsive Therapy. I swilled the words around my brain but they didn't make sense. Was it some sort of museum of psychiatry? I'd seen documentaries about that being used years ago but they didn't use it any more. Did they?

"If you cause me one more minute's effort," the consultant said. "One more complaint from the staff. One more time when you decide you fancy a trip outside. This is where you will be half an hour later."

My eyes must have shown her that her threat had hit home because she smiled – a cross between a sneer and a grin.

"I'll ask one of the nurses to introduce you to some of my ECT patients," she carried on. "Especially just after they've been down here. Take note and adjust your behaviour because I really don't have the time or inclination to deal with you for much longer."

The consultant turned on her heel and marched away, leaving me to scamper after her or be left behind in this nightmare maze of corridors. When I returned to the ward I looked around me at the other patients. Did they know about the rooms downstairs? My attention turned to two ladies I'd known for a few weeks now and chatted to. I hesitated to call them friends but they were as close to that as anyone I'd interacted with since I came here. Christine was usually a talkative, smiling breath of fresh air but now she was standing by the wall with a vacant expression on her face. Her denim jeans were stained dark around the top of the legs and I realised with a jolt that she'd wet herself. Linda was an older woman who loved to take on everyone else's cares and worries and dispense the wisdom of her life experience. Now she was sitting nursing a cold cup of tea in the dining room, looking around as if she had no idea where she was.

"Don't worry they'll be back to normal by this time tomorrow." One of the staff had noticed me studying the two women. How had I not noticed this phenomenon before? Christine or

Linda would disappear for an hour or so each week and then spend the next day in a world of their own. Was it a last resort treatment or simply that a day's respite from their usual problems made it worth undergoing the treatment? I tried asking them both the next day but neither of them knew what I was talking about. But from that day onwards my only aim was to get out of that place without being subjected to the treatment in the downstairs room.

I've since attended both Christine and Linda's funerals. Both took their own lives, though Linda's family refused to accept the verdict of her inquest. I've attended the funerals of three other patients who were at the clinic at the same time as me – all gone before their time. The worst one was Christine's though. I'd bumped into her in town a week or so before she died. That would have been about six months after I left the clinic. I stopped to say hello and after a moment she recognised me and gave me one of her huge smiles that could light up a room. She seemed happy and more talkative than I'd ever known her – telling me all about her girls. Her two teenage daughters were doing well at school and they were all living with Christine's mum for now. The next thing I knew I saw her death announcement in the local paper while I was waiting for a dentist's appointment. The funeral was next day and I was there sitting at the back watching her daughters follow the coffin in. They were in their school uniforms, a teacher accompanying them and each had been allowed to bring a friend to support them. Imagine that at the age of thirteen or fifteen. Your best friend chooses you to go to their mum's funeral with them.

But going back to that day in the clinic when I was brought face to face with what my future could be if I didn't "behave". I became the model patient, giving the staff no excuse whatsoever to find fault with me. Within a couple of weeks they couldn't justify keeping me any longer and my advocate arranged a meeting with a social worker to talk about where I would live when I left. The social worker barely managed to cover her bewilderment at my situation. Her usual clients were people who had been in and out of the clinic for years and relied on the benefits system to fund rented accommodation in the community. A few years ago she had worked out a slick system for passing people along the conveyor belt from hospital to supported housing and then independent living. With the brutal spending cuts imposed on social care that was now simplified as none of the supported housing existed any longer. The only thing that complicated our relationship was that I didn't fit her client profile. Daniel was refusing to allow me to live back at home but he was prepared to be generous with money until our divorce went through. Frighteningly quickly my social worker had found me a privately rented apartment.

The great day finally arrived and I was discharged from the clinic, clutching a paper bag of medication and my overnight case. The final hoop I'd had to jump through was to meet with my consultant one last time. I was terrified she would veto my release, given her usual attitude to dealing with me, but then I realised she was just as keen to get rid of me as I was to go.

"This is just one of those tick the boxes things I have to do for every patient I discharge," she said. For once she was speaking to me like a human being and it wrong footed me for a moment. "I've already filled in the forms so let's just chat for a moment so everyone thinks I give a damn." She laughed without her face cracking a smile.

"Okay," I said, willing time to move faster so I could get out of that room and breathe.

"So, what are your plans out in the big wide world?"

I couldn't meet her eye but I certainly knew the answer. "It'll take me a while to get used to being on my own," I started. Then in as stronger voice, "I'm going to find a job and then one day, hopefully not too long away, I'm going to be allowed to be a mother to my children again."

"Oh yes, the children. Well, good luck with that." She looked as if she knew a secret and was determined to keep it from me. "And what does your husband think about that?"

"I have no idea. I've come to terms with the fact he doesn't want me in his life any more. But he can't stop me seeing the children forever. It's not as if I've committed a crime or anything. Now look, I want to go."

I left the room without looking back but I could feel the sneer on her face burning into my back. What had I done to make this woman hate me so?

****

Daniel had worked with the social worker to organise all my clothes and other essentials to be waiting for me at the apartment. The social worker dropped me off, leaving an emergency number and a handful of leaflets and that was it. I was on my own. I'd promised myself that once I left the clinic one of the first things I would do was put together an official complaint about the bullying and intimidation I'd suffered. Now that I was out and I could get some perspective about the situation, I realised that most of the staff had been dedicated and kind.

It was just a couple of the nurses and that complete monster of a psychiatrist who seemed to have taken against me and made it their mission to make my life a misery.

One of the senior nurses in particular had taken me under his wing in the days before my discharge from the clinic. He'd spent hours chatting to me, making me focus on the positive side of everything and encouraging my plans and ambitions for the future. Only once had he been negative. After I left the clinic he phoned me to let me know they'd forgotten part of my medication and he was happy to bring it round on his way home. I made him a cup of tea and we chatted. He felt more able to be honest outside the ward environment.

"You need to be prepared for one thing," he said. "From now on whenever you have a physical illness the medics will see your diagnosis from the clinic on your records and it will cloud their judgment. I'm not trying to upset you – it's simply how it is."

I knew he was speaking from experience. He'd shared with me that he'd suffered mental health problems himself in the past and had struggled to return to his current work and to be taken seriously by people in all aspects of his life. He was trying to help by making me be realistic about what I faced in the outside world. Ian had been faced with discrimination and bullying from colleagues in an environment where they really should have known better.

But as I stood at the window of my new home looking out over the town, all my anger and resentment towards the clinic staff melted away. I had a choice to make. I could waste the rest of my life thinking back to the terrible time I had just endured. Or I could look forward, learning from what I'd been through but not being defined by it. Looking at it that way there really was no choice. Whether it was the medication I'd now been on for some time starting to do its job, or whether my naturally practical personality had kicked back in, it was time to move on.

First day of the rest of my life and all that. Fresh start.

****

2013

I'd been living independently for nearly six months and the divorce was almost sorted. The one thing giving me nightmares was what Daniel was planning for the children. I was convinced that behind my back Daniel was applying for sole custody due to my "mental instability" and that in his version of the future I would only be allowed supervised visits with the children for a couple of hours each weekend. The thought of not being able to touch my children without a stranger looking on appalled me. I hadn't seen them for such a long time and since that August day the previous year when I'd been admitted to the clinic my chances of living with them had diminished. Daniel refused to talk to me about them. In fact he was determined to keep all contact via lawyers so I couldn't even try to sway him by meeting to discuss things.

Once the divorce went through I'd be able to find somewhere nicer to live – somewhere with a room where the children could stay when they visited. I acknowledged that I wasn't able to care for them full time yet. It would be a while before I could do that. But surely their mother should be allowed to look after them part time? However I seemed to be the only person who thought so. It felt so unfair. I hadn't put a foot wrong since leaving the clinic – not a single

episode that could point to unstable behaviour.

I researched the family court liaison service who could make a decision on the arrangements

for the children. I was determined to state my case calmly and clearly and come away with an

offer of something more than weekly meetings in a contact centre. But the rug was about to

be pulled from under me just as it was in that ward round meeting when I'd thought I was

going to be allowed home. Every time I tried to make contact I was fobbed off by someone

saying their service couldn't help me. Eventually I turned up at their office only to be asked

to leave. I sat in their reception area refusing to go until someone dealt with my case.

It took them two hours to get me out of that room. It was only when I overheard someone

suggesting they should ring the community mental health team that I moved, walking towards

the exit as if I was wading through porridge. I ignored their offers to phone a taxi for me and

walked the three miles to where I lived. I don't know how long I sat staring out of the sitting

room window too stunned to even think about what had happened. I know it was days before

I bothered to shower and change my clothes.

Then I surprised myself. In a burst of energy I transformed myself, hair washed and face

made up, wearing clothes I'd bought to cheer myself up at Christmas but had never worn. It

was as if I'd emerged like a butterfly and it wasn't just the clothes or the cleansed body. My

mind felt as if it had been rebooted by the frustration of being unable to arrange a meeting the

other day. Was this the bipolar kicking in? Having set off downwards for days was my brain

telling me it was time to go high? I vaguely thought that I wouldn't be aware of it if that was

the case. But it was a totally new experience for me and I was going to make the most of it. I made myself a to-do list and attacked it enthusiastically. Number one was find a job. Somebody should have warned the world I was on my way.

Once I put my mind to it, it didn't take me long to find a few jobs I could apply for that would make use of my previous experience. I was over qualified for them all but I didn't care and I'd come up with a believable story to explain why I was back-tracking in my career. This isn't the time to be modest – I have a great CV. From my first class degree in business and law through to my several years' paralegal experience, I knew I was employable. Interview invitations arrived for three of the jobs I'd applied for but there was one I really wanted. If my recent history had taught me anything it was not to get my hopes up so I tried to treat all the interviews equally. They were all arranged for the same week, within a couple of days of each other. I was offered the first one on the spot but asked for time to think it over. The second one didn't go quite so well but they still rang me later that day with an offer. I was tempted but I wouldn't have forgiven myself if I didn't hold out to see if I was offered the one I really wanted.

Things were obviously looking up at last. My third and final interview, for the job I'd convinced myself was perfect for me, went like a dream. You know when you walk into a building you've never been to before and it somehow feels like home? That's the feeling I got when I walked into their office building. I was interviewed by the head of the organisation and the HR/Finance manager. They weren't big enough to have a separate department for each. The boss flicked through my portfolio of qualifications and certificates for various extra training I'd undertaken. Then came the inevitable question.

"Any organisation like ours would be lucky to have you. But why are you applying for posts that you're clearly over qualified for?" The HR woman shot a glance at her superior that clearly said she didn't want him to put me off.

I can't remember my exact answer but whatever I said must have gone down well. They offered me the job there and then and I accepted, making a mental note not to forget to politely turn down the other two later. The HR manager gave me a quick tour of the place, introducing me to some of my future colleagues. That feeling of coming home increased with every room we went in and every person we spoke to.

I couldn't wipe the huge grin from my face. Here was the fresh start I'd been looking for. My chance to show everyone they'd been wrong to write me off. As usual my thoughts raced ahead and I could see myself as part of this dedicated team. The work they did was so worthwhile and exactly the kind of detailed work that suited me.

I pretty much skipped out of there and even a frustrating journey on public transport back to my flat didn't dampen my mood. Now I had a job I could look for a reasonably priced car to enable my commute. I got off the bus a couple of stops early and went window shopping at a nearby car dealership. I could feel an excitement rising in me that I had to damp down. Was this how it would be for the rest of my life? Worrying whenever I felt happy that I was heading towards that dreaded rollercoaster again?

The words of Ian, the nurse from the clinic, came back to me. His warning about medical professionals not taking me seriously because of my past mental health issues echoed in my head but I closed the thoughts down. Mistakenly, as it turned out.

My euphoria went on for several days until out of the blue I received a call from my GP's

surgery. Could I go in later to talk to the doctor? Well that was a first. After all the battles

with receptionists I'd had in the past to get an appointment, now I was being called in. I

didn't think much of it. Probably some sort of follow up after six months out of hospital. But

I came out of that appointment broken and crying. I should have realised there was something

wrong when I was sitting in the waiting room. The receptionist kept giving me sidelong

glances and she'd barely been polite when I booked in. At last my name was called and I

walked down the corridor still innocently thinking this was just a routine appointment.

"I've been asked to give a medical report saying you're suitable for a job you've been

offered." The doctor wouldn't meet my eye. "Unfortunately if I provide that report then I

suspect your job offer will be withdrawn."

"But why? There's nothing in the job description that could be harmful to me." I could feel

hot tears starting to prick the backs of my eyes but I refused to let them through.

"No. But it does mention working with vulnerable people at times. And following the report I

was sent by your consultant when you were an inpatient, I'm afraid I can't sign off on that."

There was no discussion allowed. My light at the end of the tunnel had been extinguished just

like that. Still fighting back tears of frustration, I told him not to bother with the report. I'd

withdraw my acceptance of the job and return to my hermit-like existence. But if I had to do

that, I wasn't sure I'd survive very long.

I screwed up my courage and rang the person who'd made the job offer. He was very understanding after I explained how my life had been over the past year, but without a medical report he would have to withdraw the job offer. I could hear the reluctance in his voice which made me feel slightly better but I knew he had no choice.

Then the next part of my roller coaster experience happened. Just half an hour later the HR manager phoned me back. She'd had a word with her boss and convinced him to take me on despite my doctor's negative opinion. I wouldn't let myself believe it at first but she carried on to explain.

"You should've told us about your diagnosis up front," she said. "My husband suffers from the same condition and I have to say you seem to be coping admirably. We have to put that stuff about vulnerable people into the job description to cover ourselves but most of the time the people you meet in the course of your job will be anything but vulnerable."

How I wished we were face to face rather than talking on the phone. I wanted to hug her and make her understand what a huge favour she was doing for me.

That was my turning point. The first time someone had shown confidence in me for such a long time. And believed in me knowing all the facts. But even though things are changing and a mental health diagnosis doesn't carry the same stigma it used to, I met with the two people who had interviewed me and asked them to swear that they wouldn't share their knowledge of my condition with anyone else. They understood and I trust them both to keep their word. If my secret was to come out in the future I would have to face up to it But I can't begin to explain how good it felt, right at that moment, to have people believe in me again.

There was a pile of paperwork to sign to seal the deal. I couldn't wait to start work, even

asking if I could start the next day which they found amusing. We agreed on a start date in a

fortnight's time and I let myself start to believe I could begin to rebuild my life at last.

And that is how I, Meredith James, became a Miscarriage of Justice Investigator at Nothing

But Truth.

Chapter Ten

I had been lost in the mists of reminiscence for longer than I realised but there was still plenty of time before I was due at Starbucks. I was pleased to find that thinking back over those dark times hadn't upset me as much as it usually did. It looked as if I was finally coming to terms with what I'd been through and moving on. Usually when I found myself thinking about those times I tried to use the "thought stopping" technique I'd been taught by one of my counsellors. It's a way of coping with the over thinking that can threaten to dominate your life when you have the type of condition I'd been diagnosed with. When I became conscious of my thoughts racing or obsessive thinking I pictured a huge white billboard with the word STOP written on it. The very act of imagining the billboard dragged my thoughts away from whatever they were stuck on. It often worked but not always.

Today, although I hadn't picked up on the fact I was over thinking my bad times, at least the thoughts hadn't dragged me down. Maybe it was something to do with the fact that the prospect of what I had to do later, meeting Paula Reed, was worse than the memories.

I packed my iPad away and took a deep breath before setting off towards my rendezvous with Paula Reed. I would be very early but planned to spend some time bringing my notes up to date while I waited for her to arrive. But as I pulled into the car park and found a space near Starbucks I spotted the white Merc parked a short distance away and cursed as I realised my chance to do some work had disappeared.

Glancing in the rear view mirror I saw that my hair was a mess and my face was shiny after

the trip into Manchester. Realising I didn't even have a chance to freshen up I cursed again.

No doubt Paula would be her usual well-groomed self even after a full day's work.

Entering the coffee shop I looked around. The place was much busier than I'd expected it

would be at this time of day. I started to wish I'd suggested meeting at the office instead. The

moment I thought that, though, I realised it would have been impossible. Too many people

around who might wonder what we were discussing.

Paula was sitting on a sofa deep in conversation on her phone. I walked over and mimed

"Drink?" at her but she waved me away, pointing at her full cup on the table. While I waited

for my own drink I watched Paula winding up her phone conversation. A hollow feeling in

the pit of my stomach reminded me I hadn't eaten since breakfast but I didn't want to wolf

down any of the tempting pastries while talking to Paula. Finally I was served and went to sit

opposite her. As expected, Paula looked as immaculate as she had that morning. I hated the

low comfy sofas in here, preferring to sit on the wooden chairs arranged round small tables,

but it was too late to suggest moving so I did my best to arrange myself comfortably but

assertively. Paula may have suggested this meeting but I wasn't going to let her dominate it.

"Thanks for agreeing to meet me, Meredith," Paula said, her familiar calm and rich tone

triggering memories I didn't want to confront. At least nowadays I did have the choice of

whether to agree to meet Paula. There had been a power shift in our relationship, no matter

how small it might be. I had to try to remember that.

"You said we needed to talk." I could already hear myself coming across as the sullen

teenager summoned to face a disappointed parent. I needed to nip that in the bud and

concentrate on talking to Paula as if I was her equal.

"Yes. The thing is I wanted you to know I had no idea we'd be working together if I took

over Michelle Ashe's place at Nothing But Truth. What I mean is, I didn't deliberately seek

out the opportunity to see you." I didn't believe a word of that but managed to keep the

disbelief off my face.

"Okay. Well, if that's all then it's fine. I'm good at being professional. Keeping work and

personal stuff separate. So there's no problem. Nobody else at Nothing But Truth needs to

know about our...connection."

Paula smiled. "Exactly. But it's not quite that simple."

"Why? What's the problem?"

"Well, I suppose your interpretation of our connection, as you call it, is regarding your stay at

the clinic a few years ago."

"Obviously. What else could it be? Unless you mean the way you did your best to stop me

getting this job. But to my mind that's tied into my stay at the clinic. As you call it."

I held Paula's stare as a few moments passed with no further comment. Then Paula sighed

and seemed to be searching for the right words to carry on.

"You've been looking into challenging the arrangements for the children, haven't you?"

I was shocked. It was as if Paula could read my mind, just as she'd been able to at the clinic. She was the only person who talked to me about the girls back then. And now it seemed as if Paula knew, or had guessed, my plans to speak to a solicitor about my options. Now that a few years had passed since Daniel took the children away from me I was sure the situation could be reviewed. But why would Paula Reed care? Surely she had no say in my future any more. I didn't need to confirm that Paula's assumption was correct; the horrified look on my face told Paula all she needed to know.

"Well, you need to think very carefully about how you proceed," Paula said. "The children are happy with Daniel. They don't need you crashing back into their lives. They barely remember you. If you want to be a good mother to them just walk away."

"What? Why is this any of your business? You ruined my life and I've done my best to climb back from the depths you pushed me into. I've built a place for myself in the world where I have respect and status. Things I thought I'd never have again. How dare you come along and threaten that?" I had to make a conscious effort to control the volume of my voice. I could feel the telltale signs of losing control of a situation. I took some deep breaths and started to feel better but Paula seemed determined to chip away at my self control.

"You have respect and status at Nothing But Truth, I've seen that in the short time I've been involved there. But how much respect would your colleagues have if they knew? You obviously haven't been quite as open and honest as you like other people to be have you?"

"Jeremy knows everything. And he knows I can do my job. You can't threaten that."

"I didn't say I could. But all it would take would be a few well chosen words dropped into the conversation around the coffee machine..."

"Hang on. I get that you could ruin things for me at work. If everyone found out about my diagnosis I'd probably leave, you're right. I mean, all the talk about the stigma of mental health reducing is wonderful but I'm not sure it's as rosy as people think. You should hear the way some of my colleagues talk about clients with a mental health problem. But I'm not one of those campaigning types who can put their hand up and admit to what they've been through. So, like I say, I'd probably leave and try and find something else. Would you follow me and ruin things again? Is this some kind of personal vendetta against me?"

Paula shook her head.

"Then why? And what on earth does it have to do with whether or not I can see my children?" My voice had risen again and a few of the other people in the coffee shop were surreptitiously listening in to the conversation. I tried to control my anger. "Tell me."

"The thing is, Meredith, it's not just Daniel and the children who will be affected." My puzzled expression urged Paula on. "I thought you must somehow know. Maybe a mutual friend had told you? I know Daniel hasn't bothered to tell you, even though I've nagged him to."

I was aware of a chill rising up my spine as Paula's words competed for my attention –

mutual friend – Daniel hasn't bothered – I've nagged him. My brain was jumping ahead,

guessing what was to come, but it was so awful that I was still denying the possibility. Not

even in my worst nightmares had I imagined this.

"I'd better just spit it out," Paula said. Although her words implied she was reluctant to

deliver the blow, the light in her eyes said she was enjoying every moment. "There's

something I didn't tell you while you were at the clinic. It wouldn't have been appropriate.

But Daniel and I knew each other before your arrival there. A long time before. Old flames, I

suppose you'd call it. Then, long after you left the clinic, long after your divorce, in fact, we

met again at a fund raising event we'd both been invited to and attended alone. It took us both

by surprise. Anyway, the thing is, I've been seeing Daniel for a while now. We're engaged.

I'm going to be the girls' stepmother."

****

I couldn't move. The only thing I wanted to do at that moment was get up and leave the

coffee shop. I couldn't think any further than getting outside so I could breathe. Instead I was

paralysed. Staring at Paula as if I could will her to take back the words she'd just said. It

wasn't possible. How could the two people who had, separately, wrecked my life years ago,

now be joining forces? Then after a few moments a more reasoned response started to creep

over me. What was it that Paula herself had always told me in our clinic sessions? Oh yes –

"It's not always about you, Meredith." That was it. When I was overreacting about something

that had happened on the ward, the psychiatrist would put it into perspective. Not everything

was about Meredith.

In fact she'd gone much further than that. By the time I left the clinic my self esteem had

been whittled away bit by bit until I thought nothing was ever about me. That I didn't deserve

to be considered in any decisions that were made. It had taken months to climb back up to a

level where I thought myself worth caring about. Now I lived in a kind of middle ground

where I tried to maintain control over my work and home lives. But in any situation that

involved others I saw myself as firmly at the back of the queue.

So as I sat there, Paula not saying another word, I began to look at the situation from Paula

and Daniel's viewpoints. They'd rekindled their relationship long after I left the clinic,

apparently. Take me out of the picture and why shouldn't these two successful, intelligent

people have fallen for each other? But there was just a niggling doubt at the back of my mind.

What if Paula was playing games with me like she used to? The doubt must have shown itself

on my face.

"You need proof?" Paula asked, reaching her phone from her bag. She flicked through some

photos before handing the phone to me. The picture displayed on the screen showed Paula

and Daniel holding hands, Paula displaying her left hand with its diamond ring. I glanced at

Paula's hand now and saw the ring. Strange I hadn't noticed it before. My reaction to seeing

Daniel in the photo surprised me. I would've expected to feel at least a pang of jealousy but

there was nothing, which was a relief. I couldn't stop myself asking the next question.

"Do you have any photos of the children?" I hardly dared let myself hope I might be about to

see a picture of my girls. I'd thought about trying to contact Daniel to ask for photos but had

known he would just ignore me.

Paula reached for the phone and switched it off. "I do but I don't think Daniel would be happy if I showed you them. Maybe another day. Let me talk to him about it first. He doesn't even realise we're working together."

Hardly working together, I thought but let it go. It wasn't as if the steering group met that often. Thankfully Paula and I shouldn't need to cross paths too often before Michelle Ashe was able to return.

"Look, I need to go now," Paula said. "But what I was saying earlier. It wasn't meant to come out so aggressively. It's just that I don't think any more upheaval would be good for the children at the moment. If you'll just agree to hold off trying to see them for a while. Maybe until after the wedding. Then I'll back you up in any discussions with Daniel. I promise."

I stared at this woman who had promised me other things in the past. Or more accurately threatened. Could she have changed? I didn't have any choice but to agree to her suggestion. And now all I wanted to do was get home.

****

I slept in the children's room that night. It was a restless sleep full of dreams about Paula playing the part of the wicked stepmother in various fairy tales. I couldn't see the children's faces but they didn't seem to want to escape their wicked stepparent who spent most of her time searching for photos of me and destroying them.

I woke feeling more fatigued than when I'd gone to bed.

Chapter Eleven

2013

Dawn Rothwell had sat in the public gallery of the court throughout every day of her brother-in-law's trial. She'd been surprised, but relieved, that the prosecution hadn't called her as a witness. She'd been interviewed by the police, of course, in the early days of their investigation. She hadn't been able to tell them much. The last time she'd seen Karen had been at their father's funeral years ago. And that was the specific question the young detective constable had asked her. When she had last seen her sister. When it turned out to be so long ago they seemed to lose interest in Dawn. Hadn't bothered to ask if they'd been in touch since.

When two police officers had turned up at Dawn's home that day in August last year, investigating Karen's disappearance, Dawn had initially been bewildered that they'd thought she might be able to help them. They'd told her the bare minimum about the circumstances surrounding the case and they'd only stayed about half an hour. It was clear that the sisters weren't close – understatement of the year – and they were wasting their time. They politely told her they would keep her informed and left as soon as decently possible. When she heard on the news that the police were questioning someone who was clearly John Mitchell, Dawn wasn't surprised.

It was only when Dawn herself was asked to visit the police station and answer some further questions that she started to worry. What if they'd worked out she had a motive for getting rid of her sister? She'd already told them they didn't get on well. Should she turn up with a lawyer or would that make her look like she had something to hide? Of course she did, have

something to hide that is, but it wasn't to do with her sister's disappearance. So far there had

been no hint that they were trying to connect what had happened to other members of the

family. Dawn just had to hope it would stay that way.

In the end she'd gone to the police station alone and it was soon obvious the police were just

collecting background information to build a case against John. Well she was perfectly happy

to help on that score. Sadly there was nothing to back up what Dawn told them so the police

couldn't put it forward as evidence. The positive side to this was Dawn being told she

wouldn't be needed as a witness.

Dawn was glad she'd been left out of the trial, apart from as a spectator. She was happy to be

in the background of the case for now. She'd been determined to show up every day though.

She'd always wondered, when she watched the news, how come all the victim's family

members manage to get into the public gallery each day at a trial that's bound to attract a lot

of attention. Well, in her case it turned out that being friends with one of the court ushers

helped. It had been quite an effort though, keeping up appearances. There had been a couple

of days when she felt like she really couldn't be bothered, but she'd dragged herself there.

And, of course, she'd needed a different outfit every day. There was no way she was going to

give the Prestbury social gossips an excuse to criticise her.

Anyway, she'd been there. Every single day. And she'd stared at her brother-in-law for

almost every minute. She hardly knew John Mitchell. She and her sister had been estranged

for so long she couldn't remember the last time she'd even seen him. She'd emerged from the court each day exhausted by the effort of concentrating on both what was being said and watching his every move.

Was it possible to wish for something so hard that you forced it to happen? If so, John Mitchell would be found guilty. And it wasn't from any sentimental desire for justice for her sister that Karen was wishing so hard. She'd been doing some research. If someone was convicted of murder they couldn't inherit from the person they'd killed. Which basically meant that if John went to prison for Karen's murder, all Karen's assets would pass to Dawn as her closest living relative.

Dawn had wiped her internet history after every search for information about the process. It wouldn't look good if the police decided to backtrack and investigate whether Dawn had a motive to get rid of Karen. The last search she'd done had been just yesterday when she'd narrowed down a list of lawyers based in Manchester. As soon as the verdict came – and it just had to be guilty didn't it? – Dawn would be on the phone to Harlowe Martin, the firm of solicitors who seemed to the best at what she wanted. When a person went missing it usually took seven years to have them declared dead but if a jury had decided that person had been murdered, a judge could declare them dead immediately. Then it would be a relatively smooth process that would lead to Dawn inheriting what was left of everything their father had left to Karen.

And there was another source of concern. She had no idea what was left of Karen's inheritance from their father. But she was willing to bet it was more than she herself had left. She laughed at her choice of words. Willing to bet. In the years since their father's death Dawn had managed to gamble away almost all her inheritance. It was only when her husband had finally given up trying to talk sense into her and threatened to leave that she saw the light. She'd been seeing a counsellor for her gambling addiction and attended a support group at least once a week. If only she'd confronted it sooner. But now there was a solution in sight.

She'd seen the possibility of turning her fortunes around as soon as she heard Karen was thought to be dead and John had been arrested. If it made her some sort of monster that her first reaction to the news was relief then so be it. There was never going to be a tearful reunion between the sisters. Too much had been said and done for that. She'd never liked John Mitchell so she didn't spare a second's thought for him. A plan for her future laid itself out before her but it all hung on the outcome of the trial.

Step one of the plan had been to start divorce proceedings. If her darling husband thought it was acceptable to use threats to leave to get what he wanted, she could do without him. His tantrums about her gambling had snapped her out of the downward spiral she was in but he'd also made her realise she could have a far more interesting future alone. And more importantly, if they were going to divorce she wanted to do it before she inherited anything from Karen. Dawn had always been the practical sister and it was time to put all her talents to the test.

Some people would have hesitated before behaving this way but they hadn't grown up with her father and sister. Dawn had convinced herself she deserved to come out on top at last. Karen had always been Daddy's Girl. No matter how much their father had tried to hide it Karen was his favourite. For every time Dawn had been pierced through the heart by something that made the favouritism obvious, she planned to make the most of this chance to turn her life around.

Ever since Dad's funeral Dawn had been trying to deny what Karen had told her that day. It was something that made sense of his favouritism towards Karen and it had shocked Dawn to her core, making her question everything she had believed in all her life. It was typical of Karen to choose that day, the day that should have been set aside for celebrating Dad's life and coming to terms with his death, to drop her bombshell. At least she waited until after the service and the wake, when most people had left, to take Dawn to one side. Dawn was trying to clear away all the uneaten food and would have appreciated some help, but it never would have crossed Karen's mind to share the workload.

"We need to talk," Karen said and Dawn agreed. There was a lot of paperwork to sort out and they needed to agree a date to meet with the solicitor about the will. Dawn had been having nightmares that revolved around everything being left to Karen, in spite of the fact that Dawn was the older sister. Dad had told them years ago that his will made it clear everything should be split equally between the sisters but Dawn had never quite believed it for some reason.

"Yes, we have a lot to sort out," Dawn said. The sisters had never been close and this polite exchange was an example of how they always dealt with each other.

"No, I mean we need to talk now," Karen said. "You know I've been working on the family tree?" Dawn vaguely remembered Karen telling her about it the previous Christmas. Karen had been swept up in the enthusiasm for genealogy after watching the TV series Who Do You Think You Are? and she'd been in touch a lot more regularly than ever before, asking for anything Dawn could remember about grandparents and aunts and uncles.

"Yes, it's a shame it wasn't finished before Dad..."

"Oh, I showed him most of it last time I visited him in hospital. He helped clear up a few gaps and questions I had. Anyway, never mind. The important thing is this. Well two things. First, Mum and Dad's wedding date and your birth date don't make sense. Not unless you were on the way before they were married..."

"Hardly shocking these days," Dawn interrupted.

"I didn't say it was. But when you add it to the other thing I've found out, it is."

"What other thing?"

"Well, it's not strictly connected to the family tree. I mean you wouldn't document blood types on there." Karen smiled slyly.

Dawn knew something was about to be said that could change her life forever. "Why are you talking about blood types?"

"I noticed on Dad's hospital wrist band it had his blood type as A. And the thing is, it reminded me of when we were kids and you were doing a science project. You needed to know all our blood types. Mine's A and so was Mum's – I remember from when we used to go and give blood together. And it turns out Dad was A too. Yours is B. It means he couldn't have been your father."

Dawn sat down with a bump. Of all the times for this to come out, this had to be the worst. In just a few days time the solicitor would read Dad's will and his assets would be split between her and Karen. If Karen made this discovery public would she end up getting everything, leaving Dawn with nothing? Was that why she was bringing it up now? So much in Dawn's precarious financial situation depended on the inheritance she was expecting.

Amazingly Karen had been satisfied with letting Dawn into the secret, or part of the secret at least, of her parentage. All their lives Karen had looked for ways to upset Dawn or show her in a bad light. This would keep her happy for a long time even if she had nobody to share the knowledge with who'd be bothered. She'd never shown any sign of trying to challenge Dad's will or tell anyone else about it. But from that day onwards the two women hadn't met or communicated, apart from a couple of phone calls. Karen hadn't even turned up to the solicitor's office to hear the will read.

It suited Dawn to break off her ties with her sister. Or rather her half-sister, she supposed she should call her now. If anyone was going to cast any doubt on whether Dad died of natural causes it would have been Karen. She never accepted anything at face value. The family tree stuff was a case in point. Who on earth went down to the level of blood types when they were researching their family tree? Well, Karen obviously. But no normal person would have.

Dawn had cared for their father for the last two years of his life. When his health had declined there was just one thing he was adamant about – that he didn't want to end up in a nursing home. So Dawn's spare room had almost been converted into a hospital room towards the end and it was only in those final days that he had actually had to go into hospital. District nurses and other care workers had helped but a lot of the strain had fallen on

Dawn. By the time Dad died she had to admit, if only to herself, that it was a relief. She didn't know how much longer she could have gone on like that.

She was sure Dad had known the end was close. One day when they were alone in his room, Dawn flicking through a magazine while, she thought, Dad was dozing, he surprised her by speaking for the first time that day.

"Dawn, I want you to promise me something."

"Anything, Dad. What is it?"

"If they end up taking me away – taking me into hospital – I want you to, to..." Dawn strained to hear as his voice started to fade. And then he really was asleep.

Dawn sat watching him for a while. He looked so peaceful when he was asleep and the pained expression on his face relaxed. She wondered what he'd been about to say. Was he going to ask her to help him die? It was what it sounded like he was building up to. Dawn couldn't sleep that night for thinking about her dad's strange little speech. The more she thought about it the more she decided she was right.

The following day Dawn had to call the doctor because her father had taken a turn for the worse. While she was waiting for her to arrive Dawn spent some time searching the internet and found several helpful websites. By the time the doctor had arranged an ambulance to take Dad to hospital, Dawn was sure she would be able to carry out his request.

Dad hung on long enough for both his daughters to visit him several times but then the inevitable happened, hastened by what Dawn had learnt on the internet. The ward was so short staffed there was nobody around to see what she'd done. And she didn't feel bad about it – she was fulfilling her promise to her dad after all. He'd made it clear that he wanted her to help him on his way, so to speak. He'd always hated hospitals.

When Dawn returned home that evening she immediately set about clearing the spare room of all its medical paraphernalia. She knew she wouldn't rest until it was all in the garage awaiting collection. On the bedside table she found a scrap of paper with a scrawled note in her father's handwriting: Dawn, don't forget you promised, if they take me in hospital, to record Countdown for me each day. Dad x

****

The day after the guilty verdict was delivered at John Mitchell's trial Dawn Rothwell was at the offices of Harlowe Martin in Manchester waiting for her appointment to talk to a solicitor about having Karen Mitchell declared dead. She'd worried that her haste might be interpreted negatively but in the end she didn't care. The sooner things were in motion the sooner she'd have money in the bank again. The ink was barely dry on her husband's signature on the divorce papers and that was another source of worry. Could he challenge their settlement when he found out Dawn would be inheriting from Karen? They'd managed to negotiate a so called amicable fifty-fifty split of everything (or nothing in their case). Dawn was starting to wonder if he'd met someone else, so keen did he seem to be out of the marriage.

The young man who came to fetch her from the reception area looked barely old enough to

have left school, never mind to have qualified as a solicitor. He was pleasant enough though

and certainly easy on the eye and Dawn enjoyed a little harmless flirting as they travelled up

in the lift. As it turned out, though, the young man was just there to show her to the right

office and the man she ended up dealing with was way up at the other end of the age scale.

Not unattractive though – a bit of a look of Tom Jones about him.

"Good morning, Mrs Rothwell. I understand you'd like some advice about declaring someone

dead." No beating about the bush here, Dawn realised.

"That's right. You might have been following the murder trial that finished yesterday?"

"Of course."

"Well the victim, Karen Mitchell, was my sister." Dawn wondered if she should dab at an

imaginary teardrop at this point but decided against it. She'd got through the trial by sitting

poker-faced in the courtroom, no sign of emotion. She was obviously good at it so she was

going to keep it up.

"I see. Well if you've done any research at all you'll be aware that to be legally declared dead

a person needs to have been missing for seven years."

Dawn's heart fell. She was sure she'd read that there were exceptions for murder cases.

Thankfully the lawyer's next words echoed her thoughts.

"But with someone having been convicted of the person's murder, it's likely a court would consider an application much sooner."

"Sooner?" Dawn said. "Or immediately?"

The lawyer sighed. Dawn worried he was trying to keep an expression of distaste from his face. But this was no time to be polite or worry about etiquette. This was her future she was trying to protect. And she was sure the solicitor's distaste would be wiped away by the fat fee he would be charging her.

"I can draw up the paperwork immediately if that's your wish?" He asked an assistant to bring Dawn some tea while he went to an inner office to prepare the necessary documents. Dawn sipped her tea from its delicate china cup, wondering if the refreshments would be added to her bill. Ever since her slide into worrying about debt she seemed to consider everything in terms of its cost.

The meeting was over far more quickly than she'd expected. Dawn signed a few papers that the solicitor's assistant brought through from the outer office, the assistant signed as a witness, and Dawn was back outside less than an hour after she'd arrived.

Dawn decided to make the most of being in the city centre. She didn't get into Manchester much these days and she'd always loved the shops and restaurants. Unfortunately all the cards in her purse were over their limits so she had to make do with window shopping for now. She wondered how long it would take the legal system to process the paperwork she'd just signed. A few months had been the solicitor's guess. She could wait a few months. As she walked between the exclusive shops around King Street she made a determined effort to

ignore being so close to one of the largest casinos in the city. She could feel a pull like a

strong magnet and for once she was grateful for having no cash or credit available to her.

Dawn checked her phone to find the nearest Gamblers Anonymous meeting and saw there

was one that afternoon she could go to on her way home. She sighed with relief, knowing she

needed help today. Maybe the trial had had more of an impact on her than she thought. Or,

unlikely though she thought it could be, was she finally grieving for her sister instead of

seeing her death as an opportunity? No, she was sure that wasn't it. Ever since Karen had

dropped her bombshell about Dawn's paternity, Dawn had stopped thinking of her as a sister,

even though they shared the same mother.

Whatever the cause she had to fight the temptation to find a way to gamble. She'd closed

down all the accounts linked to apps on her phone but there were constant invitations to

reopen them. How would she be able to resist when she had money again?

Chapter Twelve

Ever since my meeting with Paula Reed I'd been unable to focus on one thing at a time. I knew it was in danger of affecting my work but whenever I tried to concentrate on the case I found myself, within minutes, distracted by what Paula had told me. Paula's presence at Nothing But Truth was in danger of sending me spiralling downwards and I didn't know what to do about it.

I decided to take myself out of the situation for a few hours so I'd have a chance to think. Without planning where to go in advance I set off in the car and found myself heading south west towards Wales. It was something I'd done many times before when I was struggling to cope but when I thought about it sensibly I realised it wasn't just going to be a few hours of a trip. I quickly phoned the office on my hands free phone to let them know I'd be unavailable for the day. It wasn't as if anyone was expecting to see me but I was happier having made the call.

That feeling of obligation, of having to explain myself even when nobody expected me to, was one of the things that were dragging me down. Maybe I should think seriously about moving on to a different job. I'd already been approached twice recently by people I'd come across in the course of investigating a case. But no sooner had the thought entered my head than I realised I couldn't bear the idea of being hounded out of my dream job by Paula Reed. And the thought of giving Paula the satisfaction of having got rid of me made me even more upset.

I was reminded again of how much I missed having Mick around. A lot of the time we simply shared the apartment and went about our own activities and interests. It was nice, though, to have the option of talking things through with him. I glanced at the phone menu on the dashboard and considered ringing him, but it always worked better when I waited until I had my thoughts in some sort of order first. That's if he even wanted to speak to me. Oh, why did everything in my life have to be in turmoil at the same time?

There were any number of lovely spots on the north Wales coast I could have chosen to park up and go for a walk but I decided to drive on until I reached Colwyn Bay. Memories of childhood holidays always made it feel special there. Parking in a pay and display, I walked on the beach for an hour, breathing in the clean air until I started to wonder what had been so terrible after all. This always put things in perspective and by the time I returned to the car I'd settled my mind. Wouldn't do any harm to stick another hour's ticket on and go for a fry up though.

Eating the giant meal in the cosy cafe I repeated to myself how I was going to go forward. I would not be forced out of the job I loved. I would stand up for myself. And I would focus on the Mitchell case until either John Mitchell was a free man or the case had to be closed for lack of evidence. Simple.

****

"Are you sure you need to go up there again?" Jeremy asked. "At this stage in an investigation don't you usually arrange for the client to phone you for updates rather than a face to face meeting?"

He was right, I knew. And I was finding it hard enough to convince myself my motives were above board without worrying about what Jeremy thought. I wasn't going to fail at standing up for myself at the first hurdle though.

"I think I need to see his reaction to some of the stuff I've found out. You know I've been having my doubts for a while. I can't shake off the feeling he's not telling me the whole story." And yet I still felt a magnetic pull compelling me to sit across a table from John Mitchell and it wasn't just to gauge his reactions. I was so confused about my feelings toward this man and I wanted to use this visit to confront them once and for all.

Jeremy rubbed both hands over his face. He was probably worried by the possibility I might unearth a lie when talking to John Mitchell and he knew dropping the case at this point would jeopardise his deal with the TV company. But he hadn't completely lost his grip on his fundamental belief in Nothing But Truth's mission – to campaign for truth and justice.

"Okay. But this has to be your last visit unless there's a damned good reason otherwise. And make sure the cameraman goes with you, at least to the prison entrance and back. The producer was on the phone earlier complaining about the number of times you've gone off on your own. Your video diary stuff is good but not good enough apparently."

Thankful that the TV producer's requirements had distracted Jeremy's attention from my reasons for visiting John Mitchell, I left his office quickly before he could start lecturing me about professional boundaries. I left the building and headed home to prepare for the next day's trip up to Cumbria.

****

"Some parts of life in here are such a cliché. I'm the guy everyone comes to if they can't read. I'm one of the most educated apparently. So I spend half my time reading letters to lads or writing replies for them. It's straight out of an episode of "Porridge" except it's far from being funny. And I'm next in line for a job in the prison library. The daft thing is before I came here I can't even remember when I last read a book. Sorry if I'm going on a bit but I'm not exactly spoilt for choice for intelligent conversation in here."

This was the most relaxed John had been during my visits so I thought it best to let him carry on, just prompting him a little so I could understand more about his time inside. But even as I thought it I realised the conversation was going beyond the usual boundaries of my role.

"Is there anyone in particular you get on well with? I don't suppose you'd call each other friends in here but..."

"Oh yeah. The bloke I've been sharing with for the last few months is someone I could've seen myself being mates with on the outside. He's a good laugh – always ready to crack a joke if he sees you down in the dumps."

"Well that's good."

"Yes, except he's getting out tomorrow." John laughed. He'd told me before how whenever he experienced something positive these days it was soon snatched away. "I'll actually miss him, and I never thought I'd hear myself say that about anyone in here. Never seen anyone

change from not being able to read to devouring books so fast. Heaven knows what's wrong

with the schools in this country."

I realised we were half way through the visit and I hadn't even started talking about the

investigation yet. If someone was observing us they'd be forgiven for thinking John and I

were on a date rather than a prison visit. It was time to pull myself together. I could examine

my own feelings later and I didn't think I was going to like my conclusions. But for now it

was time to do what I'd, officially, come for.

"John, I need to update you on the case – let you know where we're up to. The thing is we've

hit a bit of a dead end. With Sam Raynor having died soon after your conviction, your theory

about Sam and Karen having an affair goes nowhere. There's nothing to back it up at all. Sam

was acting on Karen's behalf with the finances but all her files are in order. There's nothing

to suggest their relationship was anything but professional."

John snorted with derision. "You've followed up everything she was doing with the money?"

"Yes. Shortly after your conviction Dawn Rothwell got solicitors on the case and they were

responsible for tracking down all the money and transferring whatever was Karen's to Dawn,

once Karen had been declared legally dead."

A fleeting look of hatred passed over John's face before he managed to control his expression

again. "Yes, I know. If I supposedly murdered my wife then her sister didn't have to wait

long to have her declared dead. Nothing I could do about it stuck in here. Oh, I asked my solicitor to put up a fight but it seems Simon had washed his hands of me. My case didn't look good on his record. Funny how he's crawled out of the woodwork again now there's the prospect of an appeal. And lots of publicity from the documentary. All of this even though Karen's never been found." I noted John's use of "Karen" rather than "Karen's body". It seemed he was the only person who believed his wife was still alive somewhere. I remembered the first time we'd met when he'd told me he didn't think Karen was dead. He obviously still felt the same way.

Walking back to the car park after that visit I gave myself a good talking to. I'd finally admitted to myself that there was an attraction between me and John Mitchell but Jeremy was right. It was time to be professional and build back up the boundaries I usually kept between my clients and myself. At least Jeremy couldn't complain about me not bringing a cameraman today after all. Chris had cried off because he wasn't feeling too good and I hoped that would be a good enough excuse for Jeremy. All in all I was feeling much more positive and professional. And it wasn't just Jeremy's advice that had brought me to my senses. Despite the current state of my relationship with Mick, I knew my feelings for him went far deeper than the spark of attraction I'd felt for John.

Two years was too long a time to spend with someone not to put up a fight for the relationship. All those thoughts I'd had at the beginning of our separation sounded stupid even to myself. What did it matter who made the first move to get back together? As soon as I had a chance I was going to tell Mick I wanted him back. If that meant some compromises about work then I'd have to start being a bit more flexible.

Happy that I'd finally wrangled my feelings into some sort of order, I drove back to Cheshire more optimistic than I'd been for ages. And I'd managed to wrap up my early morning visit with John in time to catch Popmaster on the car radio. Respectable scores of 24 and 21 added to my good mood. But that was only going to last as long as it took me to reach the office.

****

John Mitchell walked back to his cell as slowly as he could. The officers were short staffed and he was unlikely to be allowed out for more than an hour or so later. He'd enjoyed talking to Meredith James again. Before Nothing But Truth became involved in his case he hadn't had any visitors and it hadn't really bothered him. Now, though, he was getting used to speaking to normal people again. And to having hope of getting out of here at last. That other woman from Nothing But Truth – Michelle something? – had been the first one to come. But that hadn't been a visit so much as an assessment.

John had spent hours wondering how to act when he met Michelle. Ashe, that was it. Michelle Ashe. A psychiatrist, or psychologist or something. He was desperate to pass whatever test she was doing so that Nothing But Truth would take him on. In the end he'd realised all he could do was be himself, or rather the version of himself he'd invented the day he left home. And whatever he'd said must have been what she was looking for because he found out within a few days that they would be going ahead with an investigation for him.

Reaching his cell, John lay on his bunk to think through that assessment again. It would occupy his mind for a while and help to get him through the rest of the day. Michelle Ashe had been younger than he expected. He knew she must have done years of university and medical school to reach the level of a qualified psychologist, yet she looked as if she was in her early twenties. She had a manner that put him at ease immediately but once she was in assessment mode she was focussed on getting what she wanted as quickly as possible.

There had only been one part of the process that wrong footed John. He'd expected the session to deal solely with the circumstances of his supposed crime but Michelle barely touched on that. Then she wanted to know all about John's family background and childhood. He gave her all the stock answers he'd developed over the years to deal with casual enquiries from people he met. That both parents had been killed in an accident just after he left school. That he had no siblings or other family. That usually brought an end to any chit chat about relatives. But not a word of it was true.

His parents were alive and, presumably, well – he'd never heard any different. They lived in Cumbria with his disabled younger sister. Various aunts and uncles lived nearby and helped out looking after Victoria whenever they could. They were a close family. He wondered whether they admitted to anyone that convicted wife murderer John Mitchell was a part of them? None of them had gone to Manchester for his trial. He'd asked Simon Johnson every day whether they'd been in touch but there had been nothing.

He couldn't blame them. He'd never felt part of the family. Not since the terrible day of Victoria's accident. That's what they always called it. Her accident. John was eight years older than his sister. He'd decided one day to take her for a walk in her buggy to the path around the lake near where they lived. Everyone said it wasn't his fault. They all blamed Grandma for not watching the children closely enough. When John's uncle pulled Victoria from the water he thought she was dead but she wasn't. Partial drowning they called it when he overheard it being discussed. It had caused brain damage and his sister would require lifelong care.

John wondered if he'd done the right thing, lying to Michelle Ashe about his family. But it was too late to worry about it now. When he got out, maybe he'd go and visit them. Try and rebuild some bridges. It was strange to think how close to them, geographically speaking, he'd been all this time.

****

It had been a nightmare drive back – the M6 was at a crawl for miles around Preston. I was starting to regret squeezing in the, not totally necessary, visit. Walking towards the building I checked my phone and saw I had three missed calls. I'd forgotten to switch on the Bluetooth that allowed my phone to work through the car audio system. One missed call from Richard Ferguson, one of the legal experts on the steering group, and two from Susie, who'd left a voicemail. Although I'd be seeing her within minutes I listened to the message.

"Hi Meredith. Just wanted to give you a heads up that Richard Ferguson is waiting in the office to see you. Seems a bit agitated. See you soon."

I couldn't imagine why Richard would want to meet me without any warning and he hadn't left a message when he called. I nipped into the ladies' to freshen up after the drive, then went in search of coffee on the way to my desk. Richard was sitting on a chair pulled up to the next desk, in conversation with a reluctant Susie. As always she was snowed under with work and she looked relieved when she spotted me. Richard saw me at the same moment and stood up. I was shocked at the change in his appearance since I'd last seen him. Richard had always looked young for his age but not today.

"Meredith, I'm sorry to turn up unannounced but could you spare me a few minutes? In private."

I was even more curious now. If whatever Richard had to say couldn't be said in front of Susie, who knew everything that went on in the organisation, what could it possibly be?

"Of course. Let's go and see if the boardroom's free."

We sat at the large table, me in my usual end seat and Richard to one side. He looked as if he hadn't slept the night before, his eyes red and tired. He took a deep breath before he started to speak.

"I won't beat about the bush, Meredith. It's about the email threats you've been receiving. I know who they're from."

If I'd had time to guess what Richard was going to say it would never have been that. I wasn't even aware that anyone here at Nothing But Truth, apart from Jeremy and Susie, knew about the threats. I was speechless for a moment before Richard's words sunk in.

"Well, that's good, isn't it? Tell me who it is and I can let the police know."

Richard shook his head slowly. "It's not that simple."

"Why?"

"Because, without realising it, I'm involved." He rubbed one of his large hands across his eyes. "The person who sent the emails. I...we've been having an affair."

I felt like I'd fallen into some sort of parallel universe where everything I thought I knew was turned on its head. Richard Ferguson had been married forever to his childhood sweetheart. Never a rumour or hint of him cheating on his wife. I tried to absorb the shock as I thought back to all the times I'd been to parties at their home. They loved hosting gatherings of Richard's colleagues and I would have bet everything I owned on them being faithful to each other. And I would have lost, apparently. I wasn't sure how to react but one look at Richard's devastated face stopped me judging him and made me want to help.

"Tell me everything."

"It only started a few weeks ago. A client of mine from a while ago came back to ask for more advice. I was already in a bit of a dilemma because I should've declared my involvement in the Mitchell case. To be honest, at that first meeting when we discussed it I hadn't read the files. And my memory's not what it used to be." I tended to forget how old Richard was, but looking at him now I was reminded. He looked as though he'd shocked himself at how neglectful he'd been. He carried on, "By the time I realised I should excuse myself from the case I didn't want to admit I hadn't done my homework. Stupid. I know that now."

I felt as though I was still missing something. "Hang on. What do you mean by your involvement?"

"When Karen Mitchell was declared legally dead, I was the solicitor representing Dawn Rothwell."

The implications of Richard's words sped through my brain this time. "Dawn Rothwell? It's her that's been threatening me?" I reached for my phone to contact the police. The sooner Dawn Rothwell was arrested for threatening behaviour the better. But Richard put his hand over the phone, preventing me from picking it up from the table.

"Please, Meredith. Hear me out. Dawn's blackmailing me. If you go to the police she'll tell my wife about our...relationship. When she realised the emails weren't working, that you were carrying on investigating John Mitchell's conviction, it seems she decided on a different way of stopping the investigation. She thought she could blackmail me into convincing Jeremy to drop the case. When I told her I didn't have that much influence she asked me to at least make any police action against her disappear."

"So you want me to let her get off scot free? After all the weeks of anxiety she's caused me?"

"I'm begging you Meredith. I've never been unfaithful before and I never will again. Do you think I deserve to lose my marriage over a, well a fling? And if you ever need any legal advice you know I'll do anything I can to help you."

I felt sick. "I need some time to think. But in the meantime I think the least you can do is resign from the steering group, Richard." I didn't wait to hear his reaction.

****

I ignored Susie's obvious curiosity about my meeting with Richard. I knew I had to contact the police and ask them to drop their investigation into the emails and the longer I put it off the harder it would be. But at least this was something I didn't have to do in person. I fired off an email to the address where I'd been forwarding the abusive messages. Just a quick couple of lines saying the messages had stopped and I felt like I was wasting their time carrying on with the investigation.

I knew how I would have felt, receiving such an email after putting in so much effort on a job. I cringed as I thought about my contact reading it – they would feel as if I'd taken them completely for granted.

A couple of hours later my phone rang. The caller name showed it was Mick and a quick burst of adrenaline coursed through my system as I answered. I'd been close to ringing him a few times over the past week, and had only this morning resolved to sort things out with him, but if I'd been thinking he might want to talk about our relationship I was about to be disappointed.

"I've just had one of the tech guys on," he said, obviously trying to control the tone of his voice. This was one very unhappy DCI Mick Bannister. "Do you realise how much time and effort their team has put into this? Do you?"

I wasn't sure if he really expected an answer and decided to just let him rant on. I'd learnt early on in our relationship that trying to interrupt him when he was in full flow was pointless.

"And now you decide what? You're bored with it? Suddenly it doesn't matter to you so they should just drop it? You realise they only took this on so quickly as a favour to me? What do you think will happen next time I ask them for a favour? I'll be right at the back of the queue, that's what."

"Have you finished?" I asked. It seemed he had as he didn't answer. "I received some confidential information this morning that made it clear the person who'd been harassing me won't be doing it any longer. I thought it was in everyone's best interests if the investigation was dropped. I wasn't trying to cause you a problem or make you look bad but if that's what's happened then I'm sorry."

"Seriously, Meredith? Confidential information? Well, that lets me know where I stand doesn't it? We should do you for wasting police time" And he hung up.

Chapter Thirteen

An hour later I was still trying to get over the way Mick had treated me on the phone. I felt as if I'd been slapped rather than just shouted at. His reaction to what I had done was in danger of taking away what little hope I had of a reconciliation. I heard my phone beep alerting me to an incoming email. Hoping it would be something that would distract me I opened the app immediately. The new message was from an address I didn't recognise but it wasn't the victimavenger one I was so used to.

I read the message twice before taking in its significance. It was some sort of cryptic clue to finding some evidence. It didn't specifically mention the Mitchell case but why would anyone have bothered to send it unless it was connected to something I was working on?

My first reaction was to contact the tech team at the police station, the ones who'd been helping me with the threatening emails. But how would they react? It wouldn't surprise me if they treated me like the boy who cried wolf. It took me ten minutes of tying myself in knots about the best thing to do before I realised there was only one professional course of action and I had to just bite the bullet and do it. I rang my police contact.

"Hi. Look, I know I've wasted loads of your time with those emails but I've just received one from someone else that looks like a real lead in the case I'm working on." It sounded weak even to my own ears.

"Hi, Meredith." I could tell from his tone of voice that he wasn't pleased to hear from me but was trying to be polite. "The case you're working on? That'd be a case that the police investigated and the courts got a conviction, would it? Well we've got direct orders from DCI

Bannister to do everything by the book from now on. No favours, okay?"

"Okay, I understand." Disappointed but not surprised, I ended the call. I spent the rest of the

day and most of the evening trying to solve the riddle in the anonymous email. By the time I

went to bed I'd cracked it and knew what it meant. It was directions to a bank in the city

centre and a code to access a safe deposit box.

****

I didn't feel guilty about following up the tip-off without informing the police. I had tried and

they'd fobbed me off. I wasn't going to ignore what could be a vital link in the case just

because my police contact was too busy to talk to me. I'd done all the hard work tracking

down the bank where there would be a safe deposit box that matched the codes I'd been

given. I would turn over whatever was in the box to the police eventually, of course I would.

But first I would find out whether it helped John Mitchell's case.

I phoned Cameraman Chris. This was something that just had to be captured for the

documentary. Fortunately he'd recovered from whatever had ailed him the previous day and I

picked him up on the way into the city centre. For once I drove all the way into the city and

parked in a multi-storey car park. The charges made me wince but this wasn't the time to be

worrying about that sort of thing.

It was a five minute walk to the bank and before we went inside I took a deep breath. I'd

never been into a bank vault before but I'd seen them in films. There was a queue a mile long at the enquiry desk. Whoever said technology was taking the place of banking in person had never been here. Eventually I managed to speak to someone and I was whisked through a door by a member of staff. The room that housed the safe deposit boxes was huge, each wall lined with what looked like locker doors of varying sizes. I was left alone with the box that matched the codes I'd been given. My heart rate quickened as I tapped the numbers into the keypad on the front of the box. I took a few deep breaths before I opened it, telling myself to calm down. It might be nothing.

I wasn't sure what I'd expected to find in the box. But it wasn't this.

Chapter Fourteen

A key. And written on the brown cardboard tag attached to the key a postcode and a house number. Apart from that the box was empty. Chris hadn't been allowed inside the bank vault with me. He was waiting in the street outside, browsing shop windows, and I should have gone straight out to show him what I'd found. But first I sat on one of the chairs in the main banking hall and opened the maps app on my phone. It only took a few seconds to find that the postcode related to a property on the outskirts of Blackburn, Lancashire. My thoughts were racing. Could this be where Karen Mitchell had spent the past few years? Hiding away less than fifty miles from her former home. Well people often said the best place to hide something was in plain sight. But surely Karen would have come forward or moved on from any hideout she'd used back in 2012.

There was only one way to find out how the Lancashire address fitted in. I met up with Chris and we returned to my car where I did a quick piece to Chris's camera about what I'd found. Then it was time for one of those awful drives where the camera was trained on me the whole time and I was expected to give a running commentary of the thoughts going through my head. At least Chris made it easy for me. He was used to this kind of work, having been part of the documentary team for years. He often joked about how easy his working life was now, compared to the years he'd spent as a news cameraman. I was able to relax and talk to the camera as if nobody else was there.

"Okay, I'm going to follow up on the key I found at the bank. I'm not sure if I should have made the police aware of what I'm doing but after my last run in with them I think I'll go it alone for now. Of course the tip off I received, that led me to the bank box, may have nothing at all to do with the case. People contact me for all sorts of reasons and they're not always helpful." I laughed at my own understatement.

It took some time to negotiate the city centre traffic but eventually we made it to the motorway links that would take us to Blackburn by the most efficient route. The postcode from the key label was programmed into my map app which would lead me straight to the property. The further I drove, though, the less certain I was that ignoring the police was such a good idea.

"When we arrive I'll contact the local police," I told the camera. "But I'm still going to give the property a quick look over before I call them. I have a key – it's not like I'll be breaking and entering." I wasn't sure who I was trying to convince. Myself mainly.

As I pulled up in the small square surrounded by stone cottages, I thought I saw someone coming out of the tiny garden in front of the one we were interested in. I couldn't be sure, though, as the front gardens seemed to be shared between all the cottages on that side of the square.

I headed to the front door of the stone cottage confidently, a cover story of being an estate agent ready in case any neighbours stopped me. Cameraman Chris was just a few metres behind, keeping the camera trained on me. He'd get some shots of the outside of the building later if we found anything useful.

I opened the door, pushing firmly when I realised there was a pile of junk mail and leaflets behind it. At last I managed to squeeze through and opened the door wider for Chris. The door led directly into a small sitting room, sparsely but comfortably furnished and with a large TV in the opposite corner to the door. There was a musty smell and a patina of dust on all the surfaces but the place seemed like any other property that had been empty for some time.

Walking through to the kitchen I started to feel an odd sensation. I might have called it a premonition if I believed in such things. Whatever it was I was glad I hadn't come here alone. I gave what I hoped was a confident smile to the camera then walked further into the room over the slate tiles. Chris flicked the light switch, hoping to improve the light quality for his filming but there was no power.

"Hang on a minute, Meredith," he said. "Let me just attach an extra light to my camera otherwise this is all going to look as if we're filming at midnight." There was a small window in the kitchen but it didn't allow much daylight through.

I waited then looked towards the spiral staircase in the corner of the room. It looked as if Chris might struggle to climb it with his large camera.

"I'll nip upstairs while you sort that out," I said, already halfway up by the time I'd said it. I popped my head into each of the upstairs rooms – two bedrooms and a tiny bathroom. Only one of the bedrooms was furnished, with a large bed, wardrobes and dressing table. One incongruous note was the dirty looking sleeping bag on the bed. There was a laptop set up on the dressing table, switched off. The bathroom just had a minimal amount of toiletries and a couple of blue towels.

I went back down to the kitchen. In other circumstances I might quite like it here. Not a thing out on the work surfaces. Everything put away in the cupboards. Yes, I could live with a kitchen like this. Chris gave me a thumbs up and I started looking in cupboards, then laughed.

"It's not as if I'm going to find Karen Mitchell in one of these cupboards. What is she? Hide and seek champion 2012?"

Chris spluttered with laughter then cursed silently, knowing he'd be in trouble for making a background noise. We were both still trying to stop ourselves laughing when I reached for the handle of the large chest freezer in the corner of the room and pulled it open. And suddenly we weren't laughing any more.

****

There was probably an official description for the state of what I found in that freezer, but the only word I could think of was "soup". We had no way of knowing how long the power had been off at the cottage but it must have been a long time. The remains were still identifiable as human but that was mainly due to the sodden clothes almost floating in the large white metal box that had become Karen Mitchell's coffin.

I knew the police and CSIs would refuse to confirm it was Karen until they'd carried out tests but it would be an impossible coincidence to find anyone else's dead body here. I'd called the police seconds after opening the freezer and Chris and I had left the cottage immediately for fear of further contaminating the crime scene, and also because the stench in the kitchen was overpowering. It had crossed my mind that I should call an ambulance too but then I'd wiped that thought from my mind. Now the only thought that kept running through my head was that I was glad we were in Lancashire and not Manchester. No chance of it being Mick Bannister who would respond to my call. And yet a small voice was telling me that Mick was the one person I did want to see. The one person who could comfort me after the horror I'd just experienced.

Once the local police and crime scene investigators moved in I would have liked to go home and put some distance between myself and the grisly scene in the cottage kitchen. But Cameraman Chris was adamant he was going to stay put and film the remains being taken out of the building.

"This scene will have a huge impact in the film," he said. Unlike me he'd been able to return to normal within a few minutes of filming the contents of the freezer. But since he'd had experience filming in war zones and the aftermath of terrorist attacks all over the world, I supposed he was immune to the shock of witnessing dead and damaged bodies.

I knew I had no choice but to wait with him. I'd had it drummed into me often enough by Jeremy how important it was to keep the TV people happy. Chris was on the phone to his director now and I decided I should make use of this waiting time to make a few calls of my own. First I spoke to Jeremy to let him know what had happened. His reaction was the same as mine had been once I'd recovered from the initial shock.

"What are the implications for the case?" Jeremy didn't beat about the bush for once.

"I think it'll depend on whether they can determine when she died. I hate to say this, Jeremy, but finding Karen Mitchell's body might not do us any favours. It might just strengthen the prosecution's original case and mean John's conviction can't be challenged."

"Well, I'm going to need you to step up your efforts to find something else to exonerate him. We can't afford to lose this one, Meredith."

I came off the phone worried by my boss's attitude. I'd never before known him try to steer a case towards a positive conclusion if the evidence was against it. He'd always been the unbiased observer, directing the rest of the organisation but never insisting on what they should find. Things must be worse that he'd let on if he was worried that losing one case would affect Nothing But Truth so badly.

The question of how the time of death would be determined was nagging at me so I decided to speak to Alex Rogers, the pathology expert on the steering group. I had watched enough episodes of CSI to know that what I'd seen in the freezer would not be easily analysed. Fortunately Alex answered on the first ring.

"Hi, Meredith," Alex said. "How's it going?" I filled her in on what had happened, doing my best to describe the barely human remains I'd seen. "From what you say I don't think they'll be able to give a definite date, never mind time, of death. Especially if the body was frozen for some time before the power failed." It was confirmation of what I'd guessed.

"Thanks, Alex. I don't suppose you have any contacts at the Lancashire Police forensic lab do you? It'd be good to get an early idea of their findings."

"I do actually. I'll get in touch and I'll let you know as soon as I hear anything." It was times like this when the steering group came into its own. It wasn't always what the group members knew so much as who they knew that helped. An unofficial heads up about a piece of evidence could be extremely useful.

A few minutes after finishing the call and going to wait in my car for Chris, I saw a black van pull up close to the cottage. The coroner's staff had arrived to take the body away, although how they would do so was a mystery. I soon had an answer to that. The men who'd arrived in the van wheeled a trolley containing the large chest freezer, and presumably its contents, out of the front door and loaded it into the back of the van. Chris filmed the van driving away then spent five minutes or so shooting some footage of the surrounding houses. At last he seemed satisfied and jumped into the car looking pleased with himself and whistling.

"All in a day's work," he said when he noticed my pained expression. "I don't suppose we could follow the van and film it being unloaded at the other end?" One look at my face was enough to answer his question.

I dropped Chris off at his office on my way back home, wondering if I would ever become so hardened by this job that I'd shrug off horror so easily.

****

I let myself into the apartment and headed straight for the shower. All the clothes I'd been wearing were destined for the washing machine as soon as I'd cleansed my body. It might have been my imagination – after all I'd only been in that kitchen with Karen Mitchell's

remains for a few minutes – but it felt to me like I'd carried the stench of death and decay

back with me.

At first I was surprised by how badly the experience of finding Karen Mitchell's body had

affected me but then I realised it was a highly unusual situation for me. I was used to dealing

with the details of horrific crimes but always in the form of crime scene photographs, witness

testimony and forensic reports. The difference in this case was that for weeks there had been

nothing more grisly than pictures of some blood in a kitchen. Now I had seen a murder victim

at close quarters I was finding it hard to process.

As I allowed the powerful jets of hot water to beat down on my back, massaging some of the

tension away, I thought about how important this development was to the case. And I

wondered again who the anonymous emailer was who had pointed me towards the key to the

cottage. It seemed odd that in the years since Karen Mitchell went missing, and with all the

publicity that had surrounded John Mitchell's trial, it had taken until now for that person to

come forward and provide the information that led to Karen's body being found.

I'd given a statement to an officer at the scene about how we'd come to find the body but I'd

probably have to go back up to Lancashire in the next few days to give a full statement. I

made a mental note to request that one of the officers from Lancashire should come to me

instead. Although I was used to driving up and down the country, that trip was one I could do

without repeating. I would be busy for days following up on the implications for the case of

finding Karen's body.

Dressed in pajamas though it was still only early evening, I wandered through to the children's room and lay on one of the beds. I often found it easier to think clearly in this room, surrounded by the things I had bought in anticipation of a day when the girls would be allowed to visit. But now, after Paula Reed's threat to expose my mental health history, I wasn't sure if that would ever happen. I'd pressed pause on my plans to get legal advice about a fresh attempt to make contact with the children but now I felt like a coward for doing so. Would it really be so terrible if my colleagues at Nothing But Truth found out about what I had been hiding since I started work there?

It had taken me a long time to come to terms with my diagnosis of bipolar disorder. Shortly after starting my job at Nothing But Truth I had convinced myself I didn't need the medication I was prescribed and I weaned myself off it. But within months I felt myself being dragged down into depression. I'd had the insight to be able to go to my GP for help, admitting I'd stopped taking my medication. I had switched to one of the other doctors at the group practice after the situation with the medical report for my new employer. I was much happier with the new GP but you could never guarantee being seen by the doctor of your choice so I'd been anxious about going at all.

Of course, the overworked doctor's practice wasn't entirely blameless as they should have been monitoring the drug levels in my blood but I took the responsibility on myself. Within a few weeks of being back on an adjusted dose I was on an even keel again, though I refused the offer of additional medication in the form of antidepressants. I could still remember what happened when I went too high. It might feel great at the time but it wasn't worth the embarrassment and potential consequences of being out of control.

I tried not to think about that time too often but sometimes I couldn't resist it. It was like pressing on a bruise to see if it still hurt – and of course it always did. It was the only time I'd ever seriously considered taking my own life. I mean, actually made a plan for how to do it and come within a few moments of carrying out that plan. I don't know what stopped me but at that time, and for a long time afterwards, I felt as if the world would be a better place without me. I wouldn't have believed anyone who told me I could get through another day, never mind weeks and months, and find a time when I would feel happy again.

Now I accepted that I would need medication for the rest of my life. And I knew that losing those incredible highs that came with my condition was definitely a price worth paying if I was protected from the lows that were literally life threatening. But having come to terms with all this, was it now time to take the next step and admit the truth to friends and colleagues? I didn't feel emotionally strong enough to make such a decision. I would keep my plans for the children on hold until this case was over. Until Paula Reed was, hopefully, off the scene as far as work went. But if she was to marry Daniel, did that make us related in some way? That thought made me laugh and I was relieved to find I could react with humour in the circumstances. I decided to go in search of a glass of wine to celebrate.

As I sipped my drink the apartment felt far too quiet. I missed Mick so much. Would he ever be around to have a heated debate with again? To be fair our discussions over a bottle of red usually ended with us both laughing at ourselves. For the umpteenth time I wondered where Mick was right now. Was he feeling miserable, camping out on a mate's couch? Or had he already found somewhere else? Someone else?

****

It was two days after Karen Mitchell's body was found when Alex Rogers phoned me.

"Good news, bad news time," she said.

"Okay, bad first."

"Like we thought, they won't pin down date and time of death except to say it was between the date she was last seen, 3rd August 2012, and some time in the following year."

"Very helpful." I wished I could bite back the sarcasm as soon as the words were out of my mouth. Alex was doing me a favour and didn't deserve it but the news was so frustrating. At least I wouldn't have to worry about trying to make small talk with Alex when the work part of the conversation was finished. Alex didn't do small talk.

"They won't confirm cause of death yet either but, unofficially, the skull shows evidence of a blow from a heavy object, likely to have caused a catastrophic head injury."

"Again, doesn't help us."

"I know. But the good news is incredibly good."

"Go on." I held my breath.

"They examined the clothes the body was wearing. And in a pocket they found a small piece of paper – damaged by being submerged in the, er, remains. But their documents expert has processed it and found it to be a till receipt with a date on it – 13th February 2013."

"That's the day John Mitchell started his prison sentence."

"Exactly. Meredith, I think you have your compelling evidence for an appeal."

Chapter Fifteen

The TV crew manager had been pestering Jeremy for weeks, ever since the new evidence had been found, to find out when the appeal hearing would be. He didn't understand how slowly the wheels of the justice system turned at times. Jeremy didn't want to frighten him by telling him how long some past cases had taken.

"I understand the pressure you're under to finish the documentary but you have to believe me when I say I have absolutely no influence over the appeal date whatsoever." Jeremy was using his most placatory voice down the phone line but it didn't seem to be having the desired effect. He was totally fed up of running around in circles trying to keep the TV people happy.

"If it doesn't happen soon it's going to completely throw out our whole schedule for the next year. It'll be old news and nobody will give a damn."

Jeremy eventually managed to get the guy off the phone and turned his attention back to me.

"Sorry about that. If I reject any more of his calls he'll turn up on the doorstep. He's becoming my stalker." Jeremy shook his head, only half joking.

"It's ok and I don't want to take up any more of your time but I just don't understand why you don't want me at the hearing."

The appeal would take place in London, at the Royal Courts of Justice, and Jeremy had

emailed earlier to let me know he'd be attending along with John Mitchell's legal team. It

was normal procedure for Jeremy to take the limelight at this stage of a case, win or lose. As

the head of the organisation he had perfected the role of figurehead.

"What I don't understand, Meredith, is why you thought we'd do things any differently in

this case." Jeremy sighed and ran a hand over his thinning hair. "Actually, I do understand

but it would be wrong of me to indulge you."

"Indulge?" I was shocked by the word which was so out of place in our professional

relationship.

"Yes, indulge. I'd have to be blind not to have noticed how close you've become to John

Mitchell and I should have stepped in and nipped it in the bud. I don't know why he's had

such an effect on you but you need to put things into perspective. You've never come with

me to a Court of Appeal hearing and we're not going to start now."

"You're not going to start quoting budget cuts are you?" I gave a frustrated snort, then

instantly regretted it when I saw the look he gave me. Had I gone too far? Then, fortunately,

his face relaxed into a smile.

"Don't play dumb with me, Meredith. You know exactly what I mean. Do I have to send you

on a "professional boundaries" training refresher?" Jeremy's lighter tone told me he was

pulling my leg now. But the subtle warning hung in the air. No matter what excuses or

denials I tried to make I had to admit it to myself. Without even noticing I had started to think of John Mitchell differently to other clients. And it had to stop now. Because there was

another thought trying to edge its way into my brain. The flipside of the spark of attraction

that I had stopped trying to deny when I was dealing with John Mitchell. The thought that had

been whispering to me most nights lately when I was trying to sleep.

There was a niggling little doubt in my mind and it grew a little every time Jeremy Parker

reminded me that we absolutely had to find something that would mean John Mitchell would

win his case. What if? My thoughts kept asking me. What if we're working to free a guilty

man?

****

When I reached home my head was throbbing with the warning of a migraine. I knew the

only way to stop it evolving into a full blown headache with visual disturbances was to lie

down in a darkened room. It was a good excuse to hide from the world for a few hours but it

also happened to be true. If I ignored the warning I would pay for it with two or three days of

pain. Something John and I have in common, I thought, remembering his explanation for

going to bed early the night Karen Mitchell disappeared.

Lying on my bed willing myself to sleep I knew if I carried on thinking about work I'd have

no chance of switching off my brain. I let my thoughts flow towards anything but work but it

was a case of out of the frying pan into the fire. My brain had homed in on Paula Reed and

Daniel. They weren't wasting any time with their wedding plans. Susie had let slip that the

wedding would take place on Friday at Manchester Town Hall. Although Paula had only

been at Nothing But Truth a few weeks she had invited several people to the reception that would be held at a restaurant in the city centre. All the steering group members were invited but of course I was excluded.

"I didn't expect an invitation," I'd told Susie, my tone belying the words. "I mean, Daniel hasn't even spoken to me since the divorce."

"And I can tell you're not bothered," Susie said with a laugh. She was the only person I could talk to about this and it did me good when Susie treated the situation so light heartedly. My tendency to over-think things could lead me to blow a situation up out of all proportion. In this case, though, I was sure I would have been justified in being "bothered" as Susie put it. I really wasn't, though, but there was no way I could convince Susie.

Now, lying in the dark in the middle of the afternoon, I realised there was one part of the wedding arrangements that I was bothered about. Very bothered. I decided I needed to find an excuse for a trip to Manchester on Friday. And if I happened to be passing the town hall or the very expensive restaurant where the wedding reception would take place, well it would just be a coincidence, wouldn't it? And it would also be my chance to see my daughters for the first time in years. As long as nobody saw me what harm could it do?

****

The afternoon nap had done the trick and I was up and about again by four. I gave Susie a quick ring on the pretext of checking if I had left a client file out on her desk (of course I hadn't). I managed to steer the conversation towards the wedding, knowing Susie wouldn't be able to resist the chance to carry on our last gossipy conversation about it. By the time we hung up I knew the time of the ceremony at the town hall and what time the wedding party

were due at the restaurant. I could time my "coincidental" stroll around Albert Square so that

I was able to get a good view as they made their way from the ceremony to the reception.

I somehow managed to concentrate on work all day Thursday without getting too excited

about the prospect of seeing the children. But there was no way I was going to get any sleep

that night. I tried everything to induce sleepiness but despite a warm bath and half a bottle of

wine I was still wide awake when it got to two o'clock.

I gave up trying to sleep at about six and tried to have some breakfast, managing a couple of

mugs of coffee before deciding to get a head start on the rush hour traffic. There was plenty

to do in Manchester to pass a few hours. I kept checking that my phone was fully charged – I

planned to take lots of photos as long as I could do so without drawing attention to myself. I

genuinely didn't want to spoil the occasion and it would be a shame if Daniel spotted me and

things turned nasty.

The wedding was to take place at two o'clock. I travelled into Manchester by my usual route,

leaving my car at Sale and catching the tram into the centre. I was far too early as I'd known I

would be. To kill some time I went to Waterstones and browsed all three floors of my

favourite bookshop, then had a leisurely lunch in the cafe there. Although I'd been unable to

eat at breakfast time I found I was ravenous now. I checked the time on my phone. Still only

one o'clock.

I decided to head towards the town hall – I'd be able to see people as they arrived and maybe

take a few quick photos before the ceremony. A short time later a taxi pulled up and two smartly dressed men jumped out. I gasped when I realised one of them was Daniel. I hadn't given much thought to how I'd feel, seeing him again after so long, and was relieved that after the first shock I felt nothing. Then I had to stifle a laugh as I saw he was accompanied by Anthony, his best friend, who'd been best man at our wedding. What was he offering – two for one?

I was as sure as I could be that, tucked into a doorway a few metres from the main entrance, I wouldn't be seen. I watched as Daniel and Anthony walked up the steps and into the building. A few minutes later another taxi drew up. They'd obviously decided not to bother with wedding cars. Everything about this wedding felt a bit rushed. This taxi deposited Paula – looking her customary well-groomed self in a cream suit and clutching a small posy of roses – and a woman I'd never seen before. The resemblance between the two women suggested she must be a sister. The taxi crawled away into the city centre traffic, the driver scowling as though he hadn't received a tip.

The two women made their way to the entrance leaving me confused. Where were the children? I'd expected them to be bridesmaids, excited at their role in their daddy's big day. Or at least to be attending the wedding. But there was no sign of them. Disappointed didn't come close to describing how I felt. It hadn't crossed my mind that the girls wouldn't be involved in the wedding. I'd been so excited at the prospect of seeing them, even just a glimpse in the distance, and now I was deflated and on the verge of tears. At least I could still feel some emotion despite the numbing effect of my medication.

I thought about finding a coffee shop and sitting for a while until I felt better, but instead I headed for the tram stop. There was no point hanging around when the whole point of my being there had gone.

****

All the way back on the tram I brooded about my pointless mission. Right up to the moment I'd realised the children weren't included in the wedding party I had felt as though what I was doing was perfectly rational. It was only when I was walking away that I started to doubt myself. I could feel myself falling back into a frame of mind where I saw her every action as a symptom of my mental health condition. It was like walking a tightrope between what a "normal" person would do and being completely unbalanced. I promised myself that once the Mitchell case was over I would look up one of the counsellors that had been recommended to me again. There was something about my situation regarding the children that was starting to worry me. Something beyond the fact that it was odd I was still unable to have contact with them. At times I felt close to understanding but it was always just out of reach. A thought that I couldn't quite grasp and examine rationally.

The other thing that had unsettled me was seeing Anthony for the first time in many years. I smiled as I thought back to that other wedding day when he had been Daniel's best man. His nerves about making a speech had turned him into a trembling wreck who kept dashing to the loo every ten minutes. And in the end everyone agreed it had been a great speech. Our wedding had been the full monty church do – Daniel's mother had insisted on it. Apparently she hadn't bothered to attend today's which was odd since her whole world had always revolved around her son.

But that day all those years ago had been magical. No matter how awful things had become in the years that followed, I couldn't look back on my wedding day with anything but pleasure. All the people I loved, and Daniel's mother, gathered in one place and I was the star of the show. For once in my life I had revelled in being centre of attention. My parents hadn't been able to pay for the whole wedding but they'd come to some arrangement with Daniel's parents and they'd really gone to town. Strangely, whenever I thought about Daniel's parents it was only his mother I could fully visualise. His dad was just a vague, faceless outline. And it wasn't as if I had wedding photos to look back on. When Daniel had sent all my things to my flat when he removed me from his life he, or maybe his mother, had kept the wedding album. Perhaps he'd thrown it out. And my own parents had never even seen the photos.

Thinking about my parents almost dragged me down again. My wedding day was the last time I'd seen them before they were killed in a car accident. I'd been away on honeymoon and they'd left the day after the wedding for a "cheap and cheerful" holiday in Scotland. Cheap and cheerful was my mum's favourite phrase and it described almost every aspect of my parents' lives. It was days before anyone managed to contact me to break the news of their deaths.

So whenever I thought back to my wedding I limited myself to thinking about the actual day, rather than the awful time that followed it. A lot of thought had gone into every detail and I knew that although Daniel's parents had held the purse strings, my own mother had helped with the planning. The church was beautifully decorated with flowers chosen to cause the least possible problems (I had always suffered terribly with hay fever). My dress was a scaled back version of something a Disney princess would wear. The reception afterwards, in one of the town's best hotels, went from a delicious afternoon meal to a riotous evening disco. It really had been the best day of my life, only slightly spoilt when I overheard my new mother-in-law moaning to another guest. I'd spent about ten minutes trying to negotiate the small toilet cubicle in my voluminous wedding dress when I heard the familiar tones of Daniel's mother's voice on the other side of the door.

"They don't have a thing in common. God knows what he sees in her."

I didn't hear the reply but the damage had been done. After months of trying to find a way to get on with Daniel's mother I decided there and then not to waste any more effort. Remembering that comment about having nothing in common sent me reminiscing further back in time to when Daniel and I first met.

Day one of my university course in business and law saw me arrive ten minutes late for my first law lecture. The disapproving lecturer made a show of telling me that tardiness would never be allowed in court and pointed me towards one of the few empty seats. The young man sitting next to me gave me a sympathetic look as he moved his books to one side to make room. It was only weeks later that Daniel pointed out to me that it had been him I'd sat next to. He was studying law and our classes sometimes coincided. I'd been so mortified I'd barely even looked at him. So much for love at first sight.

Those first few weeks of term saw me settling in to student life and settling in to the flat I was sharing with Hannah, my old school friend. Although I could easily have commuted to Manchester University from my parents' home I'd seen this as my chance to move out. Daniel was living in one of the halls of residence having moved down from The Lake District where he'd attended a private school. He spent those first weeks pursuing every female within a mile's radius of the university. It was his first taste of freedom and he intended to make the most of it.

It wasn't until our second term that I noticed Daniel. I had thrown a surprise party for Hannah's birthday and Daniel was the only other person that turned up. I knew his reputation by now and expected him to make an excuse and leave within a few minutes but instead he stayed and by the time we had a few drinks down us the three of us had a great time. It was only later – much later – that Daniel confessed he'd fancied me since that first day in the lecture theatre. We finally got together later that term and were inseparable until the end of the academic year. Then we had to face up to the fact that, as his mum was to state a few years later at the wedding, we really didn't have much in common. We agreed to split up for the summer rather than trying to keep things going when I would be working all summer and Daniel was going off for an extended family holiday.

Reunited in the October, neither of us wanted to be the one to admit they'd spent the whole summer pining for the other. In the end Hannah became fed up of us both pouring out our hearts to her. She almost literally banged our heads together and told us to stop being so stupid. We were obviously made for each other so why make things so difficult? From then on we took her advice and even when I was on my placement year, and afterwards when Daniel's course finished a year earlier than mine, we stayed together. Of course, with hindsight I could now see that he had never kicked his habit of pursuing other women but I refused to waste time and brain cells wondering who.

After picking up my car I headed home. It had been a complete waste of a day and I was

determined to work all evening to make up for it. And to keep my mind off Daniel and Paula.

Mr and Mrs James. I wondered if Paula would use her married name. Probably not as she had

such a wonderful reputation as Dr Paula Reed. But if she did decide to change to James, I

would have to look into the possibility of reverting to my maiden name. I'd only stuck with

the surname James after the divorce because I wanted to keep the same name as my children.

Which reminded me. Regardless of the threats Paula had made, I was going to try again to

gain access to my children. I didn't doubt that Paula meant what she'd said about exposing

my psychiatric history. But in the years I'd spent at Nothing But Truth I'd built up a

reputation for being excellent at my job. It was time to trust that my colleagues would see

past my diagnosis and if they were going to judge, that they'd judge me on my actions, not on

Paula's words.

****

Despite my best intentions of getting on with some work on the Friday night, I had ended up

falling asleep over my evening meal and then dragging myself straight to bed. I put it down to

a sleepless night on Thursday and the stress of the day on Friday. I'd made up for it over the

weekend, barely leaving my bed except to forage for food and wine in the kitchen. Is there a

world record for watching box set episodes? Because I'm sure I could attempt to break it. I

enjoyed my couple of days of total laziness so much I worried I was getting used to Mick not

being there.

On Monday I woke early. The realisation that I wouldn't have to see Paula Reed - James? –

again for at least a week, as she was away on honeymoon, sent me dashing to the shower feeling more energetic than I had for months. I decided to go into the office each day of

Paula's absence and make the most of it.

"It's good to see the old Meredith back," Susie said when she spotted me already at my desk.

That made me smile. I knew Susie would have worked out why I was there working away

before anyone else had arrived. As usual a spot of displacement activity was helping keep my

mind off what had happened the previous week.

Halfway through the morning I received a call that shed a new light on the whole

investigation. Alex, the forensics expert from the steering group, was on the line.

"Hi, Meredith. My contact at Lancashire forensics has just sent me something you might find

very interesting." There was a pause, and what she said next made me realise she'd thought

long and hard before calling me. "The thing is, John Mitchell's defence team aren't even

aware of this yet. I need to know I can trust you to keep it totally confidential – otherwise it

might be inadmissible as evidence for the appeal."

"Of course you can trust me, Alex." I was trying to think of anything I might have done that

would make Alex doubt me but I couldn't come up with anything. "I'm dying of suspense.

You can't keep it from me now, it'd be too cruel." I knew Alex would be able to tell from my

voice that I was half joking.

"Okay. Well, when the CSIs searched the cottage they didn't find much apart from a lot of

clothes in Karen Mitchell's size, a laptop that had been wiped of all its content and a pile of

books and DVDs. It looked as though she was using the cottage to hide out in. But hidden in one of the books was an unfinished letter. It was dated January 2013 and started 'Dear

John'."

I felt the familiar surge of adrenaline that came with a new lead on a case. "Is there any way I

can get a look at it?" I knew there would be a delay of several days, if not weeks, before

John's defence team got their hands on it and, hopefully, passed a copy on to Nothing But

Truth.

"My contact scanned it and emailed it to me. There's not much he can do to determine

whether Karen Mitchell definitely wrote it. He kept going on about how in the old days he

might have been able to trace the typewriter a letter was typed on. I don't think he was being

serious but you never know. His job now is apparently to try and lift fingerprints from it but

he's not hopeful. I'll forward it to you but, Meredith...you know how important it is to keep

this under wraps."

"I do. Don't worry." I ended the call and spent the next ten minutes refreshing my emails,

growing more and more frustrated when the message I was expecting from Alex didn't

arrive. At last it was there and I opened the attachment. Just a single page of closely spaced

text. It looked as though the paper had been repeatedly folded and unfolded.

January 2013

Dear John

I'm not sure if I'll ever send this but I've been thinking for a while that you deserve an explanation for what's happened. If everything's gone to plan by the time you read it I will be lying on a beach somewhere very hot. Somewhere people can't be extradited from. I'll have to come up with a way of getting it to you without giving away where we are. Maybe a nice elderly lady from a cruise ship will visit our beach on a day trip. Maybe she'll agree to take my letter and post it when she gets home. My life consists of a lot of maybes at the moment. I don't even know where to address this letter to. Whether you'll be back at home or in a prison somewhere.

As I write this you are about to go on trial for my murder. How weird is that? You must be wondering how on earth you've ended up in this situation. You probably don't think you've done anything wrong.

Sam would kill me if she knew I was planning to send this. Sorry, figure of speech! But she's done so much planning and hard work. All those times I met with her, when you thought we were just sorting out the finances, we were coming up with a way to have a future together. A future without you or any of the things that have screwed us up in the past. She's the love of my life, John. Sorry if that hurts your ego but that's the way it is. When she told me how she felt about me it was the happiest day of my life.

But, and it's a big but, my conscience won't allow me to let you rot away in prison for life. Sam thinks it's a wonderful idea – the best part of her clever plan. But I never meant for it to go that far. I wanted us to leave the country and then let the police know I'm alive. When I tried to talk about that to Sam she wasn't happy. Reminded me of all the reasons we're doing this in the first place. All the abuse you put me through in recent years. Started saying we should scrap the whole plan and split up. I couldn't let that happen so I just went along with whatever she wanted. But once we're far away, living a life of luxury together, I'm sure she'll change her mind. She won't mind when she eventually finds out I've sent this letter that will get you out, if you've been convicted.

Anyway, I suppose I need to mention what we did. So you can show it to your lawyers and they can get you out. We set the whole thing up. We knew the police would suspect you of killing me if I disappeared, especially with the blood and everything. Since then I've been hiding away, climbing the walls, and Sam comes to visit when she can. Sometimes I think it'd be okay if we just stayed here, but the weather's awful and I can't even go for a walk in case someone recognises me from the news.

I read the letter through three times, making sure I had understood its implications. It looked as though Karen had been interrupted before she could include all the details of what she and Sam Raynor had done, and printed off the letter unfinished, but nevertheless it was startling.

Hopefully by now the content of the letter was being followed up by the police. Reading between the lines it seemed obvious that Karen Mitchell had been murdered by her lover, Samantha Raynor. But that word "seemed" never sat well with me.

It wasn't until much later that I had one of those penny dropping moments that made me feel as if I'd been really dumb. I'd been thinking about that letter and wondering why Karen would print it off unfinished. And then it dawned on me. There hadn't been a printer at the cottage.

I phoned Jeremy straightaway, as I would always do when I found something important. But after I explained what it was about, for once he didn't sound pleased to hear from me.

"Meredith, how many times have I told you? It's your job to find evidence for an appeal. Not to question it once you've found it. That's up to the police."

Once the call was finished I thought about it for a while. How many times have you told me that, Jeremy, I thought. None, that's how many. You've always told me to question everything. Jeremy was obviously under more pressure from the funding cuts than I'd realised.

****

I decided on the Tuesday it wouldn't do any harm to schedule a visit to John Mitchell. I hadn't had chance to speak to him since his wife's body was found and it had been nagging at me ever since. I had always been good at convincing myself that things "wouldn't do any harm" when they were exactly what I wanted to do anyway. If Jeremy objected, which no doubt he would after his previous warnings about boundaries, I would justify the visit by saying I'd needed to bring the client up to date. Jeremy knew I didn't like relying on a brief phone call and preferred speaking to clients face to face. As usual I was rehearsing the justification of my actions, which should have warned me that it was doubtful if I should be doing it in the first place.

The one thing I mustn't do was mention the letter Alex had allowed me to see. There had been no official notification to John's defence team about the letter yet and it was vital that nothing happened to jeopardise it as potential evidence. If nothing else, though, the content of that letter had got rid of any doubts I might still have had about John Mitchell's guilt. It would be good to be able to visit him without the feelings of uncertainty hanging over me.

Instead of tying myself in knots trying to work out whether what I was doing was sensible, I asked Susie to contact the prison to find out if a short notice visit booking was possible. I was in luck. If I could get there by twelve it would be fine. Then I had a brainwave. If I took the cameraman along with me Jeremy couldn't object. There'd be lots more footage for the TV company to choose from when they were editing the documentary.

Cameraman Chris was available and glad of the chance to get out of his office for a few hours so we set off for Cumbria. It was a gloriously sunny day and for once the M6 was relatively clear of traffic. The added bonus of being in the car while Popmaster was on made the morning pretty perfect in my opinion. I trounced Chris on both rounds of the quiz and had to rein in my laughter at the expression on his face.

We were halfway there when I started to question my good mood. Yes, the weather was great and so was the company. Chris could tell some wicked stories. But there was a niggling feeling starting to force its way into my thoughts. I realised with a jolt that I'd forgotten to take my medication all the way through since Friday night when I got back from Manchester. I'd been so tired that night I'd fallen into bed without even thinking about my tablets. I was sure I hadn't taken any since. That was four missed days. And I'd been drinking quite heavily, for me, over the weekend which wouldn't have helped matters.

"How d'you fancy taking over driving if I pull in at the next services?" I asked Chris.

"Yeah, fine." He was so easy going. I loved working with him.

We grabbed coffees at the services and I surreptitiously reached out a couple of tablets from my emergency supply in my rucksack. I knew I mustn't try to "catch up" doses I'd missed but I needed to start again as soon as possible. There was no way I was going to risk the side effects of being off the drug. Four days was risky enough. My tablets were meant to be taken at bedtime because they caused drowsiness so that's why I wanted Chris to drive. I hoped he wouldn't be in trouble for not filming the journey but he laughed when I mentioned it.

"There's only so much footage of cars speeding along the motorway we can use," he said. "And I'm sure there'll be another chance to do some filming of you driving another day. It's not a problem."

What I hadn't bargained for was that Chris seemed to be unable to drive without singing along to the car radio. In the end I decided, if you can't beat them join them and, switching the radio station to one with continuous oldies, I sat back and enjoyed being chauffeured for a change. It was good to have something to take my mind off the stupid mistake with my medication.

****

While Chris went for a wander around the neighbourhood of the prison to stretch his legs, I

underwent the usual sign in and search procedures as if I was in a trance. How could I have

forgotten to take my medication for so long? Part of me was glad that the effect this time

seemed to have been to elevate my mood but it could easily have gone the other way. I

wasn't sure I'd survive another episode of depression and that's why I was usually so vigilant

about taking my tablets each night. I'd have to start setting an alarm on my phone to remind

mer. Maybe I was being too tough on myself though. I had noticed that one of the side effects

of the medication was that it affected my memory. I was fortunate since that was the only

effect I'd noticed. Other people had all sorts of unpleasant side effects to put up with. None

of them as bad as the alternative of returning to the rollercoaster mood swings though.

John Mitchell was seated at the table waiting for me as usual. His face creased into a smile

when he caught sight of me.

"Well, this is a pleasant surprise," he said.

I pulled myself together so John wouldn't notice anything wrong. If there was one rule I was

determined to stick to, it was that I never ever brought my health problems into work. My

mind was flitting between my medication and Karen Mitchell's letter, neither of which I

could mention to John.

"Yes, well I thought it was worth coming to update you on how things are going. There's

nothing major since last time we spoke, apart from a couple of things your defence team are

dealing with, but..."

John interrupted her. "But you couldn't resist the temptation to see me again." I was shaken at first but the glint in his eye showed me he was winding me up. This wasn't how I would expect a husband who'd recently had confirmation that his wife had died, to act. But if playing the joker was his way of coping, who was I to judge? I decided to play along, if only to cover up the fact that I had just lied to my client by saying there was nothing major to discuss.

"Of course, there's that too," I said, keeping my voice as light as I could. "But, seriously, let's go through what I've been doing for the past couple of weeks. That way you'll be right up to date in time for the appeal hearing."

The hour's visit sped past. Just before the prison officer came over to tell John to move himself, I realised I couldn't let him go without saying something about Karen.

"John, I'm so sorry about your wife," That was all there really was to say.

"It was you that found her, I hear," he said gruffly. At last there was a small sign of emotion about him.

I was relieved that the exchange was cut short when John had to get up and leave the table. It wasn't as if I could have said Karen looked peaceful, or as if she hadn't suffered. Any of the usual things people say to the bereaved.

I had found it a useful exercise to remind myself exactly where the investigation was up to. That probably wouldn't be enough to justify it to Jeremy though. Hopefully he'd be informed about the letter soon and that would take his mind off what I'd been up to. And that couldn't

happen too soon. After watching John go back through to his wing I met up with Chris and

we drove back southwards. Jeremy had left me three voicemails by the time I returned to the

office and I headed in to see him before going to my own desk.

"I know, I know," I got in first. "It wasn't a strictly necessary visit. But Chris the cameraman

appreciated the chance to get some more shots around the prison. Said his director would be

eternally grateful." The magic words about the TV people being kept happy calmed Jeremy

down and he let me go with a gentle warning to watch my step.

"But Meredith – if we weren't so close to the end of this case I'd be seriously thinking about

taking you off it."

****

I decided to work from home for the rest of the week after all. I realised I was walking a

tightrope with Jeremy at the moment and it was best to keep out of his way. For once

working from home was stretching things a bit as a description. Without really being

conscious of it I had given myself a few easy days, doing a bit of background research and

catching up on correspondence. It was just what I needed after several weeks of long days

and stress. By the time the following Monday came around I knew I had to show my face at

the office again. Surely the documents expert would have passed Karen Mitchell's letter on to

John's defence team by now and that would generate plenty of work for me.

The sight of a suntanned Paula getting out of her car was just what I didn't need that morning. Remembering my resolve to treat Paula as an annoying but unavoidable part of my job, I forced a smile.

"Had a good time?"

Paula's expression changed from her resting face of a slight frown to a beaming grin.

"Oh, it was wonderful, thanks. Went much too fast though."

"Time to grab a coffee before whatever you're here for?" I found the words hard to say but I had an ulterior motive for asking. What newly-wed could resist showing off their wedding photos?

We sat at my desk, steaming mugs of coffee beside us, and Paula reluctantly handed over her phone so I could browse the photos. Susie gave a little cough and I beckoned her over so she could look too. We gave all the appropriate oohs and ahs.

"No bridesmaids?" I asked at last. "I thought you would have wanted the girls there." No matter how many times I had thought about this, I couldn't understand their absence from the wedding. Paula looked at me as if she didn't understand the question. Then Susie had to run back to her desk because her phone was ringing.

"Yes, it was a shame the girls couldn't be there. Chickenpox. Awful timing. So they had to stay at home with Daniel's mum." Paula glanced over to where Susie was now deep in conversation on the phone. "Listen, Meredith. I know we said we'd talk about the children after the wedding. But I'm asking you again. Please don't bother Daniel about them at the moment."

"Bother Daniel?" I was taken aback by the choice of words. "All I want is to be able to see them occasionally. Why should that bother Daniel?"

"I don't have time to get into this now. But please. Let's keep all talk about the children out of the workplace too. It's not really very professional is it? I'm here to see Jeremy. I might as well tell you as it'll be common knowledge after our meeting. Michelle Ashe isn't coming back. The stress of caring for her mother has made her ill and she's under doctor's orders to offload some of her work commitments so this one's had to go. I'm to become a permanent member of the steering group here in her place." My face must have given away how I felt because Paula carried on. "There's no reason why we can't work together, Meredith. And Daniel and I have discussed our future and decided I will give up my clinical work. A couple of little jobs like this will suit me down to the ground, especially since I'm..." She paused.

"You're what?" I asked. Might as well get all the dreadful news out of the way at once.

Paula sighed. "I wanted to talk this through with you properly, not just blurt it out. But the thing is, the reason we brought forward the wedding..." Paula was uncharacteristically stuck for words. Then she apparently decided to simply say it. "I'm pregnant."

Chapter Sixteen

After hearing Paula's bombshell news I had managed to stay in the office for a couple of hours, walking around on autopilot. In the end I realised I had to get out of the building. Pregnant. I hadn't seen it coming but now I looked back over the past few weeks I should have done. The quickie wedding was the real giveaway, though in this day and age who bothered whether you were married when you had a child?

Daniel, that's who. I remembered his attitude to family life all too well. He thought a proper family meant a man and a woman who were married and a couple of kids. He was lucky Paula was prepared to take on the couple of kids he already had. I was finding it more and more difficult to think about the children. Was I feeling guilty because they were being landed with such a horrible woman as a stepmother? But why should I feel guilty when I had no power at all over what was happening?

I drove away from the office, wondering where to go. Not home. If I went home I'd end up spending the rest of the day lying on one of the beds in the children's room.

****

Jeremy had called a special meeting of the steering group to keep everyone up to date with developments on the Mitchell case and to let them know what other cases were on the horizon. They always had to make sure they were up to speed with the details of all potential cases and Susie had been busy for days preparing briefing notes. They could have been sent out electronically, of course, but the group worked best when they could discuss things around the table.

Before the meeting the group members helped themselves to coffee and as they started to make their way to the boardroom Sergeant Dave Harris tapped Alex Rogers on the shoulder and asked her to hang back for a moment.

"Alex, is there any chance we could, er, if you're free that is, er, maybe this evening..." Alex wasn't sure if Dave was trying to ask her out but he was certainly struggling.

"I'm free, Dave. What did you have in mind? A drink or..."

Dave's face broke into a broad grin of relief. "Yes. A drink. That would be great." They arranged to meet at a local bar at eight, then made their way in to join the rest of the group. It was only as she was settling into her seat and exchanging pleasantries with the others that Alex had an awful thought. What if Dave wanted to meet her because he knew about the confidential information she'd been passing to Meredith? He'd never shown any interest in Alex before and it seemed like too much of a coincidence that he would suddenly want to meet for drinks. Alex's stomach was in knots for the rest of the meeting.

By the time eight o'clock came around Alex had worked herself into a state of anxiety which was very unlike her. She was usually cool and calm in any situation. But if a police officer had found out what she'd done it could mean the end of her career. Should she ring Meredith and warn her? No, better to wait and see what Dave Harris had to say.

Dave was a few minutes late, finally arriving a little flustered and full of apologies, blaming

traffic. A few minutes later they were seated by a window looking out at the main street of

the village. It was a great place for celebrity spotting if you were into that kind of thing,

especially if you were a football fan. As it happened neither Alex nor Dave was interested in

football or celebrities. Alex wondered if she should jump in and declare that what she'd done

was justified. She took a breath to speak but before she could get the words out Dave spoke

first.

"Alex, you don't know how long I've been trying to get up the courage to ask you out."

Alex hoped Dave wouldn't misinterpret the relief that must be written all over her face. He

was a nice enough guy but Alex wasn't looking for a relationship at the moment. She knew

she came across as stand-offish but really it was just that she enjoyed her own company.

Her stress and worry at the thought of Dave knowing about her leaking evidence from the

Lancashire forensic lab had taught her a lesson. In future she would stick to doing things

strictly by the book. She had wanted to help Meredith and she was sure it had been

appreciated but it wasn't worth the anxiety.

Now all Alex had to do was try and let Dave down gently. A little speech about how great it

was to be able to go out for drinks as friends should do the trick. Alex wasn't as socially inept

as everyone thought. By the time they left the bar she'd convinced Dave being just friends

was his idea all along.

****

Jack Hill was struggling with a dilemma different from anything he'd come across at work before. When the Nothing But Truth steering group had voted to go ahead with the John Mitchell case, Jack had done what he always did – looked into every aspect of the case. Not just the files of information the group members were given but his own research too.

In the course of this he'd been searching for background information on everyone connected to the murder of Karen Mitchell. He'd been using his Harlowe Martin laptop to do most of his online research and a quirk of the software flagged up a connection between his workplace and one of the names he had entered. It seemed that Dawn Rothwell, Karen's sister, had been a client of Harlowe Martin in 2013. Intrigued by the coincidence, Jack delved deeper and found the details of Mrs Rothwell's application to have her sister declared dead.

None of that was a problem, of course. Harlowe Martin were a big firm with a great reputation. It was no surprise that Dawn Rothwell had chosen them. The thing that was giving Jack a headache was the name of the solicitor she had dealt with. Richard Ferguson. Why the hell hadn't Richard declared his involvement and stepped away from the case? Jack was surprised but most of all he was disappointed. He'd looked on Richard as a mentor over the short time he'd been on the steering group. Now it looked as though Richard either had something to hide or had been negligent and hadn't realised the connection to Dawn Rothwell. Either way it didn't look good.

Jack struggled with the knowledge he'd discovered for days before deciding there was only one thing he could do. Confront Richard and urge him to come clean.

****

The appeal date was set. The defence legal team had already presented the new evidence of the dated receipt found on Karen Mitchell's body and the letter found hidden in a book at the cottage. Together the two documents had led to the appeal. The actual hearing should be a straightforward review of that new evidence and whether it made John Mitchell's original conviction unsafe. After just a few hours he would either return to prison to carry on with his life sentence or he would walk out of the court a free man with his conviction quashed.

John didn't sleep the night before the hearing. He'd been brought down to London earlier and was temporarily housed in the remand wing of the nearest prison to the Royal Courts of Justice. He lay on his bunk listening to his cellmate snoring until the grunts became the backing soundtrack to the images of his future he could see in his mind's eye. The scenario where he went back to prison in Cumbria, defeated and humiliated wasn't allowed to feature. Instead he entertained himself imagining how he would campaign to find Karen's real killer. The copy of the letter that his lawyer had shown him a few days ago had his defence team fired up. All his team agreed it looked as though Samantha Raynor had lured Karen into a relationship and framed John in order to steal the couple's money. The fact that Sam was also dead complicated matters but apparently shouldn't stop John's conviction being overturned.

Maybe they'd commission a sequel to the documentary they'd been making about his fight to clear his name. They'd be sure to be interested in a follow up. What was it Meredith James had said last time he spoke to her? Something about how the TV director had said John was the most photogenic subject they'd ever had. He could become a minor celebrity – one of those people who pops up on Sky News to comment on the day's newspapers. His specialist subject could be miscarriages of justice.

As the sky outside the tiny cell window started to lighten John began to think about more practical matters. Somewhere to live. He wasn't sure he could face living at the old house. He knew it had been closed up since his conviction. There had been some legal wrangling over whether it should be included in the inheritance Dawn had prised from him. A half smile played over John's face as he thought about the pleasure he would take in wresting everything back from Dawn. He'd asked Meredith to get one of the Nothing But Truth legal experts looking into that for him and their opinion was favourable. Providing she hadn't managed to spend it all John should be able to retrieve whatever was left.

He knew he should feel bad wondering about money when it wouldn't bring his wife back, but he salved his conscience by thinking about how unusual his situation was. He hadn't been allowed to grieve for his wife at all. Worse than that he'd been blamed for her death and punished for years. Surely he could now console himself with the prospect of a comfortable life ahead. He didn't know the exact amounts involved but from what he remembered Sam Raynor saying, he should be very well off.

Sounds of activity outside on the landings permeated the thick cell door and John swung his legs round and got up from his bunk. He grabbed his towel and toiletries and was ready when the door opened.

"Rise and shine," the officer said, jumping back slightly when he saw how close to the door John was standing. Without a word John set off towards the showers. Had to look his best today. He started to whistle, a little off tune, "Oh what a beautiful morning".

****

I had finally come to terms with the fact I wouldn't be accompanying Jeremy to London. In fact, the more I'd pondered my worries and doubts about the case I'd felt relieved not to be involved. I planned to spend the day at the office, catching up on paperwork and sorting out my files. Not that they needed any sorting out as I was always meticulous about leaving everything written up and double-checked with Susie regularly that everything was up to date. But it was my excuse for being there and I was sticking to it.

"We can have a long gossipy lunch at our desks," Susie said gleefully when I told her what I planned to do with my day. "When Jeremy's away his underlings will play."

I knew how hard Susie worked, especially now she had to deal with admin for the whole team, and I knew Jeremy wouldn't begrudge us a couple of hours' break at lunchtime. The CEO himself had left for London on the last train out of Stockport the previous evening. He would have stayed over in the cheapest hotel he could find. He always practised what he preached so keeping costs to a minimum was important. However, he'd let me know how confident he was about the outcome of the appeal.

"Two first class tickets back on the five o'clock from Euston." Jeremy flourished his phone that showed the ticket confirmation. I knew he wouldn't have booked them if he hadn't known he could cancel at the last minute but I appreciated the gesture and the camera crew loved it. It was odd how we'd all got so used to the TV people being there that we sometimes forgot about them. Fortunately they'd all travelled to London on the same train as Jeremy. I knew Chris lived in London and was looking forward to a night in his own bed. Today the rest of the Nothing But Truth staff could relax a little without worrying about everything they said or did ending up on film.

Of course the appeal judges could make the hearing run over into another day but it was unlikely in this case. The legal team were more confident than I'd ever seen them, both about the decision and the fact that the hearing was unlikely to take more than a few hours.

"What do you think John Mitchell will do after the hearing?" Susie broke into my thoughts and I was taken aback by how closely her question mirrored my own musings.

"Well if Jeremy's bought him a train ticket I suppose he plans to bring him back here." I registered my increased heart rate as I said the words. "It'll be mid-evening before they get back though. Are you planning on hanging around?"

Susie laughed. "You're joking aren't you? I'll be on the starting blocks out of here at five. It's the first chance I've had to leave on time for months and I'm not missing it. Do you have any idea how much earache I've been getting from Scott for the hours I've been putting in?"

I was aware that once Susie got home her hard work didn't stop. Susie and Scott's only child had special needs and, though she was now school age and attended a specialist school, Susie's evenings were taken up with paying constant attention to her daughter. There was little respite at night because her daughter's condition meant she rarely slept longer than a couple of hours at a time. Susie had confided a while ago that the strain was affecting her marriage so I could understand why she wanted to head home as soon as she could.

"I sometimes take for granted my flexible hours," I said. "You should speak to Jeremy about working out a similar arrangement for your role. He knows you'd get the work done and you wouldn't take advantage."

"Yeah, maybe. But, you know, sometimes having the excuse of pressure of work gives me a way of escaping home." Susie's eyes briefly brimmed with tears. It was the first time I had heard her say anything that remotely sounded like she wanted to escape her home life.

It crossed my mind that this might be a good chance to tell Susie about my situation with the children. It would distract Susie from her own problems and it might do me good to be able to share for once. I'd felt myself becoming more friends than colleagues with Susie for a while. But in the end I couldn't bring myself to say the words. I was so used to keeping that part of my life hidden I couldn't break the habit. It seemed like, of all people, Paula Reed was the only one I could talk to about the girls.

"I'm sorry," Susie continued, snapping my attention back to her. "I'm just tired; don't take any notice of me. There is something I've been thinking about, though"

"Oh, intriguing. Go on."

"Well, I've been getting a bit bored with this job. I could do it standing on my head. I've always fancied the investigator role. Like you say, the hours are more flexible and it's certainly a lot more interesting than what I do."

"How can I help?"

"Last time I brought it up with Jeremy he gave me his usual answer. He reckons good admin staff are worth their weight in gold and doing anything else would, how does he put it? Oh, yes, it would blur my boundaries."

"That's rubbish. He just doesn't want to lose you as PA because you're so brilliant at it. And you're right, you'd be a brilliant investigator too. But with all the stuff about budget cuts I can't see him considering it at the moment."

"Exactly." Susie looked defeated.

I thought for a moment. "How about if I gave you some unofficial training sessions? We can make a start while Jeremy's out of the way and then slot some in whenever you can get away from home. And in the meantime, how about we arrange that girls' night out we're always talking about?"

The smile that spread across Susie's face was the only answer I needed. I wondered whether to try and encourage Susie to open up more about her home situation, but I could tell she didn't want to dwell on her own problems any longer. I made a mental note to make sure I gave her an opportunity to offload whenever we had one of our "training sessions", which I was now looking forward to immensely. But almost immediately I started to wonder if my idea was such a good one after all. I found it hard to delegate, always feeling as if I'd rather do things myself. What if I trained Susie but then couldn't hand things over to her? Susie would think I didn't trust her to do the job properly.

For now I asked Susie to check that all my reports were up to date, to give her something to take her mind off what had been troubling her before we started to talk. After half an hour I brought Susie a coffee and tackled the subject of how my obsessive compulsive traits affected my work. It didn't surprise me that Susie understood straightaway.

"Let's just see how it goes, shall we? As long as Jeremy gives it the go-ahead I'm still keen to have a go. I promise not to be thin-skinned if you promise to try and hand over some jobs to me."

"Deal," I said, thinking for the millionth time how lucky I was to work with someone like Susie. We were opposites in almost every way but somehow made a great team.

For the next few hours, I buried myself in proofreading reports and checking budget figures – exactly the sort of detailed work that appealed to my need for perfection in everything I did in my job. With luck it would keep me busy until Jeremy returned. I sent up a silent prayer that he wouldn't be alone.

****

For the first time in a long while John Mitchell was feeling nervous and unsure of himself. It was such an alien feeling he wasn't handling it well. He'd arrived at the court building with two security guards and then been handed over to meet with his legal team in a small room near the court where the hearing would be held.

"Are you okay, John?" Jeremy Parker asked. It was the first time John had met the boss of Nothing But Truth. He didn't know what he'd expected but it was something a bit more imposing than this guy.

"I'm fine. Didn't sleep too well."

"That's perfectly understandable. Well, let's hope we're out of here in a few hours and you can catch up with a couple of hours sleep on the way back up north."

It wasn't tiredness bothering John, it was these odd feelings of nervousness. He realised suddenly what the problem was. The lack of control he'd suffered from all these years in prison had been magnified a hundred times today. People he'd never met and would never meet again were about to decide the rest of his life. Once he'd put his finger on the problem he felt instantly better. He switched it round. There was nothing he could do to change what was about to happen. They'd already made the decision – the hearing was so they could announce it. There was no point worrying about something he couldn't change, so he didn't. Was he turning into some sort of Buddhist?

When his name was called they made their way into the court room. John sat where he was told to and watched as his defence team set up camp on one of the tables. A fleeting thought about who was paying them all passed through his mind but again he refused to worry about it. If he walked out of here free it would be worth any amount. If he didn't – he wouldn't really give a damn what happened to them.

The head judge started reading out a statement that contained their decision. This was it.

****

While John Mitchell's future was being decided in London, Jack Hill and Richard Ferguson were halfway round the most exclusive golf course in South Manchester. It was a glorious day and the course was busy. Richard had been a member of the club for years and Jack had rung him a few days earlier, asking if there was any chance of a round. They'd always got on well – Richard reminded Jack of his late father and Jack was like the son Richard and his wife had never had. Richard had a suspicion that Jack was letting him win this morning.

"Come on, lad, out with it. What's up?"

Jack considered pretending there was nothing up at all. If he didn't say anything they could just carry on as they always had. But he knew that would be wrong. He needed to clear the air with Richard, no matter what the consequences. While he was lining up to hit his ball from the next tee, he decided it was now or never.

"I know, Richard," he said.

"Know? Know what?" Richard's heart rate shot up and he felt the familiar burning pain in his chest that was there more and more lately. He knew straightaway what was coming but that didn't stop him panicking. Flashes of memory like scenes from a film flitted through his brain. Dawn Rothwell had been the most exciting and, yes, flattering thing that had happened to him in years. He had to admit, to himself if nobody else, that he hadn't needed much tempting when she suggested meeting up. He'd tried to explain away some of the guilt by telling himself he hadn't had much opportunity for sexual gratification in recent years. He and his wife had been childhood sweethearts and, though they'd enjoyed a good physical relationship for years, she had lost interest in that side of their marriage far sooner than he had.

When he'd first met Dawn a few years ago, when she came to him about her sister's estate, there hadn't been a hint of attraction from her. That should have given Richard a clue when she contacted him recently and suggested getting together. And yet there hadn't seemed anything fake or forced about their short-lived affair, which had amounted to just a few afternoons spent in budget hotel rooms. Dawn was either a brilliant actress or she'd enjoyed the encounters just as much as him. But there he went again – making more of it than he now knew it was. Just a set up so Dawn could blackmail him.

How on earth had Jack found out? And what would he do with the knowledge? Richard decided to take the initiative and hopefully, in doing so, neither of them would have to spell out exactly what it was that Jack knew.

"Look, Jack. You're a young man with a brilliant future ahead of you. Unfortunately I'm an old man with an average past behind me. Learn from my mistakes. If I could take back what I did I would. But you have to be realistic in the legal world. I'm going to step down from Nothing But Truth. I've already had a word with Jeremy and there's a couple of people from Harlowe Martin I recommended he might want to choose from for my replacement."

Jack looked embarrassed. He didn't know what he'd wanted to achieve but it wasn't this. Although Richard's full time legal career had already ended, Jack knew how proud he was of his involvement with Nothing But Truth. And what would he do with himself? But he could see that the decision had been made and he knew Richard well enough to realise he would never change his mind.

"I'm sorry, Sir," Jack said. Where on earth had the "Sir" come from? But it seemed to fit the situation. "I just stumbled over what had happened and I didn't know what to do. But everything you've taught me was telling me to come out and talk about it. Not to sweep anything under the carpet. But just for my peace of mind – was it deliberate or just an oversight when you didn't declare a conflict of interest in the Mitchell case? With Dawn Rothwell having been a former client I mean."

No mention of the affair. The relief was overwhelming. He could, hand on heart, tell Jack that he had simply been careless or negligent, depending on how you looked at it. All that was left to do then was to reassure his protégé.

"You've done the right thing, son. I'm proud of you. Now come on, we'll be in trouble if we hold up the game any longer. Oh, and I know Mrs F is hoping I'll be able to persuade you to come back with me for dinner later."

****

Pam Philips might have been only a lay member of the steering group but, in the absence of a particular field of expertise she had to concentrate on, she was able to notice more about what was going on than the other members. She'd been aware for a while that things were not as they should be but she'd put it down to the changes in the organisation necessitated by a lack of funds. Now though, she was sure there was more to it and she phoned Jeremy Parker, knowing she'd have a captive audience while he was on the train back from London. After a brief discussion about the result of the appeal, Pam switched the subject to the reason for her call.

"I'm not sure how long the steering group can carry on like this," she said. Pam always got straight to the point and the difference to Jeremy's beating about the bush style could sometimes be comical. Lately, though, there had been few opportunities for laughter. She carried on, "I'm not one to gossip but it seems like there are lots of cliques forming and separate meetings being organised. I've seen it happen at other places I've worked and I have to say it's time for some strong leadership to put things back on course."

"You're right, Pam, but I'm not sure what I can do about it."

"I know they'll all groan and complain but I think we need one of those away days we used to have. Do you think the stretched budgets can run to it?"

"Let me think about it. The documentary director mentioned something the other day about doing some filming for a follow up. If they'll pay for it we'll do it. In the meantime I need to concentrate on what I'm going to say to everyone about today."

Chapter Seventeen

"I'd invite you over for a glass of champagne to celebrate – but is that in bad taste considering champagne was the last thing Karen ever bought?"

It felt like we were surrounded by a mob of reporters and I only just caught what John had said.

"Let's go inside and talk in my office," I shouted above the noise. "Or would you rather enjoy your moment and we'll speak later, or another day?"

I had learnt from previous cases that I needed to keep a distance from a client who had just had their conviction overturned. It was a highly charged emotional situation and clients sometimes saw their relationship with me as more personal than it was. These coming hours and days were when this was most important. I couldn't let John Mitchell see that I'd been attracted to him, even for a moment. He had a period of adjustment ahead of him and he would need professional help to cope with it but not the kind of help I could offer. My role in John Mitchell's story was over but standing in front of dozens of reporters this was not the moment to clarify that point.

Jeremy had already made a statement and told the reporters nothing further would be said tonight but when he went inside the building John Mitchell had stayed outside on the steps to allow the photographers to do their job. Jeremy had sent me down to coax him inside and at last I seemed to have managed it.

"Okay, show me your office then. I'd love to see where you masterminded my release."

John's manner was making me feel uneasy, though I couldn't put my finger on why. Who

knew how they'd react in a similar situation?

As we made our way through the main office towards my desk, Jeremy intercepted us and

guided John towards his own office. I thought I might faint with relief. Although I'd stayed

behind to greet them all I could think of now was putting some space between myself and

John until he'd adjusted to his new situation. I hurried over to my desk planning to grab my

laptop and rucksack and leave. But just as I was stuffing the computer into the bag my mobile

rang. Dawn Rothwell's name was showing on the screen and I was too intrigued to reject the

call.

I knew I was sometimes too tolerant for my own good. When Dawn Rothwell's breathy voice

pleaded with me to see her urgently I should have ended the call and ignored her request. But

whether it was the euphoria of winning the appeal or just my nature, I instead invited Dawn

to the office. It was late in the day and most people had already packed up and gone home but

I knew Jeremy was still there. I didn't like being the last one in the old building but I knew

the procedure for securing the building if necessary.

By the time Dawn arrived it looked as though I would, after all, be the one locking up for the

night. Jeremy had come over to my desk to say goodnight and another well done ten minutes

earlier.

"Where's John?" I asked him. I hadn't seen John leave Jeremy's office.

"Oh, he said he wanted some fresh air and to stretch his legs. I expect he just wants to enjoy his first hours of freedom."

That seemed very odd to me. Someone who'd just been released after several years in prison wouldn't usually want to be on their own. But who was I to say how John should react? "Where will he stay tonight? Surely he's not planning to go back to his old house?"

"No, no. I told you about the deal he's signed up to with one of the papers? Well they've got him a room at a hotel in Manchester. I slipped him some cash so he should be able to get there okay and I'll catch up with him in a couple of days. The TV people will want him."

"Of course. Okay goodnight then. I've got Dawn Rothwell coming in to see me. Shouldn't take long."

****

"Thanks for seeing me," Dawn said. "And let me just say again how sorry I am about all the trouble I caused." I was proud of myself for not immediately saying "It's fine, don't worry." It wasn't fine. By rights I should have reported Dawn to the police for the harassment aimed at me over the last few months. Why had I let Richard convince me not to?

"What was the urgent matter you wanted to talk to me about? It's late and I'm shattered. I could really do without this."

Dawn ran a hand through her curly hair and looked as if she was trying to find the right words. "The thing is, even though he's won his appeal and he's out now...I still think John's guilty." I sighed. I'd stayed behind and waited for Dawn for this? The woman was obviously in denial. But now Dawn had started she couldn't shut up. "There's evidence that didn't come out at his original trial because there was no proof..." I held up a hand.

"If there was no proof then it wasn't evidence," I said. Dawn shook her head.

"Karen contacted me months before she died. She never told John or anyone else she'd been in touch. Everyone thought we hadn't spoken since Dad's funeral. But she rang me and told me about the emotional abuse she'd been suffering throughout her marriage. She'd contacted Women's Aid but used a false name so like I said there was no proof. I didn't know what name she'd used or even which refuge she'd contacted."

I tried to be patient. "I know how desperate you were to keep John in prison, Dawn. But you have to face facts. He's out now and his appeal went through all the proper procedures. Whatever you think, in the eyes of the law John's an innocent man." The defeated expression on Dawn's face stopped me continuing with what I'd been about to add. That John Mitchell would most likely receive a large compensation payout for the years he'd spent in prison, as well as probably claiming against Dawn for the inheritance she'd received from her sister's estate.

"What I don't understand, though," I said. "And perhaps you can explain it. Those messages from victimavenger started weeks before I began looking into John's case. I thought at first they were from someone connected to my previous case. How did you know Nothing But Truth would be investigating John's conviction?"

Dawn's face betrayed an internal struggle. She'd already admitted to sending the messages but she wasn't keen on helping me understand the premeditation behind her actions. In the end she obviously realised she had nothing to lose.

"The TV documentary. They started preparing the ground for their film months ahead of any work you were doing. As soon as your PA started preparing a file, Jeremy Parker was in touch with the TV company so they could get a head start." I thought back to that steering group meeting when Jeremy had told us the TV people had contacted him. A little economical with the truth perhaps. Dawn carried on. "They had to get consent from various people, including me, to include them in the documentary. They contacted me and came round for an introductory chat and I was horrified to realise how confident they were that John would win an appeal and have his conviction overturned. But I couldn't come out and say so without looking like a monster who wanted to keep an innocent man locked up. That's when I came up with the idea of putting you off the case."

"But it was a waste of effort because I thought it was related to that earlier case." I thought I understood now. Dawn stood to lose everything that had come to her from her sister's estate. But actually I still didn't understand. "Hang on, if you were motivated by the prospect of losing your inheritance from Karen, I don't get it. You were both left very well off by your father, weren't you?"

Dawn lowered her eyes and sighed heavily. I thought I saw a hint of something – guilt? – on her face. "The thing is, I've pretty much spent all that. By the time of John's conviction I was already heading towards selling things off to put food on the table and things were starting to look desperate. I know this sounds awful but when I found out I could apply to have Karen declared legally dead, and inherit because John wasn't able to..."

"It seemed like a way out of your mess," I finished for her, feeling slightly sick at the thought of a sister thinking that way.

"Exactly. And because of John's murder conviction I was able to have her declared dead sooner than the standard seven years for a missing person. Although it wasn't a foregone conclusion, amazingly. The courts can decide someone's been murdered and yet still not declare them dead. Fortunately I had excellent legal advice and it all went smoothly."

I noticed that Dawn's ashamed demeanour had disappeared as quickly as it came. She seemed to be enjoying telling this part of the story. As if she was proud of being so clever as to have got her hands on Karen's money.

"And you repaid that excellent legal advisor by blackmailing him."

"It was his choice to jump into bed with me. He didn't need much persuading anyway. I don't think it was asking too much for him to do a few favours in return."

I was speechless and Dawn returned to what concerned her the most – the money.

"There was something odd, though," Dawn said. "Once all the financial details had been worked out and everything was transferred to me, it was substantially less than I would have expected. I know it came up in court that John had been spending their money like water but even so, like I said, it wasn't as much as I'd hoped for. I'm sure there's still some hidden away."

"But that's not your concern now, is it," I asked. I was finding it hard not to twist the knife and make Dawn suffer. But that was unprofessional. "All I mean is, once John sorts himself out he'll be claiming Karen's money back from you."

Dawn laughed but it was a humourless sound. "Good luck to him. After paying off some debts and, well let's say enjoying a few treats over the last few years, there isn't much left. I hope for his sake he had hidden some away like I suspected. Otherwise he's going to have to join the real world and work for a living."

I was tiring of being in Dawn's company. I'd rarely met a more self-centred person. It was Dawn who needed to face up to the real world as she called it. But somehow I suspected Dawn would land on her feet. People like her always did. Again I regretted asking the police to drop their investigation into the malicious messages. It might have done Dawn Rothwell good to have her own day in court and face up to the consequences of her actions.

But was I right to disregard Dawn's theories about John still being guilty? Although I was reluctant to acknowledge it Dawn's fears were echoing the thoughts that had been worrying me earlier. There had definitely been something about John Mitchell's manner that didn't fit with an innocent man who'd been freed after years in prison. There was an arrogant swagger about him that I had found threatening. But it would do nobody any good right now to let Dawn think I agreed with her.

"Is there someone I can call to come and collect you?" I asked. Dawn didn't answer. She just picked up her bag and left the room, her shoulders slumped and with a slightly veering gait. Perhaps recent events had affected Dawn more deeply than I had thought. Although I just wanted to see the back of her, I decided I should at least make sure she made it out of the building safely.

I stood at the top of the stairs watching Dawn let herself out of the main door, making sure I heard it click shut after her. I didn't like being in the old building alone but at least I could be sure nobody who shouldn't be there could let themselves in. When I'd started work at Nothing But Truth some of my colleagues had tried to scare me with stories about the building being haunted. Apparently the building had been used as an orphanage many years ago and there were stories of children being mistreated. Fortunately I didn't scare easily and didn't believe in ghosts. I was more bothered about living people who might want to harm me.

That thought took me back yet again to thinking about Paula Reed. If only, that day when Paula had appeared at the steering group meeting, it had instead been a ghostly apparition that I'd seen at the top of these very stairs. Shaking my head at the silly thought that was so unlike me, I went back to my desk.

I sat for a while considering what to do next. I was trying to resist the temptation to phone Mick. Now the case was finally wrapped up I might be able to take a few days off. If there

was any chance of resurrecting our relationship I wanted to devote my full attention to it.
What's the worst that could happen I asked myself, reaching across to my desk phone. I
began to doubt myself as I listened to the ringing and the tell-tale change of tone as the call
was diverted to voicemail. I couldn't be bothered leaving a message. Mick would see my
work number on his missed calls list and – then what? He'd either call me back or choose to
ignore me, which would be an answer in itself.

As I reached across the desk again to replace the receiver I knocked a neat pile of papers to
the floor then scrabbled about picking them up. My attention was drawn to a photocopy of
the receipt that had been found in Karen Mitchell's pocket and I remembered my last
conversation with John Mitchell. What was it he'd said?

"I'd invite you over for a glass of champagne to celebrate – but is that in bad taste
considering champagne was the last thing Karen ever bought?"

Only now did I realise – I hadn't told John what the receipt was for, only that a receipt had
been found. Had the items on the receipt been mentioned at the appeal? Possibly, but unless I
was mistaken there had never been any mention of champagne. Anyway, the items were
irrelevant to the appeal; it was the date on the receipt that mattered. And now I was looking at
it again I realised I was right. The receipt didn't mention champagne – just "Wines & Spirits
x 2". So why would John Mitchell assume Karen had bought champagne?

My mind raced as I tried to decide what to do. But most of my options were taken away from
me when I heard footsteps in the corridor and a voice said, "I'm guessing you just realised

something that dawned on me a while ago too. Oh, and speaking of Dawn – she just drove

out of the car park. We're all alone."

****

"John? I thought you'd left. How did you get back in?" I struggled to keep a note of fear from

my voice.

"I didn't need to get back in. I never left. I've just been having a bit of a rest in another room

while you were busy with my sister-in-law. It's okay, you can give up the effort to keep your

face impassive. I know you've just worked out what I said to you earlier doesn't fit our

version of the facts." Instead of his usual charming manner, John face was set in a grim frown

and his eyes were scanning the room.

I tried to decide whether I should make a run for the exit or try and talk John round. He

walked towards my desk and reached for the photocopy of the receipt I had been looking at

moments earlier.

"Wines & Spirits x2. Cooked chicken. Prepared salad." John read aloud. And the date, the

same as the day I was convicted. As simple as that and I had my new evidence for an appeal."

"Yes, that's how you're a free man today. Simple as that as you say. Now I'm exhausted,

John, and all I want to do is go home and recharge my batteries. It's been a tough few

weeks."

John peered at me and I could almost hear the cogs whirring in his brain. Would he believe I hadn't picked up on anything odd about his comments outside the building earlier? I didn't have to wait long for an answer to that question.

"So, you're trying to figure out how I knew the wines and spirits meant champagne when it's not on the receipt and wasn't mentioned in court."

I saw a chance to divert John's attention slightly. "Actually I was wondering why nobody – the police or anyone – thought it was odd that none of those items were found at the cottage where Karen's body was hidden. It only struck me just now when I looked at the photocopy." With an effort I kept my breathing even as I could and stared at John to watch his reaction.

"Good point. That wasn't mentioned either. Well, apart from the fact Karen's last meal wasn't either chicken or salad."

While John was considering this I was trying to work out whether I could make it to the next office where there was a window that led onto the fire escape. From there I could leave the building and hide in the grounds until I could summon help. But John's next words made me realise my attempt to distract him had failed.

"I know you've figured out I'm guilty after all, Meredith. And from a stupid slip of the tongue of all things. But I didn't kill Karen, you have to believe me. You've done a brilliant job of clearing my name and I don't want you to regret that. Should I tell you the whole story?"

I knew my best chance of getting out of the situation alive was to keep John talking while I tried to come up with a way of escaping. "Yes. Why don't you explain what you mean? Why are you guilty if you didn't kill her?"

John gestured to my chair behind the desk. "You might as well make yourself comfortable. It's a bit of a long and complicated story." He dragged another chair over and placed it at the other side of my desk. While his back was turned for a split second I pressed a call repeat button on my desk phone, saying a silent prayer of thanks that I'd disabled the sound the dialler made. Thanking heaven that his was the last number I'd dialled on that phone, I just had to hope that Mick Bannister would react to repeated failed calls from my work number and notice that it was odd for me to be at the office this late. Could I hope he might put two and two together and realise I was in danger? It was a stretch and after weeks apart the odds weren't on my side. I had no alternative but to listen to what John Mitchell had to say whilst willing Mick to somehow respond to the only chance I'd had to summon help.

"If you're sitting comfortably I'll begin." John grinned at his feeble attempt at humour. "I should only have been in prison for a few weeks. We'd planned everything meticulously."

"We?" I couldn't stop myself interrupting.

"Oh, Meredith, I'm disappointed. I know how intelligent you are but now you're letting yourself down. Surely you've worked it out by now?"

"No. I've no idea. Tell me." I hoped playing dumb would be the best approach with John at this point. Let him feel superior after his years under the control of the prison authorities. But I was actually beginning to have an idea of the true story.

"Sam. Samantha Raynor. I told you I thought she was having an affair with Karen but in fact we'd been lovers for a long time. We'd talked about a life together but first we needed Karen out of the way. Sam was the perfect woman for me. Made for each other you might say. Just a pity we didn't meet years earlier. Though I have to admit we probably wouldn't have got together then. You see the biggest thing we had in common was our love of money. And the fact that neither of us had any. Karen was the key to the money."

I wanted to ask why he didn't just divorce Karen but the answer was obvious. Money. When the Mitchells had married John had virtually nothing but the clothes he stood up in. In fact it was worse than that because he was deep in debt. Karen's father had died leaving her and her sister, Dawn, well provided for with trust funds that should have meant neither of them had to work a day in their lives. The family solicitors had insisted on John signing a prenup agreement before the wedding. At that stage, years before he met Sam, he'd convinced himself he was in love with Karen and he couldn't foresee a time when he'd want to leave her so the agreement hadn't bothered him. When Sam came along and offered an alternative future John realised if he walked away he would do so with nothing.

"It was Sam who suggested she could convince Karen to do whatever she said. Karen had been confiding in her about worries regarding my spending habits and also that she'd been thinking about leaving me or getting rid of me in some way. It wasn't a big leap from that to us planning a way of getting rid of Karen instead."

"Hang on. If Karen had left you, the prenup would have been invalid. Why didn't you push things in that direction? You could've ended up with half of everything."

"You really don't know me as well as you think you do. I'm greedy, Meredith. Why settle for half of everything when I could have it all? Anyway, where was I? Oh yes, Sam lured Karen into a relationship. Groomed her I suppose you'd call it. I don't know much about the physical side. She tried to tell me once but I didn't want to know the details. Once they were close she started suggesting to Karen that there was a way they could run away together. She started siphoning off the money from various accounts into untraceable accounts abroad. Then she came up with the idea of framing me for Karen's murder so I'd end up in prison for life. Karen fell for it completely. She had no conscience whatsoever about putting an innocent man in prison, husband or not.

"That night in August 2012 when they carried out their plan to make the kitchen look like a crime scene, I had to sit upstairs in my bedroom pretending to be oblivious to it. Sam took Karen to the cottage in Lancashire and Karen stayed there for months until my trial was over. Then, that night when I'd been convicted Sam went to a shop with the sole purpose of obtaining a receipt with the date on it. It was me that suggested buying champagne. Back when we were planning everything so carefully. Thought it would kill two birds with one stone. Murder weapon and something to celebrate with later. I'm not sure of the sequence of events after that because, of course, I was on my way to prison in Cumbria. If she stuck to the plan she will have killed Karen, put the receipt in her pocket and hidden her in the chest freezer."

I was horrified by the impassive way John spoke those words, but I managed to keep the revulsion from my face. How had I sat in front of this man at so many prison visits without seeing through his charade? Now wasn't the time to question how good a judge of character I was, but he'd really had me fooled.

"That's when fate stepped in and ruined everything. I still don't understand, though, why Sam was travelling from Lancashire to Manchester when she died. It was three weeks after she'd killed Karen. There was no reason for her to have left Manchester once Karen was dead. The plan was for her to wait three weeks then make an anonymous call to the police, telling them where Karen's body could be found. She'd planted the receipt on the body to prove Karen was still alive when I was on my way to prison. Then we'd just have to wait for the justice system to catch up with events. Since I couldn't possibly have killed Karen they'd have to release me. We would've waited a decent amount of time before, well I suppose we'd have called it starting a relationship. And living happily ever after." He said the last words bitterly.

"When did you realise the plan had failed?"

"When I'd had no news after the three weeks Sam and I had agreed on, I called my lawyer and asked if there had been any developments. There hadn't of course. And I couldn't directly ask him about Sam without arousing suspicion. He told me about her death as an afterthought before we hung up the phone. I was stunned. It was like something out of a Hitchcock movie. I was destined to be in prison for a life sentence."

"You talk as if you're innocent of any crime." I could have bitten my tongue. I was meant to be keeping him talking not antagonising him. But it seemed to be the comment he'd been expecting.

"Exactly. And that's where this place came in. But it took you lot long enough to take me on."

"We have a huge backlog of cases to look at. You're lucky the murder with no body angle caught Jeremy's imagination or Nothing But Truth might have passed over your application." A question I had been wondering about for a while popped into my head. "What about the anonymous tip off about the safe deposit box? How did you manage that from inside prison?"

Yet another expression crossed John's face. It looked as though he was proud of what he'd done. Of how he'd fooled me and the rest of us into working to free him. I realised he was patting himself on the back for how clever he'd been and that this was part of the plan he was particularly proud of.

"Well, I gave you enough hints," he said. "When you visited and I told you about my cellmate who was due to be released the next day, remember? He was a willing helper once I convinced him how wealthy I was going to be once I got out. I briefed him well. It was him who emailed you about the bank deposit box. Oh, and the letter that was going to be so useful if the receipt wasn't enough to convince the appeal judges. He took that to the cottage and hid it, but not too well."

"I never believed Karen wrote that letter." There I went again, antagonising. I really needed to learn to bite my tongue.

"Doesn't matter what you believe. I'm free now. And my helpful friend is proud of that letter. After all he could barely read and write when I met him. See – another hint I gave you. I told you how I was helping lads with their reading and writing."

"This isn't a game, John." The tongue biting thing clearly hadn't worked. "You're acting as though you've won some sort of mind game. But this is real life." And for Karen it was real death.

This situation was starting to make me question why I stayed in this job. If I could be fooled so completely by a client I had met and talked to at length several times, maybe I wasn't as good at it as I'd thought. As usual my quirky brain turned this around on me, telling me not to worry, it looked like after the next few minutes I wouldn't have to worry about anything anymore.

John's eyes looked heavy with fatigue and I wondered if I could hope he might be so exhausted he would fall asleep in the comfortable office chair. I glanced towards the office door, working out how long it would take me to run from the room and into the next office to open the window to the fire escape. He seemed to have run out of steam telling his story so my choices were now between making a run for it or trying to keep him talking even longer. I'm not that good a conversationalist I thought, pushing my chair back from the desk.

I had the advantage of surprise and it took a couple of seconds for John to react and run after me. By the time he reached the hallway between the two offices I was already at the large window struggling with the catch. I knew the window was left unlocked because fire regulations required it but the handle was very stiff in spite of its constant use by the smokers on the staff. Finally it squeaked open and I pushed the window outwards, jumping onto the metal fire escape platform.

John Mitchell hurled himself out after me before I was able to set off down the narrow steps. The weight of his body forced me against the framework of the platform and I pivoted at waist level over a guard rail. In the split second it took to register the predicament I was in, John could have saved me by dragging me back towards him. Instead he grinned as he hoisted me up by one leg and flung me over.

Chapter Eighteen

I lay in the narrow hospital bed trying not to move a muscle because every single one ached. Mick had brought me an e-reader and headphones. The reader was loaded with the top ten crime novels of the previous year and their audio equivalents. Typical of him to take advantage of me being unable to comfortably read a normal book. He would have seen this as his chance to convert me to e-books at last.

After the weeks we'd spent apart I hadn't expected him to show up but it was as if our separation had never happened.

"I nearly didn't come," Mick said, hanging his head. "I was this close to ignoring the calls like the stubborn pig-headed idiot I am."

I wished I was recording that speech because I knew he'd never admit such a thing again. Whatever we'd been going through before, Mick had turned up when I called and I had him to thank for still being alive. From what the medics had told me, if my injuries hadn't been treated so quickly it would have been touch and go. I still couldn't remember how I'd ended up sprawled in the car park or why I'd been out on the fire escape in the first place but the doctors were hopeful I'd regain my memory eventually. In the meantime I planned to do exactly as I was told and rest. This was so unlike me I suppose Mick thought they'd given me a personality transplant when they'd operated.

"I've never been so scared in my life," Mick said, holding tight to my left hand but trying to avoid disturbing the cannula needle that connected me to an array of bags of fluid. My right hand was encased in the plaster that covered my whole right arm. Both legs were plastered too, the left just at the ankle but the right all the way from ankle to thigh. I was going to be out of action for weeks if not months.

But the main concern was my head injury. Scans had shown bleeding in my brain and I'd had emergency surgery that left my head swathed in bandages. Add in two black eyes and a swollen jaw and I was barely recognisable. The only uninjured parts of me were my left arm and, thankfully, my spine.

I had known things were serious the moment I regained consciousness and realised I was in hospital and in a room of my own. I would believe I was on the mend when they moved me to one of those bays where you had to put up with a few other people you'd never choose to share a room with.

"The doctors want to speak to me for a few minutes. You'll be okay?" Mick's look of concern melted away when I attempted a smile.

"I never got round to removing you as my next of kin," I whispered.

Mick shook his head at my attempt at dark humour. We'd made each other next of kin on any official forms after we'd been together six months and assumed we'd be spending the rest of our lives together, though we'd never really discussed the future. Neither of us had any close relatives and I had been horrified to realise that Daniel was still listed for me despite our divorce. It had never crossed my mind during my brief separation from Mick to think about details like that. Now it was as if our few months apart had never happened. Having saved me after my accident, Mick was determined we'd be together forever. He strolled over to the nurses' station and a few minutes later one of the doctors who were looking after me appeared.

I was still feeling tired most of the time and I started to drift off, trying to ignore the nagging worry that had been at the back of my mind for days now. I kept thinking back to when I was told that doctors wouldn't see past my mental health condition even when they were treating me for physical ailments. Surely the extent of my injuries would divert their attention? Yet I still worried that, without a reasonable explanation for my accident the doctors might think it had been an almost successful suicide attempt.

****

"Hi Mr Bannister," the doctor said. Let's find somewhere a little quieter shall we?" Mick's heart fell as he wondered if the young doctor was going to be breaking bad news. But his fears were allayed a moment later. "Meredith's doing really well. Much better than we'd expected at this early stage."

"Oh that's good news." Mick realised there was more to come by the look on the doctor's face.

"There's just one thing we're a little concerned about. Physically, as I said, things are looking good. But following the surgery to stop the bleed on her brain we're keeping a close eye on her memory."

"She knew me straightaway," Mick said. "Chatted about things that happened a few weeks ago."

"Yes, that's good. But, and this is by no means unusual after a traumatic brain injury, she's unable to remember what happened immediately before the accident."

"Oh, yes she does seem bothered about that. And do you think those memories will come back?"

"It's hard to say. I would suggest you don't pressurise her to try and remember. From what we know so far it was simply a freak accident. There's nothing to be gained from aggressively trying to restore her memory of it. I recommend that we ask her GP to monitor the situation once her physical injuries are on the mend. There are various techniques and counselling that may help if Meredith decides she wants to try to retrieve the memories."

"Okay. If that's all I'd like to go and spend some time with Meredith before my shift starts."

"Of course. But there's just one more thing. What do you know about Meredith's children?"

"Oh, has she been discussing them? It's a while since she talked to me about them. It's sad really. Her ex refuses to let her see them. She hasn't been allowed contact since an, er, illness a few years ago. I think she still hopes to be able to try and build a relationship with them one day. She's tried a couple of times to challenge her ex's reasons for preventing her seeing them. In fact I think she was planning to get some legal advice just recently. She's been preparing a room for them to stay in so I'm sure she's more confident than she's ever been that they'll be allowed to come and stay soon."

The doctor sucked her bottom lip for a moment. "Yes, she's been telling a couple of nurses about them – pretty much what you've just told me."

"And what's that got to do with her accident or her recovery?" Mick asked, puzzled.

"The thing is, Mr Bannister, I've been through Meredith's whole medical history."

"I should hope so; if you're as thorough a doctor as you seem that's exactly what I'd expect you to do." Mick was trying to keep the mood light but he realised now that the doctor had something very serious to tell him.

"Yes, but in that whole medical history there's no mention of Meredith giving birth. Let alone giving birth twice. She does have two documented episodes of pseudocyesis or phantom pregnancies as they're commonly known. Incredibly rare. The second time it happened it led to her spending some months in a psychiatric unit. Comparing the dates of those episodes with what she told the nurse it appears she's been under the delusion that those pregnancies were real and the babies were actually born."

Chapter Nineteen

John Mitchell let himself into the apartment at the exclusive tower block in the city centre. This was the first place Sam had bought with the money she'd been siphoning from Karen's accounts. Cash sale, no paper trail. Utilities and council tax and all those details set up to be paid automatically until further notice. Just the same as the cottage in Lancashire. She'd moved in there, desperate to leave the depressing flat she'd lived in before, but as far as anyone else was concerned her address hadn't changed. John shook his head sadly. He was in danger of showing some real emotion over Sam. She really had been his soul mate. Who knew what they might have achieved together if it hadn't been for her untimely death?

He could hide away from the glare of the media here for a while until he worked out what to do next. He'd spent one night at the hotel provided by the newspaper. Given them one brief interview and then walked away from the deal and come here. It was a secure building, accessed using pass codes rather than keys and Sam had set the code to a combination of their birth dates. How romantic.

He knew there would be a media frenzy awaiting him at the home he'd shared with Karen. Those vultures could wait. They hadn't wanted to know when he was writing letters to all the news organisations protesting his innocence. Probably had him down as just another lifer trying it on. He'd almost lost hope just before Nothing But Truth got in touch and told him they were considering his case.

Every time he thought about the wasted years between when he should have been released and now he felt rage begin to boil up and he had to distract himself. It had been a brilliant plan but he realised now there should have been some contingency built in. If he was doing it again he would have found someone who would act as a backup to Sam, for a price. The risk of them going to the police would be worth it. If they'd done that he would have been out of prison after just a few months. It wouldn't have brought Sam back though. Strangely, John never had a moment's regret about Karen's death but Sam's could almost reduce him to tears. He wasn't sure if that was just grief at losing his lover or whether there might be a tiny twinge of guilt involved. He doubted it. He'd never felt guilty in his life.

John wandered into the kitchen. It all needed a bit of a clean because of a surface layer of dust but otherwise it was habitable. He'd need to venture out and gather some supplies but that could wait a while. Glancing in the fridge he saw that the only contents were two bottles of champagne and a grin overtook his features. Which one? he wondered. Which one had killed Karen and might there be a small trace left behind?

Never one to be sentimental John opened the nearest bottle and glugged a few mouthfuls. He'd dump the bottles later – didn't want to risk any future investigation finding traces of Karen's demise on them. Would he ever be able to shake off the fear of the investigation being reopened and focussing on him again? But why would it?

He headed for the bedroom and lay down to sleep. He was a free man. Conviction quashed. The comments from the police that they weren't seeking anyone else in relation to Karen's murder niggled him but he had to focus on the main point. He was free. And as soon as he could work out how to access the money he was rich. He could go wherever he wanted, be whoever he wanted.

But first of all he'd lie low here for a while. It'd give him a chance to organise selling the old place and finding somewhere new to live far away from here. He'd take particular pleasure in clawing back everything he was owed from Dawn Rothwell. Or maybe there would be a more fruitful way to deal with her.

And maybe one day soon he'd visit Meredith James.

Chapter Twenty

After speaking to Meredith's doctor and learning the shocking news that her children were, what? All in her mind? Mick stood at the nurses' station for several minutes watching Meredith through the glass window of her room. In spite of her injuries she was in good spirits and he hated that he had to go back in there now and wipe away her good mood. It crossed his mind to find the doctor again and ask her to do it. How on earth was he supposed to find the right words? The children had been such a large part of Meredith's life the whole time he'd known her, even though she hadn't been allowed to see them. He caught himself thinking the same way as Meredith. Thinking about the children as if they were alive, and he knew it was cruel to let Meredith carry on in that belief for a minute longer than necessary.

Mick went back to his position next to Meredith's bed and took her left hand in his. She smiled and it melted his heart. The pain relief must be working overtime. Would she be able to understand what he was about to tell her? She'd already suffered so much over the past few hours and he wasn't sure she was strong enough to take it in. But he knew he had to get it over with before she fell asleep. He couldn't bear the thought of it hanging over him all night. Or of one of the nurses talking to Meredith about it, thinking she already knew.

****

"Meredith, I've been having a word with the doctor and she wants me to talk to you about something, okay?"

"Hmm?" I'd been drifting off on a tide of fatigue and pain meds but something about Mick's tone of voice told me he had something important to say.

"It's about the children..." Looking back on those moments later Mick told me he couldn't remember the exact words he'd used. All he could remember was the look in my damaged eyes changing from love and trust to heartbreak. It had taken him a while to persuade me that what he was telling me was true and he'd had to stand up to me telling him to leave once the words sank in. He said there was no way he was going to leave me alone until I had taken in the news properly.

Run. Run away from here faster than you've ever moved in your life. That's what every brain cell and every nerve ending in my body was telling me. But my broken body meant I had to lie there and process the news that was turning the last several years of my life into chaos.

Eventually I stared into Mick's eyes for a full minute in silence. In that time I veered from thinking it was some sort of sick joke to realising there was no way Mick would be that cruel. I also took a few seconds to register that I was thankful for my mood stabilising medication. Well, that was unusual. I'd spent years resenting having to take tablets every day to allow me to live a near-normal life. Without the drugs, a revelation such as this could have sent me heading towards a deep depression in no time. And in the end the overpowering thought forcing its way into mind was that, really, what Mick had just told me wasn't as much of a shock as it should have been.

"I can see that you're telling the truth," I said at last, my voice breaking on the words. "And, you know what? I've been thinking for a while that there was something wrong, to do with the kids. I just didn't know what it was." Even as I said this, some of the things that had

happened over the years started to make sense. Like the time I tried to get some help from the

family court system and they said they couldn't help me. Of course they couldn't – how were

they supposed to help me gain access to children who didn't exist? And really, after all these

years of me telling myself Daniel was keeping the children from me, I should have

questioned the situation myself.

"The doctor says she can refer you for some counselling. A bit like bereavement counselling

but more specialised." I nodded. "And..." Mick didn't know how to tackle the next thing that

need saying. "Would you like me to make a start on clearing the children's bedroom while

you're in here?"

"No. I'm not ready for that. Can we wait until I've seen this counsellor?"

Mick smiled with relief. He'd thought I would lose it at the thought of getting rid of the

things in that room but he obviously thought I was dealing with it well.

"There's one more thing the doctor said." Mick held my hand tighter. He told me later he was

worried it was too soon to bring this up. "She said there's no medical reason why we couldn't

try for a baby. Well, once all your broken bones have healed." Mick smiled and stroked my

cheek gently. "Oh, and while we're being soppy and romantic – remember how you told me

you used to wonder whether to go back to your maiden name after your divorce?"

"Yes. Even more so now that Paula is Mrs James."

"Well, stop worrying about that. I think it'd be a much better idea if you changed your surname to Bannister. Marry me, Meredith."

I began to cry. Slow sobs at first but then full blown wailing. Mick looked concerned, as if he was kicking himself and shouldn't have mentioned it. I couldn't explain that the tears were a mixture of grief for my lost babies and joy at our renewed relationship. In the end I managed to sob out the words, "I would love that."

****

Later the same day it came to me in a flash what I wanted to do. I'd been thinking about it for hours. One minute it was clear and obvious and I understood what Mick had told me. Then I veered towards creating conspiracy theories where this was all an elaborate plan by Daniel so he could hide the children away from me by pretending they never existed. He could have convinced Paula Reed to amend my medical notes. Eventually the moments of clarity outnumbered the flights of imagination and all of a sudden it was blindingly obvious. The only other person who had referred to the children as if they were real was Paula herself. I had thought hard about it and realised Paula never discussed them with me when anyone else was around. She had obviously been playing some kind of sick mind game with me.

Although I had decided a long time ago not to put in a complaint about my treatment at the Pennine View clinic, I couldn't let this go. I remembered Richard Ferguson's offer of legal advice should I ever need it and I contacted him asking him to come and visit. I knew from my paralegal days that it was possible to obtain one's medical records so I asked Richard to do so on my behalf, begging him to keep it strictly confidential.

The results of Richard's search into my records from the clinic were enough to trigger an investigation into Paula Reed's work there. It appeared she had been deliberately lying to me about the children, reinforcing the idea of them being alive. She thought it would make an interesting case study for a psychiatric professional journal and didn't care about the suffering she caused.

I decided to keep the knowledge I had gained to myself for now. After all, Paula was no longer a practising clinical psychiatrist so she couldn't do the same thing to anyone else. But once I was fully fit I would find a way to confront Paula.

The other thing that had been occupying my mind was whether to try to retrieve the memories from before my accident. I had managed to remember up to being in my office speaking to Dawn Rothwell, and I suspected that Dawn could have something to do with my fall. It was another thing to set aside until I was fully fit and able to deal with it.

****

Jeremy Parker was in his office dealing with the aftermath of Meredith's accident. Some health and safety people were due soon to examine the fire escape and there was likely to be an impact on the Nothing But Truth building's insurance premiums. It had all taken a bit of the gloss off the success in the John Mitchell case but at least it now looked as if Meredith's injuries weren't life threatening.

Thinking about the outcome of the case reminded Jeremy he should really contact John Mitchell to organise interviews to wrap up the TV documentary. He dialled John's new mobile number but there was no answer so he left a voicemail.

"Hi, John. Jeremy Parker. Just to let you know the interview's been set up for tomorrow here at our office. I'm not sure if you've heard but Meredith James won't be available for the interview I'm afraid. She had an accident and she's likely to be in hospital for some time. Nasty head injury and memory loss apparently, amongst other things. I'll fill you in properly tomorrow. Hope all's well with the hotel and if you need anything at all just give me a ring back. Cheers."

John Mitchell played the message back immediately. Interesting about the memory loss, he thought. Though he'd already worked out that even if Meredith remembered everything about the circumstances leading up to her "accident" she couldn't prove anything against him. Oh how he loved getting away with things.

Chapter Twenty-One

I amazed the medics by recovering enough to leave hospital within weeks rather than months. The first thing I did after Mick helped me into our apartment was phone Jeremy Parker at Nothing But Truth. He'd been to visit me once in hospital but I knew he hated the places so I wasn't surprised when he left after about twenty minutes.

"Meredith, how lovely. I hope this is just a social call. There's no way you're coming back to work yet."

"I know. I know. Believe me I've had enough lectures from Mick on that score. No, I just wondered if we could set a target date for me to come back. In a couple of weeks maybe?"

Jeremy laughed. "I really have never known anyone like you, my dear. Of course. Put it on your calendar and we'll see you then. Oh, and by the way, your suggestion of letting Susie step up and take over your role temporarily has been a great success. I can't confirm it officially yet, but there's a chance we might be able to offer her the job permanently."

"Oh." I was taken aback.

"Sorry. Didn't mean to worry you. I meant as an additional investigator."

I had been worrying for days that Jeremy might have replaced me or decided the organisation could do without me. I sighed with relief. Then it was on to the next task I had been determined to face as soon as I got home. I wasn't used to my crutches yet, and I would need a wheelchair when I went outside, but I managed to hobble to the door of the children's

room. No, the spare room. I had to get used to calling it that.

"Mick," I shouted, and he came running, probably thinking I'd stumbled. "Sorry, didn't mean

to worry you. I think I'm ready. If you meant it about taking a few days off, is there any

chance you could clear this lot out soon?" I knew it had to be done and the sooner the better,

but I'd wanted to see the room I'd created one last time before getting rid of everything.

Mick knew better than to question whether I was sure. A nod and a smile was all that was

needed.

****

My first day back at work turned into just a few hours. I was less fit than I'd thought but at

least I'd shown my face and picked up enough information to be able to work from home for

a while. Susie and I had worked out that we could work as a team for a while – me

coordinating investigations from home while Susie did all the driving around that was needed

to follow up leads and have face to face meetings.

There was a huge bouquet on my desk and I assumed it was from Jeremy or Susie but it

turned out to be from John Mitchell "With thanks for the rest of my life". I was touched by

the gesture but had an odd "someone walked over my grave" sensation. And it only crossed

my mind later to wonder how he'd known I would be back that day.

I dismissed the question and got on with the job that was my top priority that day. Before I disappeared again to work from home I wanted a word with Jeremy. It would be a meeting that would decide whether I could continue to work for Nothing But Truth. And it was something that had come out of my counselling sessions about the phantom pregnancies and their aftermath.

The counsellor had helped me learn that the way to deal with the psychological symptoms was to face up to evidence that the pregnancies hadn't been real. My records were the best source for that. But during our intensive sessions it had become clear that someone else was responsible for implanting the deep belief in my mind that the children had been born and were still alive, right up to the time I was hospitalised after my accident.

We'd worked out that, as I had suspected, the trigger for my most serious symptoms had been during my stay at the Pennine View clinic in 2012. The counsellor was able to gently take me through the weeks running up to that time when my mental health had deteriorated, probably brought on by the stress of my crumbling marriage to Daniel James. It was while I was under the "care" of Dr Paula Reed that I had sunk back into my obsession with the phantom children. I had shared with the counsellor the results of Richard Ferguson's investigation into Paula Reed's unethical methods of research for psychiatric journal case studies. By talking to me about the children as if they were alive, Paula had set me off on a downward spiral that suited her case study needs perfectly.

When Paula had turned up to join the steering group at Nothing But Truth she had failed to mention that she had been suspended from the clinic. There had been complaints from the families of other patients with similar experiences to mine. After a few weeks in the clinic their conditions were worse instead of better. Of course, back then I hadn't had any family to fight or complain for me. Daniel had been happy to offload me the moment I entered the clinic. It still hurt me like a punch to my stomach to think back to that time. Later, when Paula had said she decided to cut back on her clinical work, it was really because she had been dismissed from the clinic. She was lucky not to have been struck off but it seemed she had offered payments to the other families so they would withdraw their complaints.

Those snippets of information had surfaced when Richard Ferguson had called in some favours from colleagues. It was his way of repaying me for turning a blind eye to his relationship with Dawn Rothwell. I knew I could probably take legal action against the clinic and Paula for the suffering she had caused. But now all I wanted to do was draw a line under those experiences.

One thing I was adamant about, though, was that I couldn't continue to work for Nothing But Truth if Paula Reed was still part of the steering group. I just had to hope that Jeremy would understand. I asked Susie to help me take two mugs of coffee into his office. Although my mobility was improving, I still couldn't manage to carry stuff and walk at the same time. In fact I was still reliant on a wheelchair much of the time. It was frustrating.

"I think we may be here for a while so I thought we could do with coffees," I said as Jeremy looked up from his laptop screen.

"I'll be with you in just a second, Meredith."

I made myself as comfortable as I could in the chair across from him. I glanced round the room, appreciating as usual the tasteful decor. I had butterflies in my stomach at the thought of the conversation that was about to take place. Jeremy was aware of my mental health diagnosis from when I first took this job but nobody except the doctors, me and Mick knew about the phantom pregnancy part. Jeremy finished what he was doing and closed the laptop, giving me his full attention.

"Now, what can I do for you?" he said, taking a gulp of the coffee I had made just how he liked it.

I took a deep breath, then told him everything as clearly and concisely as I could. I was grateful that he didn't interrupt me once – he just listened, with the occasional nod of his head, as I got it all off my chest.

"And that's why I won't be able to work with Paula Reed in future. Basically, I'll have to leave unless you let her go," I finished. I tried to read his reaction on his face but it was impossible.

"I'm so sorry," Jeremy said and I was horrified for a moment, convinced he was about to refuse my request. But then he continued, "So very sorry, Meredith. If I'd had any idea about her connection to you, I would never have invited her to join the group."

"It's not your fault, Jeremy. I should have spoken up that first day when she turned up to cover Michelle's place on the group. But I was too scared."

"Well, it's true that I've offered her Michelle's place permanently," Jeremy went on. "But in light of what you've just told me I'll be withdrawing that offer immediately."

Relief flooded through me and I thought I might embarrass myself by crying. I didn't cry easily but once I started I was one of those people who were ugly criers – red face, snot everywhere, the works. Not a good look for the office. We chatted for a few minutes before Jeremy's phone rang and I excused myself.

Next stop was an edited highlights version of the conversation for Susie, back at our desks. Since I would now be staying put and Susie and I would be working so closely, I thought it was important to be open and honest with her. It didn't surprise me that Susie's reaction was sympathetic and supportive.

"I'd like to be a fly on the wall when Jeremy fires her, though," Susie said. But I didn't want to waste another second thinking about Paula Reed. Our only connection, when you looked at it clearly and calmly, was that Paula was now married to my ex-husband. Plenty of women were in the same situation and there was no reason why I should ever need to communicate with Paula.

Emotionally drained, I was relieved to gather up all the things I needed for a whole week working from home and, with Susie's help to take everything out to Mick's car, leave the building. Mick had been as good as his word, taking some rare days off to help me but I could tell he was getting twitchy, wanting to be back with his team.

"Why don't you go in for the afternoon?" I suggested, then stifled a laugh as he tried to stop grinning.

****

After Meredith left his office Jeremy sat thinking for a long time. What she had just told him had made him see just how badly he'd taken his eye off the ball lately. He should have chased up Paula Reed's references before welcoming her to the organisation. His carelessness had caused one of his staff terrible suffering and could have damaged the organisation beyond repair. Thinking about Meredith as one of his staff was starting to feel a little inadequate. She almost felt like family to him now. He felt so guilty for putting her through a miserable time.

It was another badly needed kick up the backside after the one Pam Philips had given him regarding the steering group. He was lucky to be surrounded by people who weren't afraid to confront him in order to stop him compromising his standards and betraying the organisation's aims.

He was kicking himself now, of course, for trying to take the burden of the organisation's financial problems on alone. He had a perfectly competent Finance Manager and they'd always worked well together. Shaking his head as he realised the root of his problem he sat with his face in his hands for a few minutes. It was his ego. As he was growing older he'd started to feel defensive whenever anyone suggested delegating important tasks. As if they didn't think he was still capable. That had spread to all aspects of his job and he was only just realising it. Of course, the outcome was that he had been spreading himself too thin.

Thinking back over the past few months and the devastating cuts to the organisation's funding, Jeremy suddenly felt as if he'd been walking blindfolded to towards a cliff edge. It was as if someone had shouted "Stop!" and whipped off the blindfold, and Jeremy had looked down to see his feet about to step over the edge. If he carried on like this Nothing But Truth would be gone before the year was out. He couldn't let that happen. But had he come to his senses in time?

****

When Mick arrived home that evening I was napping on the couch. He crept past me into the kitchen but I was already half awake and the sounds of him reaching things out of cupboards made it impossible to doze off again. I went to join him, hobbling on my crutches. I'd been ordered to use them and be more mobile, otherwise my return to normal mobility would be slowed down. I had a target of walking with just a stick but that was still a way in the future.

"Sorry, I thought I'd been quiet," he laughed. It was an ongoing joke between us that even when he was trying to be quiet he sounded like a bull in a china shop. It made me think back to those weeks when we'd been apart. I would rather have Mick here creating a racket than go back to being without him, no matter how quiet it had been.

"It's fine. If I'd slept any longer I wouldn't sleep tonight." I noticed Mick had reached glasses out and was about to open a bottle of champagne. "What's the occasion?"

"Don't need one. But after what you sorted out with Jeremy today, I thought we should celebrate. What's the matter?"

I had drifted off into a trance and Mick had to click his fingers to get my attention.

"What? Oh, I don't know. Something to do with the champagne I think. I got that 'someone walking over my grave' feeling again. It's weird. And it keeps happening."

"Maybe you should mention it next time you go for a check-up at the hospital." Mick tried not to show it but I knew he was starting to worry that these episodes had been caused by my head injury. And I was thinking how weird it would sound if I went in and told the doctor I had a funny turn every time someone mentioned champagne. Within a few minutes it was forgotten as we drank our champagne and threw together an evening meal from what was in the fridge.

Later, as we relaxed enjoying the glow of the champagne, I decided it was time to bring up something we'd left on a back burner since my first few days in hospital. I'd never felt closer to Mick than in those first few days of my recovery but I kept wondering if he'd only come back to me because of the accident.

"I'll let you off the hook you know," I said.

Mick looked puzzled. "I've absolutely no idea what you're talking about."

"The proposal. I realise you might have felt pressured into making some grand gesture because I'd just been dragged back from death's door..." Even as I said the words I was hoping with all my heart that he wouldn't agree with me.

Mick silenced me with a kiss then left it a few moments before launching into an explanation. "I was stupid not to have asked you before. And I can't believe how long I let that stupid situation drag on after I moved out in a huff."

Once again I wondered how this man I'd thought I knew so well could have had such a radical change to his personality. Mick would never have admitted being in the wrong before my accident. Maybe I should start feeling glad it had happened. He carried on, his words getting more surprising with each sentence.

"I love you, Meredith. I have since pretty much the first time I met you. Your accident has made things crystal clear for me. You never know what might happen from one day to the next. And you never know when you might lose someone who's so precious to you. Well from now on I'm going to make the most of everything I've got and the most important part of that is you."

Time to quit while I was ahead. I'd only wanted him to confirm that he still wanted to marry me. I'd ended up with a bonus of finding out how deeply he felt about it. It was one of those moments I wished she could bottle so I could take it out next time I felt sad.

"I guess I'd better start looking round the bridal shops then," I said with a grin that turned to a laugh when I saw the look on Mick's face. The bridal shops in the area between where we lived and where I worked were renowned for being exclusive and expensive. "Don't worry, you know me. I'd be happy to elope."

"Quick, google the number for the Gretna Green blacksmith's shop," Mick said and I whacked him round the head with a cushion.

"You're such a cliché."

Although I'd played it down, I was looking forward to planning the wedding I wanted. My first wedding day had been wonderful but I'd had hardly a hand in organising it. If I was honest, I realised that back then I had let myself be bullied by Daniel's mother into agreeing with everything she suggested. I was older and, supposedly, wiser this time. Now my accident was behind me and I was on the mend physically, what could spoil my second chance?

Chapter Twenty-Two

The documentary makers had agreed to fund the team building day Pam Philips wanted. But they wanted it to take place quickly so they could add it on to the end of the film. Everyone agreed it would be a good way to show off the organisation as a whole rather than just me and Jeremy. There was a slot available in the schedules in a couple of months' time and the producer didn't want to miss it.

And that's how Jeremy, Pam and a reluctant selection of steering group members and staff ended up on a coach to The Lake District the following week. Jeremy had been determined to show how disability friendly the organisation was and had put pressure on me to join them, wheelchair and all.

"Mick's not going to like it," I'd said. But I did like the idea, very much. I was going stir crazy in the apartment and couldn't wait to be out there doing something normal. Pam had broken it to me that I wouldn't be allowed to join in most of the activities but that didn't bother me. I would take my new e-reader and find somewhere to sit in the sunshine and read while the others were doing all the physical stuff. I'd never enjoyed that sort of thing anyway, but I was looking forward to being involved in the afternoon's planned discussions about the organisation's future.

The documentary makers had insisted that John Mitchell should join in the day. They were paying for it after all so they were calling the shots. It was the first time I had seen him since the day he was released from prison and although Jeremy had told me I'd seen John at the office that evening, I couldn't remember a thing about it. He made a point of sitting next to me on the coach so we could catch up. I knew I had to be polite but I felt uncomfortable being so close to him. Although my memory of just before the accident was still blank, I could remember how I had felt about John during prison visits and how I had been unable to decide whether or not he could be trusted.

"And you really don't remember a thing from just before your accident?" John asked, staring into my eyes as if he was searching for something more than what he had asked.

"Nothing at all. The last thing I remember is seeing you and Jeremy on Sky News just after the appeal hearing. I think I remember every word of the statement he read out and how he ended by saying you both had a train to catch."

"Yes, that's right, he did." John narrowed his eyes. "But that's the last thing?"

"Yes. I must have known you'd both be coming back to the office a few hours later so I hung around. Jeremy's told me I spoke to you outside where there was a crowd of reporters."

"Yes, I remember. Then you went back in and I decided to stretch my legs and get some air, once the reporters had left."

"Oh, hang on," I said. "Dawn Rothwell came to see me. I remember that too, though it comes and goes."

John sighed. "Let's forget that for now. Time to look forward instead of back, eh?" We spent the rest of the journey in an awkward silence while some of my younger colleagues tried to start up a sing song at the back of the coach.

We arrived at a large hotel on the banks of Lake Windermere. In previous years the Nothing But Truth staff had stayed here for team building weekends. In theory they had been for "planning meetings" but they'd always turned into more of a fun break. I smiled as I thought back to some of those times. I sometimes forgot how long I'd been working for the organisation and it was a shock to realise I'd been here at least three times before. For some reason those past trips had always been in the middle of winter so we'd spent most of the time inside in front of a roaring fire. Now we were here in glorious weather, it was a shame it was just a day trip.

Everyone piled off the coach but John hung back to wait for me as I was lowered from the vehicle on the wheelchair lift. I liked the way he simply waited for me rather than trying to fuss about and help. The awkwardness I'd felt earlier started to fade away and I was looking forward to the next few hours.

Pam Philips had excelled herself organising the day in such a short time. Everything was planned with military precision and before long I found myself alone as I'd expected. I wheeled myself onto a decking area and asked a waitress for coffee as I settled in to read. I had the latest Peter James thriller to start and I couldn't wait. As I turned on the reader I became aware of no longer being alone. Glancing to my left I saw John Mitchell sitting at the next table smiling at me.

"Sorry, I didn't want to interrupt," he said.

"It's fine, but shouldn't you be with the others?"

"Not wanted until after lunch, apparently. We're going to film a discussion group about my case or something. No point me joining in what they're doing this morning as it's all stuff that's internal to Nothing But Truth." It seemed they really were doing some team building and planning this time, then. I felt a pang of envy as I wondered what I was missing. But, reminding myself that I'd be involved later and I had decided to be polite, I realised I was going to have to say goodbye to my pleasant solitary reading session.

"In that case come and join me," I said, sighing inwardly. I really did want to start my book but there was no polite way of saying so. I was beginning to realise that John was displaying all the signs of over-attachment to me that I'd been worried about. It seemed as though it was only because I'd been hospitalised and then confined to home that he'd kept his distance from me. And now he wanted to make up for it. I would have to tread very carefully.

I knew what Jeremy would tell me. Put up with it until the documentary's been finished. Don't do anything to upset him. But that was easier said than done. And really it would be double standards wouldn't it? Throughout the investigation Jeremy was forever telling me to remember professional boundaries. Telling me off for getting too close to John. But he'd changed his tune since John's release.

"Do you fancy a little walk beside the lake?" John asked and I looked down at my wheelchair and pulled a face. "I mean, I could push the chair, obviously."

I looked longingly at my coffee that had just arrived. "Just let me drink this and I'll be with you. Or would you like one?"

John went inside to order a coffee, coming back with a tray containing his drink and two plates with a doughnut on each.

"Couldn't resist," he said. "Fancy one?" He held out one of the sugar-covered cakes to me and we sat looking out at the lake while we drank and ate. I hadn't had much of an appetite lately but the doughnut was delicious and I polished it off in no time. I could feel myself relaxing and knew it had been the right decision to come today. It was such a peaceful place even when the rest of the town was full of tourists. The ferry trips that crossed the lake constantly were just far enough away not to be bothersome.

"Shall we set off before we take root here?" John said. He seemed restless and perhaps that wasn't surprising as it was still only a short while since he'd been released from prison. This place must seem like heaven to someone who's been locked up inside for years.

There was a pathway between the woods and the lake and John set off along it pushing me as we chatted about what he planned to do in the future.

"It's top secret for now," he said. "But I've been talking to Jeremy about joining Nothing But Truth."

That was a complete surprise. Of course, I hadn't been around the office lately but I would have expected Susie to have ferreted out gossip like that. Her change of role from PA to investigator was obviously going to damage our ability to find things out.

The path was getting bumpier now and I started to think we should be turning back but I was feeling decidedly woozy and couldn't find the words to explain what I wanted to John. I felt as though I could fall asleep at any moment. Was it the fresh air after being cooped up at home for so long? Whatever it was I wanted to go back to the hotel – I wasn't feeling at all well. But when I tried to speak it came out as an incoherent moan.

"It's fine, Victoria," John said soothingly. "Don't you worry about a thing. We're just going for a little walk. I'll take care of you." Victoria? I was alert enough to notice him getting my name wrong. What on earth was going on?

John hadn't noticed his slip of the tongue. As he pushed the chair towards a slope just ahead, I started to pass out but revived slightly when a shout came from the direction we had come from, near the hotel.

"Hey, watch out! That path's dangerous."

John snapped his head round but then seemed torn between carrying on along the path and responding to the shout. In the end he dragged the wheelchair back along the path, putting on a good act of being out of breath when we reached the decking at the hotel. Pam Philips was standing there watching him, an odd expression on her face.

"Thank God I saw her," John panted. "I managed to get to her just before she reached the slope. I don't know what's happened but she's out for the count."

There was a brief debate about whether to phone an ambulance for me, which I heard as I started to come round and I shook my head, so they simply lay me on a sofa in front of the fire in the hotel lounge.

"What happened?" I asked, still groggy but physically unharmed.

Pam explained that I'd been found on the path towards the lake. John Mitchell had disappeared having told Pam the camera crew were expecting him.

"John saved me from rolling into the lake?" I asked. I was still confused. Hadn't we set off for a walk together?

"Yes, seems he's been a bit of a hero this morning," Pam said. "No doubt the TV people will want to film a reconstruction." She saw my horrified expression. "I'm joking." But we both knew she might actually be quite right.

****

The rest of the day passed off without incident. I was adamant I would not take part in a reconstruction of my rescue by John but I did thank him when we were alone for a moment.

"No need for thanks. You saved my life when you got me released from prison. Just returning the favour."

When I told Mick about the incident later his analytical mind went into overdrive.

"What made you pass out?" he said. "Do we need to get you checked over by the doctor?"

In the end we compromised. I made a call to my doctor and described what had happened. The doctor ran through a few questions before asking what I'd had to eat that morning. I told him what I'd had for breakfast and we discounted that as a cause. It wasn't until a couple of hours after the phone call that I remembered the doughnut I'd eaten just before the lakeside walk. It had been covered in sugar and icing sugar. A suspicious person might think it was the ideal item of food to use to disguise a crushed sedative tablet.

I shook the thought from my head. Where on earth had the idea that John could have tampered with the cake come from? I was aware that paranoid thoughts like that could be a sign I was heading for a relapse with my mental health. Maybe I should think about asking to be referred for some more counselling. But for now I needed to think about today's events rationally. Like John had said, he considered that the Nothing But Truth investigation had saved his life by resulting in his release from prison. He saw me as the person who had achieved it. Why would he want to harm me?

******

I had hoped that my brush with danger would be quickly forgotten about but for days afterwards I received messages, phone calls and even flower deliveries from colleagues checking if I was okay. Eventually I started ignoring incoming calls and listening to messages in batches. Every single one of them mentioned what a hero John Mitchell had been, saving helpless, wheelchair-bound little me from a watery grave. Well, they weren't quite so dramatic but that was the gist of it.

If I hadn't already decided to forget my suspicions, all the calls would have brainwashed me into doing so. It seemed John Mitchell could do no wrong. Then, when I had almost come to the point of deleting emails without reading them, I spotted one from a Diana Mitchell. The surname caught my attention and I opened the email. The message was brief but too intriguing to ignore:

Dear Ms James. Please excuse me contacting you out of the blue. I found your address on the NBT website. I am John Mitchell's cousin and I heard about what happened at the Lakes Hotel the other day. I need to speak to you. Diana Mitchell.

I sent a reply inviting Diana Mitchell to meet with me. Mindful of personal safety and keeping my home separate from work, I suggested a local cafe the following day. A reply came back immediately confirming the meeting.

Diana Mitchell was a lot younger than her cousin – mid-twenties at the most. There was a slight family resemblance between the attractive young woman and John Mitchell. Something about the eyes. We waited until the waitress had brought our drinks before discussing anything more important than the weather. Then Diana took a deep breath.

"You're going to think me very strange for contacting you," she said. "But after what I heard the other day I simply had to. My friend works at the Lakes Hotel and she's been telling everyone who'll listen about the drama. She overheard someone say the guy, the "hero", was called John Mitchell and she asked if he was a relative. Obviously it's a common name but she described him and it's definitely my aunt and uncle's son. Not that we've seen him for donkey's years but..."

It seemed she was never going to pause for breath. I put a hand on Diana's arm and asked her to slow down.

"Just rewind a minute, please," I said. "I know everyone's saying John saved me the other day but really it was just a near miss of a thing. I'd wandered onto a dangerous path in my wheelchair. He stopped me before I could roll towards the lake. Why would that bring you rushing down from Windermere to speak to me?"

Diana took a few deep breaths. "Yes, I can see it seems odd. The thing is he's always been the black sheep of the family." She stopped as if not sure how to go on.

"I suppose his conviction for murdering his wife didn't help," I said, then bit my tongue for sounding so flippant.

"To tell you the truth nobody in the family was speaking to John for years before that."

I had read all the files about John's background in the early days of the investigation. Both his parents had been killed shortly after he left school. I remembered thinking it gave us something in common. There was little about his extended family and nothing that would suggest he was cut off from them for any reason. I told Diana all this but the other woman shook her head.

"John's parents are both still alive. The rest of us live locally and we're a very close-knit family." She went on to tell me the story of John's baby sister, Victoria, and the terrible accident at the lake.

"Victoria? That's what he called me..." I stopped myself before I got carried away. It had obviously been a traumatic event in John's young life and being in the same place must have caused him to have a flashback to that other time. "No wonder he was so overjoyed to have saved me. Perhaps in some small way he thought it made up for not being able to save his sister from going in the water."

"You don't understand," Diana said. "Our grandma always took the blame for what happened. But my mum's always said John did it on purpose. That he deliberately sent Victoria's buggy down the path into the water. He was jealous of all the attention everyone was giving the baby. Well that backfired on him, didn't it? Victoria needs round the clock care so she's always had all their parents' attention. There's other stuff he did, growing up, that meant him being sent to prison didn't come as a surprise. He's no hero."

I was stunned. How come my investigation hadn't turned up any of this family background? Because I'd taken John Mitchell at his word and for once hadn't dug any deeper. If I'd caught him out in the lies about his family, I would have wound up the investigation immediately. It was my golden rule and no amount of pressure from Jeremy would have convinced me to carry on once I knew the client was lying to me.

As I let the implications of this settle in, I asked Diana to fill in the gaps in John's background. An incident in his childhood that had affected his sister forever didn't necessarily make him guilty of his wife's murder. But a pattern of behaviour might point that way. I listened as Diana reeled off a list of schools John had been expelled from.

Hearing about the schools John had attended in the Lake District made me wonder if he'd ever been at school with Daniel and Paula. It was irrelevant to this discussion but I couldn't help considering it. I tried to close down the thought as soon as it entered my head. Everything to do with Paula was still raw and it would be a while before I could think about her without immediate heartache.

"They had to send him away to a special boarding school in the end. Then, once he was old enough to leave school, he also left home. He's turned up a couple of times since but my aunt and uncle live as if they only have one child." Diana finally seemed to have run out of steam. She started to gather her things together. "Thanks for meeting me and listening. I just wanted you to know the kind of person you're dealing with. Our family closed ranks years ago and when John's trial hit the news we closed in on ourselves even further. But after I heard what happened at the hotel...well, I don't want it on my conscience if he hurts someone else."

******

I rang Jeremy Parker and asked him to see me as soon as possible. I didn't give any hint what it was about because I suspected Jeremy would fob me off. He was still desperate to make sure nothing took the gloss off Nothing But Truth's success in the Mitchell case. But the more I thought about it, the more I was sure John had intended to harm me when he set off towards the lake pushing me in the wheelchair. Hearing that his sister was called Victoria had confirmed it.

Jeremy agreed to see me if I could get to his office in the next half hour. That wasn't a problem as I'd met Diana nearby at a cafe in between my home and the office. I called a taxi and when it arrived I was still mulling over what Diana had told me. Unusually there was a traffic queue which held us up just outside my old school. It was odd how often little coincidences occurred, I thought. My discussion with Diana had brought up thoughts of Daniel's old school and now I was confronted with my own.

I was always telling myself to find a different route to the office and it seemed the taxi drivers used the same one too. When I was driving again I really would have to find one that didn't bring me past this place every time. But any alternative route would take longer so it didn't really make sense. Better to try and ignore the memories stirred up every time I saw the building. How different my life might have been if I hadn't been sent here.

All the way through primary school I had been top of the class and yet managed to be a popular child with lots of friends. All that changed when I went to secondary school. My parents had been persuaded to enter me for a scholarship at this well-known independent school. There was no way they could have afforded the fees but my primary school headmaster had been confident I could win a free place in the entrance exam.

Sure enough I'd passed the exam with flying colours. I remembered my mum parading me round all the neighbours showing me off in my new bottle green uniform. I had never seen her so proud before or since. It was only on my last day at primary school that it dawned on me I was the only one going to that school. All my friends were destined for either the nearby state school or one of the faith schools a little further away. I faced a five-mile bus journey to a school where I would know absolutely nobody.

I made a couple of friends over the years. Usually the ones nobody else wanted to sit next to. But a combination of snobbery and nastiness made most of the girls avoid the "charity case" whose parents could barely afford the uniform. Having struggled through five years and managed a decent set of GCSE results, I wanted to leave school and go to college but my parents convinced me to stay on for sixth form where my fees would continue to be paid. Seven years in a friendless environment took their toll on me and I sometimes wondered if that had contributed to my personal problems over the years. Luckily my college years were the exact opposite and one of my few friends, Hannah, had stuck with me throughout.

At last the traffic was on the move and I shook the thoughts of my miserable teenage years from my mind. I felt like a completely different person to the child who'd hated every day of her life at that school. Was John Mitchell now a completely different person to the boy who had deliberately sent his sister's buggy hurtling towards a lake?

Never had I needed to talk something over with Jeremy more. Hopefully he wouldn't immediately go on the defensive and start ranting about it not being my job to question this stuff. For once we seemed to be on the same wavelength but if I had expected Jeremy to take immediate action I was about to be disappointed.

"I understand your concerns, Meredith, I really do. But we're so close to the finish line on this. And really, who are we to say there's any connection between what John's cousin told you and the case we've been involved with?"

"I just think we have a moral obligation to alert someone to this."

"But who? John Mitchell is free because the appeal court judges agreed his original conviction was unsafe. Because of evidence we found. How would we, as an organisation, look if we stood up now and said we shouldn't have been working with him in the first place?"

I could see his point but I was determined not to let this go. I would never forgive myself if John Mitchell harmed someone else and I could have prevented it. Maybe I should talk to Mick about it. Get a police officer's perspective on the situation. But we'd agreed not to bring our work home any more. If I couldn't get Jeremy to agree with me, though, I might have to go back on that. Mick would know who to take my concerns about John's historical behaviour to. For the umpteenth time since I'd spoken to Diana Mitchell, I kicked myself for not listening to that little voice that had nagged at me throughout the investigation. What if we're working to free a guilty man, I'd asked myself. But what if his guilt wasn't only related to Karen Mitchell's death?

"How about a compromise," I said now. "If I sit on what I've learnt until after the documentary is shown, will you agree to back me up in whatever I have to do to alert the authorities later?"

"Yes, but alert them to what?"

"I know everyone's been calling him a hero since he supposedly saved me at the lake..."

"Supposedly?"

"Yes. There are too many similarities between our little walk by the lake and what happened to his sister when she was a baby. And he called me Victoria for goodness sake."

"Meredith, you have to admit you weren't really in any fit state to know what he was saying." Jeremy's voice was at its most gentle but instead of being comforted I found it patronising.

"And why was that? Did anyone think to wonder why I was on the verge of passing out, having been fine for weeks?"

"What are you accusing him of now?" I didn't like the tone Jeremy's voice had now taken. It was time to leave before I was tempted to tell him a few more home truths. We'd always got on well but there was a limit to how much insubordination Jeremy would take. If I wasn't careful John Mitchell was going to be the cause of me losing my dream job.

****

Frustrated after my conversation with Jeremy, I was pleased to find a voicemail from Susie on my mobile. Susie was enjoying being out and about but wanted a catch-up session with me on our latest case.

"If you're free I was thinking we could combine it with our girls' night out. It's never going to happen otherwise, is it?" The message ended.

I thought it was a great idea. Mick had hardly let me out of his sight for weeks, apart from the disastrous Lakes trip, and I could do with a good chat and a chance to relax. I rang back and left a message suggesting a bar in town. We communicated mostly by phone message these days and I missed the way Susie would always grab me for a gossip whenever I went into the office. I was proud of the way Susie was blossoming in her new role and I looked forward to catching up with her that evening.

We arrived at the bar within minutes of each other. Susie had come by taxi so I was pretty sure she was planning a boozy evening. Mick had dropped me off on his way to a night shift at the station and I'd get a taxi home.

After a couple of glasses of wine, we brought each other up to date on what had been happening since we last had a good catch up. I was pleased to hear that Susie's new role was still making things run smoother at home. Scott was coping better with their daughter, though he still had to call Susie back home at times.

"She's even sleeping better," Susie said. "It's as if, because I'm happier, she's picked up on it and relaxed more."

I had been thinking for a while that it was about time I told Susie everything about the clinic, Paula Reed and the ordeal of finding out my children didn't exist. So far I'd only given Susie edited highlights. But was now the right time? We were enjoying a relaxing evening and my story might spoil it. I was sure Susie and I were now close friends for life. If anyone would understand what I'd been through it was her.

"Susie, tell me to stop if you don't think this is the time or place," I started, trying not to be put off by Susie's raised eyebrows. "The thing is, I've never really had a best friend, as such, but I feel like I have now." Susie smiled now and patted my hand. The gesture gave me the confidence to go on. By the time our second wine bottle was empty I'd told Susie everything, from my miserable school days, through my nightmare marriage to Daniel and then my experiences at the clinic and the full story about why I hated Paula Reed so much.

I wasn't sure what sort of reaction I'd expected but Susie couldn't have dealt with it better. She ordered one (bottle) for the road and proposed a toast. "To the two of us, best friends from this day forward. And no more looking back."

My awful hangover the next day couldn't dull the glow I felt, knowing I'd been right about Susie. We would be there for each other, supporting through all the trials of Susie's family life and my present injuries and past traumas.

Chapter Twenty-Three

At long last the TV company boss let Jeremy know the date when the documentary of the

Mitchell case would be shown. It had been so long since Nothing But Truth had been

involved in a televised case, and because the organisation had been through so many changes

since then, Jeremy decided to make an occasion of it. Everyone was invited to a party at the

Nothing But Truth offices – there would be a big screen showing the programme "live".

Partners were invited too but I wasn't sure how to bring the subject up with Mick. He still

wasn't completely happy about me returning to work at the place where I'd almost lost my

life, so how would he feel about attending a party there? In the end I needn't have worried.

When I tentatively mentioned the party one day when we were having breakfast Mick

surprised me with his reaction.

"I can't wait to see the programme," he said. I searched his face for any sign of sarcasm but

there was none. "You all put so much work into it. Let's hope the film makers have done

justice to it." He seemed oblivious to his odd choice of words so I let it go for once. "I might

have to be on call though. Will that be a problem?"

"When are you not on call?" I asked with a wry smile. We were both devoted to our work but

it was Mick who could be called away any time of the day or night.

I was so pleased Mick wanted to go to the party, it brightened up my whole day. I still wasn't

fully mobile yet – my physio had warned me it would be months before I got there. But at

least I had finally ditched the wheelchair and crutches in favour of a jazzily decorated metal walking stick. There was no need for me to go into the office today. Once Mick left for work I went to the spare room and packed the last few traces of my obsession with two little girls who'd never existed. My counsellor was pleased with how quickly I had accepted the situation but in reality I was still working through my feelings about the whole thing.

I left the room and went to make a drink. While the kettle boiled I slipped back to the spare room. Looking in a couple of boxes until I found what I wanted I reached out two small teddy bears and sat them on the windowsill. Thoughts of those two little girls had helped me through some of the hardest time of my life. It would be nice to have something, just a very small something, to remember them by.

****

Yet again I had cause to be grateful for being able to work from home. Now that Susie was stepping into the role of investigator, I had suggested she should come round for some informal training sessions. The first and most important of these was to do with personal safety. I felt a bit of a hypocrite setting myself up as some sort of expert after the disastrous accident I'd suffered at work. But that had been a freak incident and nothing to do with the kind of thing we'd be covering today.

Although I had always loved my job, I had to concede that there were times when it put me at risk. Mick and I had countless arguments about it. But with common sense and forward planning it was possible to minimise the risks. Nobody had trained me in this. I had learnt as I went along that there were situations that were best avoided. There was no point Susie having to learn on the job if I could give her a few pointers first.

As always when we got together, we spent a good while catching up on each other's gossip before getting down to work. Susie was much happier since being allowed to move out of her admin role and being happier in her work was still having a beneficial effect on her home life too.

"It feels like Scott and I have been given a second chance at our marriage," she said. "I'm so grateful, Meredith. If you hadn't encouraged me to pester Jeremy about changing my role I'd still be stuck at my desk frustrated every day. Scott's so happy with things he's not even bothered about me going to the party."

I was as pleased as Susie herself with the transformation in her outlook on life and proud to have had a hand in bringing it about. I was also excited about the prospect of working as a team with Susie. We seemed to almost know what the other was thinking at times. It would make working cases much easier, having someone around to back me up who was on the same wavelength.

We chatted for a while about the upcoming party where everyone would be watching the TV documentary. One thing I hadn't shared with Susie was my knowledge about John Mitchell's family background and that I would be following up the information his cousin had given me as soon as the documentary had been televised.

****

Jeremy had really gone to town on the party decorations. Or rather his new PA had. Susie's replacement in that role had fitted in straightaway. She still had a lot to learn if she was ever going to match Susie's organisational skills, but give her something like this party to plan and she was in her element. My only worry as I looked around the place was how much it had all cost. Weren't we supposed to be looking for savings in everything we did? That question was soon answered when Jeremy asked for everyone's attention a few minutes before the programme was due to start.

"Thanks for coming, everyone. Before the main event I have a brief announcement to make. It's been a tough few months and I know you've all done your bit to make Nothing But Truth carry on its excellent work, regardless of the cost cutting." There were a few nodding heads and a few groans around the room. Most people seemed to be expecting to hear about another round of budget cuts and maybe even job losses. "You might have noticed I've been out and about more than usual lately. And perhaps I'm a bit guilty of not keeping you all informed..."

The nods had turned to sighs of impatience. Everyone knew Jeremy's habit of beating about the bush but the clock was ticking and nobody wanted to miss the start of the documentary.

"Come on, Jeremy, spit it out," someone called from the back of the crowd.

"Okay, okay, here it is. I've been out there banging a drum for Nothing But Truth and it seems to have done the trick. We now have enough in grants and donations to guarantee the organisation's future for at least the next three years."

A cheer went up and then everyone made their way to the boardroom where the large screen had been set up. It was a bit of a squeeze to get everyone in and a few people, including me, Mick, Susie and Jeremy, went to watch in Jeremy's office instead. I was relieved not to be in the middle of a big crowd, especially as I knew I'd be dominating most of the scenes in the programme. The editors had done a brilliant job of turning hours of random footage into a gripping and entertaining documentary. We heard a loud round of applause from the other room as the credits rolled.

I noticed Jeremy giving me sidelong glances throughout the programme. I put it down to the fact he was proud of my work but towards the end he gestured towards the corner of the room, obviously wanting me to join him there. In a whisper he broke the news that he wouldn't be able to back me up in my wish to make John Mitchell's lies about his background public. I was horrified.

"But why, Jeremy? When we spoke about it you said you agreed and understood. Don't you see how important this is to the credibility of Nothing But Truth?"

"You heard what I said earlier about donations that will secure our future? Well a major donation has come from a very grateful John Mitchell. Do you suppose he will want to be associated with us if we ruin his newly restored reputation?"

I wasn't sure if I was more upset or angry but I calmed down quickly. "Fine. You're the boss as you're always reminding me. There's nothing I can do. But don't be surprised if his own family decide to go public. How do you think it will look for the organisation when his long dead parents appear?" I went back to Mick's side, assuring him I was okay when he looked concerned. I had learnt over the years that I needed to protect myself from the effects of stress

and anger or I risked triggering another plunge into the depths of depression. Recognising

this now, I was proud of myself for how quickly I managed to put on a normal face and tried

to enjoy the party.

****

When everyone piled out of the boardroom, among them I caught sight of John Mitchell. I

was sure he hadn't been there earlier but I must have been mistaken. A jolt of adrenaline

burst through my system. It was the first time I'd been in his presence since the incident at

the lake and since his cousin had told me all about his background. Perhaps he'd arrived late

and slipped into the boardroom after everyone else. I was certain I would have been aware of

him otherwise. I took a few deep breaths and concentrated on a quick mindfulness exercise

that allowed me to put everything in proportion. I was simply at a party, surrounded by work

colleagues and accompanied by my partner. What could possibly go wrong?

It wasn't like John not to come straight over to me and announce his presence though. Instead

he was chatting to others who'd been watching the programme in the boardroom. Hopefully

that was a sign that, at last, he was starting to get used to the idea that I wasn't a friend, just

someone who had worked towards his freedom. I'd been starting to get a bit concerned about

the way he'd imprinted on me like an orphaned animal. It had happened to a lesser extent

with other clients but never as intensely as with John. It was a relief because I didn't know

how I'd be able to cope with his attention now I had such misgivings about him.

Mick had caught sight of John too and went over to speak to him. I knew he'd been trying very hard to get along with my colleagues and I supposed he saw John Mitchell in that category. Perhaps I should have confided in Mick about the new developments after all. Reluctantly I went over to join them, just as they reached glasses of champagne from a tray. Mick passed one to me and we stood awkwardly for a moment.

"A toast," John said. "To Nothing But Truth." As he clinked his glass against mine and looked into my eyes, I froze. That 'someone walking over your grave' feeling overwhelmed me but instead of going off into one of my trances everything was crystal clear.

****

While I wondered how to react to what I had just remembered, I was aware of Mick at my side taking a call on his mobile. I needed to speak to him urgently now but whatever the person on the other end of the call was saying seemed serious.

"Really sorry, love," he said a moment later. That was the station. The boss wants me in immediately."

"Of course, no, that's fine." It was an understatement to say I could have done without Mick leaving me at that moment but I knew he had to go. I looked around for Susie. If I stayed with her I'd be fine until I worked out what to do. And although I'd agreed with Jeremy not to discuss my concerns about John, I was sure talking to Susie about it wouldn't count. Meanwhile John Mitchell was watching me with a strange expression on his face.

"Everything okay, Meredith?" he asked.

"Yes. Yes, absolutely fine." I knew I must try to appear completely normal but I also knew I wasn't a good enough actress to pull it off. I headed towards the ladies', pulling Susie by the arm on my way. John Mitchell couldn't follow me in there.

"What's up, Meredith?" Susie asked. Ever since my accident people had been treating me like china but Susie had been perfectly normal with me until now. The expression on her face told me how worried she was.

"I'm okay. Listen, I just had like a flashback to before my accident. My memory's starting to come back and I'm not sure I like it, especially with all the other stuff that's come out lately."

I had Susie's full attention but just before I could explain properly what I had realised when I held my champagne glass next to John's, Susie's phone rang. This was getting ridiculous. Every time I thought I'd got the attention of someone I could rely on they were distracted by their phones.

"Sorry, Meredith, just hang on a sec. I can't ignore it, it's Scott." The call lasted just a few seconds and the look on Susie's face told me all I needed to know. Scott tended to overreact when he was left in charge of their daughter. Susie needed to go home and check everything was okay. "But I'll try and come back later, okay?"

I nodded. There was nothing I could do to stop Susie leaving when there might be an emergency at home – it wouldn't be fair. When Susie had gone, I wondered how long I could stay in the ladies' toilets before people started worrying about me. Should I go out and try

and find Jeremy? I could, but I wasn't sure I wanted to try to explain things to him after our

conversation just a few minutes earlier. He didn't seem to want anything said against our star

client who'd become our major benefactor. I hadn't sorted everything out in my own head yet

and there was really only Mick or Susie I could talk to who'd understand. What if I started

accusing John Mitchell of things and it turned out to be some sort of weird side effect of my

brain injury making me think he was responsible? But that couldn't be true, could it? After

all, John's own cousin had been accusing him of all sorts of things just a short while ago.

Several colleagues came and went, asking if I was okay as they were passing. In the end I

realised I'd have to leave the room. Mick was unlikely to come back to the party. Whatever

the work emergency was it would probably keep him at the station most of the night. I would

phone a taxi and go home. That was the most sensible thing to do.

I reached into my bag for my phone, planning to scroll through my contacts to find the taxi

number. I scrabbled about in the bag for a moment before realising I'd left my phone at

home, plugged in to charge. Of all the times! I never forgot my phone. Never. Until the one

time when I actually really needed it. Why hadn't I checked for it when Mick left? Never

mind, I could ask to borrow someone else's phone to ring for a taxi. It was too noisy in the

party room so I made my way to the building's main door downstairs. There would always be

someone hanging around the main door on occasions like this. As I reached the bottom of the

stairs, I saw Dawn Rothwell coming through the front door. Why on earth would she be here?

I was too curious about Dawn's presence to worry about leaving for now. Of course, Dawn

had been involved in the case but only in a minor way. And to put it bluntly she'd ended up on the losing side so to speak. So why turn up at the celebration party? Dawn spotted me and

hurried over.

"Thank God you're here," she said. "Listen. I know it's a bit late in the day but I've found

that evidence that shows that Karen was a victim of domestic abuse. Can you help me take it

to the police? I've no idea what to do."

I was taken aback. What evidence? Last time I'd spoken to Dawn about the case was just

before my accident. In fact for a while I had been toying with the idea that Dawn might have

pushed me. But after the memories that had flooded back a few minutes ago, when John

Mitchell touched my champagne glass with his, I knew it wasn't Dawn who was responsible

for my injuries. I glanced over my shoulder to make sure John wasn't around. Maybe going

with Dawn would be a good idea. It would kill two birds with one stone – allowing me to

leave the party and dealing with this evidence that Dawn was so concerned about. Maybe

she'd even give me a lift home once we'd sorted it.

Dawn's car was parked close to the entrance and we were on the road within minutes.

"I thought you lived in Prestbury," I said. The sought after village was in the opposite

direction.

"It's not at my house," Dawn said. And that was it. Her tone had changed from when she had

spoken to me just a few minutes earlier. A vague alarm started to sound at the back of my

mind but I ignored it. I couldn't think of any reason why Dawn Rothwell should be a threat to me. If anything, she should be grateful that I had called off the investigation into the threatening emails she had been sending in the early days of the case.

There was one thing she might have against me, of course. All that business with the email threats had been aimed at having the investigation into John Mitchell's conviction closed. Dawn seemed to have come to terms with it since but what if she'd decided John's release was all my fault? The fact that she'd been sure he was guilty, combined with the prospect of losing the money she'd received from her sister's estate might be enough for her to want revenge against me. I wished Dawn would hurry up and get to where this supposed evidence was. This evening was turning into a nightmare and I just wanted to go home. Unfortunately I was starting to realise that things might be worse than I'd feared.

We were heading towards Manchester city centre. Miles from my home and miles from Dawn's local police station. That's where she should have gone with any new evidence she'd discovered. They would then have liaised with whoever had taken on the reopened Karen Mitchell murder case. Although a statement had been made saying the police weren't looking for anyone else in connection with the murder, in reality they couldn't simply drop it altogether. It would be on ice unless new evidence surfaced. I cringed at my choice of words as I thought about all this. That moment in the cottage kitchen when I opened the freezer would stay with me forever.

Dawn pulled into an underground car park at an apartment block right in the centre of the city. We'd passed the dingy side street where Sam Raynor's office was located a few moments earlier, bringing back another milestone in the case – the moment I'd learned that Sam was dead.

"What are we doing here?" I asked as we got out of the car and walked towards an elevator.

"I told you. There's something here that's evidence of what happened to my sister."

I wasn't sure I believed her but we rode up to the thirteenth floor and Dawn let us into one of the apartments using a pass code. Opening the door to allow me in first, Dawn sat on the sofa and looked at her watch.

"You might as well make yourself comfortable," she said. "It could be a while."

I was starting to get a really bad feeling about this. What was all that stuff I'd been teaching Susie lately? All about staying safe in any situation at work. Well, I'd just ignored the majority of it and ended up in the middle of God knew what. I looked around the room. It was as if it had been furnished as a show flat. Very stylish but nothing personal about it. From where I sat I could see into the large kitchen that was full of every possible gadget but looked as if it was never used.

"Whose flat is this?" No reply.

"What are you playing at, Dawn?" No reply.

I was starting to lose patience when I heard the beeping of a pass code being entered on the door. The handle turned and in walked John Mitchell. All pretence of friendship or courtesy was gone from his face and it made him ugly. He jerked his head at the door and Dawn scurried out without a backward glance. I sat like a statue. All the stress I had been coping with during the evening seemed to have made me unable to react. While a dozen thoughts flitted through my head all I could do was stay silent and wait to find out what he had planned.

Chapter Twenty-Four

Susie was back at the party within an hour. By the time she'd arrived home the crisis was over and Scott had insisted she should go back.

"You only get chance to enjoy yourself once in a blue moon," he said. "And much as I'd like to keep you to myself looking as gorgeous as you do, it'd be a shame to waste it by staying in."

Susie didn't need telling twice. She crept upstairs to give a silent kiss to her daughter who was sleeping for once. On the drive back to the party she tried to fend off the pangs of guilt, firstly for leaving her daughter and secondly for leaving the majority of the caring to Scott. He deserved a night out too. Now that she'd changed jobs and there would be slightly more money coming in, maybe she'd look into booking a specialist babysitter occasionally.

Back at the party, after five minutes of searching, she realised Meredith wasn't there. She'd been quite agitated when Susie left so she was concerned. She tried phoning Meredith's mobile but there was no answer. She didn't bother leaving a message, knowing Meredith would call back when she saw the missed call.

Susie chatted to a few colleagues for a while but she couldn't shake off the feeling that something was wrong. Meredith was usually stuck to her phone during waking hours so why hadn't she called back? Susie thought about what Meredith had told her during their training sessions. After everything she taught her Meredith always repeated the same mantra: Follow your instincts. Well, right now Susie's instincts were screaming at her that something had happened to Meredith.

She decided to ring Mick Bannister. She knew he'd been called away for work but she also knew he'd want to be told if there was any chance Meredith was in danger. He answered on the first ring, his voice puzzled as his phone probably didn't recognise Susie's number.

"Mick, it's Susie from Nothing But Truth. Listen, I'm worried about Meredith."

It only took a moment to explain and Mick thanked her and ended the call, telling her he'd go home to see if perhaps Meredith had gone in a taxi and was now in bed.

"She puts her phone on do not disturb at night, doesn't she? Perhaps you're right," Susie said, but she wasn't so sure.

****

Mick Bannister had a dilemma. He wanted to dash home to check on Meredith but he'd been called into the station for a reason and that hadn't been dealt with yet. Then he had an idea. He opened the app on his phone that linked with Meredith's mobile and gave him its location. Within a minute he'd confirmed what he'd said to Susie. Meredith was safely at home, no need to worry.

He sent a quick text to Susie to let her know, then went back to the incident room.

******

I looked into John Mitchell's eyes and saw the truth there at last. Ever since I'd become

involved in this man's life I had felt like I was on a seesaw, one moment believing in his

innocence and determined to see him freed, the next questioning whether, after all, I had been

responsible for freeing a killer. The way he was looking at me now left no room for doubt. He

saw me as a threat to his new-found freedom and he'd do anything to remove that threat.

The moments before my accident at the Nothing But Truth building had been slowly filtering

back into my memory since earlier on that evening when we had touched our champagne

glasses together. Now those memories came back with the force of a flood. It had been John

who was responsible for my fall, not Dawn and not some careless accident or attempt to harm

myself. I tried to control my heart rate and breathing as the flashback threatened to

overwhelm me.

"I knew the moment you remembered," John said, his voice flat and devoid of emotion which

was somehow more frightening than if he'd shouted at me. "The champagne was the key

again, wasn't it?"

I tried to break away from his stare, from the magnetic pull of those eyes, but I couldn't. And

I knew it was pointless trying to pretend I didn't know what he was talking about. "Yes. I

remember. That night when I fell – it was because I'd noticed you saying something about

Karen that you couldn't have known. Unless you were involved."

John nodded. He seemed to be trying to work out what to do next. I took advantage of his

uncertainty to glance beyond him towards the apartment door. If I could try to manoeuvre my

way so that I was in between John and the door, was there a chance I could escape? But I was

forgetting my damaged legs. It was all I could do to hobble about with the aid of my walking

stick. Any thoughts of running away were futile.

More memories of that other night when I'd been stuck alone with John came back to me.

Although it hadn't ended well, I knew I'd tried to use the right kind of strategies to deal with

him then and I should do so again now. Keep him talking. Maximise the time for someone,

anyone, to figure out I needed help. Looking round the apartment I noticed the packing cases

strewn about the place.

"Are you moving out?"

John followed my gaze and looked surprised as if he'd forgotten about the boxes. "Yes. I've

sold this place. And the cottage in Lancashire."

As the implications of John's words sank in I felt chilled to the bone. If I hadn't already

discounted any doubt about his involvement in his wife's death, those words would have

settled it. As I'd hoped, John relaxed a little and carried on.

"You know, I'm even more impressed by Sam Raynor than I used to be. I've been able to sell

this place and the cottage without anyone even realising I owned them. She did such a

fantastic job of setting up fake identities and accounts. And all the cash she'd stashed away before...well, before, you know. It means I'm sitting on an even bigger fortune than I expected."

I managed to bite back a sarcastic comment about being pleased for him. I knew John's ego well and that the best way to keep him talking was to let him tell me how clever he'd been. "How did you convince Dawn to help you tonight?"

John shook his head and gave me a half smile. "When my new legal guy looked into what she had left of Karen's money, it was hardly worth taking her to court for. I didn't let her off the hook but I promised her I would if she'd do me a few favours. Oh my god, at first she thought I meant sexual favours – can you imagine?" He shuddered. "I've been watching you for a while and I had a feeling you were starting to remember things that might be a little embarrassing for me. I put Dawn on standby to help me tonight. Just in case."

"She didn't hang around for long," I said. If Dawn had stayed after John arrived I thought I might have been able to persuade her to switch sides and help me escape. But she had left as soon as she got the chance.

"You know where she'll be, don't you?"

"No. Where?"

"We're only a stone's throw from one of the most popular casinos in the city. Ever since she found out I wasn't going to claw back Karen's money, Dawn's been losing a sizable chunk of it in there every night."

"She told me she was trying to fight her addiction. Going to support groups, whatever."

John laughed. "Well it looks like she gave up on that. Pathetic isn't it?"

I stared at him. He saw nothing wrong with feeling contempt for a gambling addict while standing before me as a self-confessed murderer. I thought back to how scared I'd been years ago in the Pennine View clinic – convinced any of the other patients might harm me. Now I understood that the really scary people were walking the streets. As if sensing my heightened fear, John smiled and held his hand out to me.

"Let's go out and get some air on the balcony."

****

Dawn Rothwell was starting to have a few pangs of conscience. At least that's what she assumed it was. Having never suffered from a conscience before she couldn't be sure. Whatever it was, though, she was beginning to regret what she had just done. She tried to rationalise it – she'd had no choice after all. When her brother-in-law had announced he wasn't going to try to claw back the money she'd known there would be a catch. Her side of the bargain meant helping him deal with Meredith James. What Dawn didn't seem to have worked out, because she was so focussed on the money, was that John Mitchell's plans for Meredith were an indication of his guilt in Karen's death.

John was right when he'd told Meredith that Dawn had returned to her gambling addiction. At least up to a couple of nights ago. Then she had come to her senses. This was her chance to keep her beloved home. To rebuild her life in the community she'd lived in for many years. She'd booked some urgent counselling sessions and she would be starting back on the long road to conquering her addiction.

Although she was feeling proud of herself for turning her back on temptation, her fresh start looked like being spoilt by guilt. Whatever John had planned for Meredith it was not going to end well. Nobody could link Dawn to it – she'd been careful to make sure nobody saw them leave the Nothing But Truth office together. But the feeling of being in the wrong wouldn't go away.

And the worst part of it was that she could feel those other feelings of guilt, the ones she had buried for years, fighting to come to the surface. Nobody had ever questioned her father's death. He was old and had been ill for a long time after all. Only Dawn knew that she'd hastened him on his way, believing it was what he wanted. So why, now, was she starting to feel remorse for something she had justified to herself at the time?

As she drove down the A34 heading home, Dawn knew there was a police station just off the bypass about two miles ahead. All at once everything seemed clear. All she had to do was go to the police station and give a statement. Leave out the part about her own involvement – just tell them John had approached her for help with disposing of Meredith James. She could probably be out of there in an hour or so. She could tell them to contact Meredith's partner – what was his name? Bannister that was it. In Manchester. He'd organise rescuing Meredith and everyone would be happy. Except John Mitchell of course. He'd be heading back to prison. What was that other thing he'd delighted in telling her when he came to discuss the money? Oh yes. He had a lot of friends inside now. And they had a lot of friends outside. Friends who could hurt people.

Approaching the slip road she would need to take to reach the police station, Dawn put her foot down and sped past. She'd deal with her guilt and her conscience in her own way.

****

"Do you think I'm stupid?" I couldn't understand why Mitchell would think I'd want to go out onto the balcony with him. His voice, which up until this point had been controlled, suddenly switched to an aggressive tone.

"Far from it. But do as I say."

Chapter Twenty-Five

Shane Evans was starting to get twitchy. He'd been happy to help John Mitchell with a few errands. Shane had been released a few weeks before John and, without his own home or a job to go to, he'd been grateful for the opportunity. John had promised him he'd be well paid and, sure enough, this week they'd met for a pint and John had casually passed over an envelope bulging with cash. It wasn't until John had started to talk about his future plans that Shane became nervous. And now, thinking back over recent weeks, he was feeling even more nervous.

He'd been inside three times and he wasn't going back. He'd promised himself and he'd promised his girlfriend. Just before she closed the door in his face on his first day of freedom. To be fair she'd opened it back up a couple of minutes later and slung two bin bags full of his possessions at his feet, closely followed by a cheap sleeping bag. He reckoned if she cared enough to have kept hold of his stuff this long he was in with a chance of getting his feet back under the table. It was just a matter of time.

But with no other prospect of paid work he set his mind to sorting what he'd agreed to do for John Mitchell, during those long conversations in their cell. The first part of the money that was his main motivation for doing this would be waiting for him in a flat in Manchester. The second part of the job waited in Lancashire, and that depended on retrieving some items from a flat in Manchester first. But there was a problem. A condition of Shane's probation was that he must not visit the area where he'd committed his crimes, namely central Manchester. So his priorities were decided for him. In and out of Manchester as quick as he possibly could. Then back up to Lancashire.

He called in one of very few favours he had left with his old mates and was soon behind the wheel of a battered transit van, his bin bags stashed in the back. He had to hope he wouldn't be stopped by the traffic cops on the motorway because he had neither licence nor insurance and doubted if the vehicle was either taxed or MOT'd. Shane parked near the tower block but not in its car park as he didn't want to draw attention. The beaten up van would stand out like a sore thumb next to the luxury vehicles most of the residents drove.

He went up to the thirteenth floor, using the code he'd memorised to open the door of the apartment he was interested in. He might have only learnt to read properly recently but he'd always had a good head for numbers. He let out a whistle as he wandered through the flat. It was like something out of a film. Remembering he needed to be out of there quickly, Shane rifled through the kitchen drawer he'd been told about, spotting the keys attached to a cardboard label straightaway. One for the front door, one for the back. What was it John had said? This was a spare set of keys. John had insisted his partner should have spares of everything involved in their plan. He reckoned his partner would have had the others with her when she died in a car crash. That guy had worse luck with women than he did, Shane thought as he detached the larger back door key and pocketed it. He'd rather access an unknown property via the back door than the front. You never knew how many nosy neighbours there might be.

He looked around the apartment again, marvelling at how everything was exactly like John Mitchell had said it would be. If it wasn't for the fact he knew he'd be caught, Shane might have enjoyed staying here for a while. He let out a sigh of relief when he spotted the small pile of bank notes held together with an elastic band. There was at least as much as John

Mitchell had estimated. What was it he'd said? Sam always kept a decent stash of emergency cash just in case. Well thank you, Sam, and rest in peace and all that.

The next job was to find the laptop which was exactly where it should have been. A top of the range MacBook, well top of the range a few years back anyway. He was supposed to send an email, having signed up to a new email address on hotmail, then retype the letter and print it off. The idea was that it wouldn't look as if it had spent weeks being moved from one hiding place to another in his cell like the one that had been printed off in the prison library. John had managed to convince the librarian he was using it as part of his unofficial reading lessons for Shane. Shane had never understood why this part of the plan was so important. And as for taking the laptop and printer with him and leaving them at the next place he was due to visit – now he'd seen the quality of the laptop there was no way that was going to happen. He could get a lot for this down at his local pub. John Mitchell was being generous but this little bonus wouldn't do any harm.

Relieved now he'd decided not to bother with recreating the letter, Shane stuffed the old copy into his pocket. He carried the printer down to the van then went back up to get on with sending the email. He'd memorised the content and it only took him ten minutes or so to complete the task. Now he needed to get on with the next job. He had no control over how quickly Meredith James would work out what the email meant and act on it.

For the next part of his task Shane needed to look smart and presentable. He used the bathroom to freshen up and run a comb through his hair. He was still wearing the clothes he'd had on when he was released from prison but they looked clean and decent enough. Glancing round the apartment he wondered whether to help himself to anything – old habits die hard.

He resisted temptation, knowing that the cash he'd just pocketed would see him through a few weeks.

Next stop was the bank, just a short walk away so he left the van where it was. It only took a short time to sign up for a safe deposit box, put the key in it, and return to the van. Now all he needed to do was make it back out of the city and he could start to breathe again. It was hard work being law abiding!

On his way back up to Lancashire Shane treated himself to a mixed grill in the cafe at the motorway services. It felt like he was heaven, enjoying proper food again after years of prison slop. You were never sure if one of the inmates working in the kitchen had contaminated your meal because of some imagined dispute. He sat for a while, pondering the strange list of tasks he'd been given by John Mitchell. He was slightly curious about it but mostly just wanted to get it all over with. John had been a big help to Shane – unlocking the mystery of reading and writing that his schooling had left him with. Shane believed in John's innocence and was sure his current campaign for an appeal would be successful.

Shane almost missed the turning he wanted and the guy in the car behind him blared his horn as Shane took a left without signalling and set off down the lane to the village where his next target was located. The address he'd memorised, and that matched the address on the cardboard tag attached to the key, was just down here. Shane went round the back of the cottages and let himself in the back door, chucking the bin bags into a corner. He hadn't really thought much about where he was going to sleep that night, or for the near future, but now he climbed the spiral staircase and threw his sleeping bag onto the bed in the main room. John had told him nobody was living here so why shouldn't he make the most of it? The banks were closed by now so even if the clue in his email was already solved, nobody could access the key until the next morning at the earliest.

Within an hour Shane was stretched out on the sofa watching TV and feeling as if he might doze off at any moment. The only problem he'd had was that he was hungry. He'd hoped to find something to eat in the kitchen but the power was off in there for some reason. He was no electrician but he supposed it must be on a different circuit from the rest of the cottage. Whatever, there was no point looking in the fridge or freezer for anything so he'd phoned for a takeaway delivery, telling them to come to the back door. The mate whose van he was using had also lent him a cheap mobile and he had plenty of cash to pay for takeaways so why not? While he waited for his food to arrive he'd retrieved the piece of A4 paper from his pocket. Following John's instructions, he slipped it inside one of the books on the shelf. Job done.

Shane had brought the MacBook in with him from the van and decided to have a play about on it. It was only then that he realised the mistake he'd made. Cables. He'd left them all behind, including the power cable that had been plugged in at the Manchester apartment. He could still probably sell it but he wouldn't get nearly as much, dammit.

After a good night's sleep Shane was thinking about making a move from the cottage. After all, the whole point of the email he'd sent the previous day was to lead this Meredith James woman to the cottage once she'd found the key at the bank. No sooner had he thought about this than he heard a car pull up outside the cottage. Shit! Every instinct told Shane to get out of there now, even though it meant leaving the laptop and his sleeping bag. He hurried out of the back door, remembering at the last second to grab his bin bags, and went to open the back gate that served all the cottages' back yards. It was locked. It had been swinging open the day before when he'd arrived. He ran to the end of the row of cottages and round the side of the last one. Seconds later he was walking out of the front gate that served all the cottages on that side of the square and hurrying to the van.

As he'd predicted, his girlfriend had calmed down after a few weeks, which he'd spent dossing on various friends' sofas. When he called her and asked if they could talk she relented, which was handy since hers was the address he'd given to his probation officer. When the knock came on the door they didn't need to hear the announcement, "Police, open up," and one look at his girlfriend's face told Shane he'd just messed up his final chance with her.

Chapter Twenty-Six

John was obviously tired of my attempts to stall him. When it was clear I wasn't going to allow him to hold my hand he instead shoved me ahead of him onto the small balcony. All I could think about was that fall I'd suffered from two floors up at our office building. This time we were on the thirteenth floor. My injuries might have been bad last time but a fall from here would be instantly fatal.

Why on earth hadn't that near death experience been enough to put me off working for Nothing But Truth altogether? Maybe if I'd left the organisation John Mitchell would have tired of his obsession with me. But of course it wasn't me he was obsessed with, it was my memory. His constant fear that I would remember what he had told me that night, and what he'd done to me, was what had led to us being here now.

The time for trying to stall John was over. I desperately searched my mind for something I could say that would make him reconsider what he was doing. A thought struck me but I knew it would be a last resort. If it didn't work it was likely to incite John to harm me and there was little I could do to defend myself.

"Remember what you said to me on one of my prison visits?"

"What?"

"You said you could understand why people take their own lives when they're locked up in one of those places. If you hurt me again they'll throw away the key this time."

"Nobody knows we're here. Nobody knows I have any connection to this place."

"What about Dawn?"

John laughed. "She knows better than to cause trouble for me."

****

It looked as if Mick Bannister wasn't going to be able to leave the station before morning and he didn't want Meredith worrying. No doubt she'd be asleep by now, with her phone on silent, but at least he could leave a quick message so she'd understand where he was when she woke up.

As expected, Meredith's mobile went unanswered and when the voicemail kicked in Mick left a message that he hoped would explain what had gone on that night. He wasn't worried about confidentiality – if anyone had a right to know this it was Meredith.

"Hi, it's me. Sorry I haven't made it home but everything hit the fan after I left you last night. Listen, you need to prepare yourself for a shock. It looks as if you were right when you were having doubts about John Mitchell's release from prison. I'll tell you all about it properly when I see you, but the lab alerted us to a DNA match from a sleeping bag at the cottage where you found Karen Mitchell's body. It's flagged up a guy who's been in and out of prison a few times for burglaries. But the important thing is, until recently, he shared a cell with our John Mitchell. We've picked him up and he's singing like he's auditioning for a boy band. And if you're wondering why I'm dealing with it – he's flagged up an address in the city centre and two of my units are on their way now. Hopefully they'll be picking Mitchell up. Anyway, that's it for now. See you in the morning."

****

"Get real, John. You shove me over that balcony and Mick Bannister will be all over this." The thought of Mick choked me up for a moment but I pulled myself herself together. "He's never been convinced my first fall was an accident. If I end up dead on the floor down there he will investigate it and he will find you."

I could see John was thinking this over but he'd got away with so much he probably felt invincible. We were both on the balcony now and thirteen floors up it was wild and windy. I grasped the handle of my walking stick, surprised John hadn't made me leave it inside. If I could land a well-aimed blow at his head maybe I could weaken him enough for me to be able to get back inside. As if he'd read my mind, John reached out towards the stick but I kept a tight hold. It was now or never. The metal made contact with his temple with a sickening crunch and John staggered slightly but stayed standing. He put his hand up to his forehead to test for blood, then with a growl he launched himself at me.

****

Witness statements contradicted each other. Most agreed the first thing they were aware of was the sirens and flashing lights of several police cars arriving close to the entrance of the tower block. Some said they'd seen two people struggling on the balcony of what they later learnt was the thirteenth floor of the block.

What wasn't in doubt was the twisted body lying on the tarmac outside the building, a growing pool of blood escaping from below the coat someone had hastily thrown over it while they waited for more emergency services to arrive. A metal walking stick lay a few metres away.

The police took witness statements but opinions were split. Some said they were sure a woman and man were arguing on the balcony when one of them fell over. Others were certain it wasn't a fall but a push.

Sitting in the back of an ambulance with a blanket around my shoulders, I was the only person who knew the truth.

Chapter Twenty-Seven

We'd named the day for the wedding at last. My latest brush with death had galvanised us into action and we'd set ourselves the ridiculous target of organising a wedding in a month.

The first few days after the incident on the balcony in Manchester had faded quickly into a blur in my mind. Once I'd been checked over in hospital I was interviewed by the police. Mick had tried to spare me the experience but there was no way he could stop the standard procedure. Someone was dead after all. In the end his superior officer had to threaten to bar him from the station unless he stopped trying to interfere. He'd been taken off the Mitchell case that had arisen from the statement Shane Evans had given, once the connection to me was made. They couldn't stop him being in the building while I was interviewed though. He made a pretence of clearing a backlog of paperwork while he watched the minutes tick by on the wall clock.

I was interviewed by two officers I'd never met before. The senior officer at the station had called in help from the other side of Manchester because everyone who worked at the central station knew me through my connection to Mick. They'd been briefed about the background to what had happened and they treated me more like a victim than a suspect.

Once the interview started, I was focussed on the story I'd been over in my head a hundred times. I had no need to worry as long as I stuck to that simple description of events. Only one of the officers spoke the whole time they were questioning me. The other took notes, though everything was being captured on video. I had chosen not to have a solicitor present. I was sure there was no need.

"Ms James, can you tell us in your own words the events that led up to you being on the balcony last night?"

"Dawn Rothwell, the sister of the murder victim in the case I'd been working on, asked me to go with her to pick up some evidence that would prove the guilt of her brother-in-law John Mitchell. Mr Mitchell had recently been freed from a life sentence for the murder of his wife, Dawn's sister." I paused for breath and to take a quick sip of water. "Dawn took me to the apartment in Manchester and shortly afterwards John Mitchell arrived and Dawn left. After a short discussion Mr Mitchell forced me out onto the balcony," I gestured at my spare walking stick as if the action was subconscious. "He said he knew he was going to end up back in prison and he couldn't face that. He was going to end his life and take me with him. I managed to hit him on the head with my walking stick and then he lunged at me but he must have missed his footing and overbalanced and the next thing I knew he'd gone over the balcony rail." I covered my eyes with both hands.

"I'm sorry if this is upsetting. We need to establish the facts. We have conflicting witness statements, some of which suggest that Mr Mitchell was pushed rather than falling accidentally."

"Is that a question?" I bit my tongue. I was supposed to be projecting the image of a devastated victim who'd narrowly escaped the same fate as the dead man. Instead I was making flippant comments.

"Sorry, I'll reword it for you," the officer looked at me through narrowed eyes and I told myself again to be careful. These were experienced interviewers, trained to see through it when anyone was economical with the truth. The officer tried again, "How do you explain the conflicting witness statements I just mentioned?"

"I can't explain them. I can only tell you the truth. And if they're conflicting statements then presumably you also have witness statements that agree with what I told you." I was doing it again but this time I was sure I could see respect in the other officer's expression.

They went over what had happened several times more. I knew they were looking for contradictions in my various accounts but I was almost word perfect. At last they told me I was free to go, but they might want to speak to me again.

****

Now all I wanted to do was get on with our wedding plans, determined not to let John Mitchell ruin things from beyond the grave. Speaking of which, his funeral had been held the week after his death. Jeremy Parker had attended, feeling it necessary to represent Nothing But Truth at the funeral of a client no matter what they had done. He reported back that there were only a handful of people present, outnumbered by the press who printed ghoulish accounts the next day. Only one family member had been there – Diana Mitchell, the cousin who had travelled down from the Lake District to speak with me.

"After what she told me about the family's feelings I'm almost surprised she bothered," I said.

"I spoke to her briefly afterwards," Jeremy said. "Apparently she just wanted to be sure he was dead."

I winced but it was exactly the sort of comment I could imagine Diana making. I hoped the Mitchell family would be able to come to terms with what John had done and carry on with their own lives as they had done before all this happened.

Jeremy had spent every waking moment since the funeral trying to tidy up the mess left by the organisation's involvement in freeing someone who had now been shown to actually be guilty. He had no qualms about what I and Nothing But Truth had done – our purpose was to find evidence to allow an appeal and that's what we had done. It was up to the prosecution and police to examine that evidence and evaluate it. In this case, because of a delay in processing the sleeping bag found at the cottage, John Mitchell had been released prematurely.

However, there might be repercussions regarding the new funding Jeremy had been attracting so he was busy playing the politician again. Explaining to the generous donors how it wasn't a fault in Nothing But Truth's methods that had set a killer free. So far he was doing well and everyone was standing by their pledges and it even looked as if he'd be able to plug the gap left by losing John Mitchell's promised donation. Mitchell was probably spinning in his grave at the idea that everything from the sale of his properties would be going to his parents, who would use it to provide for the care their daughter needed. What Nothing But Truth needed now was a couple of straightforward cases that would show them off in a better light.

"All this hasn't put you off being back at work has it?" Jeremy held his breath as he waited for my reply.

"Far from it. If anything I'm more determined than ever to get on with it. Oh and Jeremy?"

"Yes?"

"There's something I need to ask you. Make sure you keep my wedding date free won't you?"

"Of course, why wouldn't I?"

"Well, with all this schmoozing you have to do I was worried you might be too busy."

"Not at all. Wouldn't miss it for the world, my dear."

"Thats's good. Because I've got a bit of a starring role lined up for you." I laughed at Jeremy's raised eyes. "Don't worry, it's a good one. The thing is, I don't have anyone to give me away and I wondered..."

Was that a tear I saw forming in Jeremy's eye? Surely not, he was always so professional and unemotional. Then he nodded and took my hand, seemingly unable to say anything.

"Right, now that's out of the way, do you want to know what Mick's found out about the aftermath of John Mitchell's death?"

"Oh, yes."

"Well, I'm fuming about this but it looks as though Dawn Rothwell's going to get off scot free. Apparently her solicitor managed to agree a deal if she told them everything Mitchell had admitted to. It all matches with what I remembered that night but can't prove. All the stuff about Karen's death and his plot with Samantha Raynor. He was so proud of himself he told us both everything."

"What do you mean by scot free though? She abducted you."

"I know. She's convinced them I went with her willingly. Which I suppose I did, except she misled me into thinking we were looking for evidence. Anyway, she's been charged with perverting the course of justice but the CPS wouldn't let the police charge her with anything more serious because they didn't think it would stick in court. So it looks like she'll be getting a suspended sentence."

"What about the other accomplice? Evans?"

"Oh, now he really was stupid to get involved. He's already back inside and looking at completing his original sentence. Then on top of that is accessory to murder, perverting the course of justice and probably half a dozen other things. I suppose it must have been greed that motivated him. Mitchell dangled the promise of a large wad of cash and he couldn't resist. I hear the officers at the station are talking about getting in touch with the Guinness Book of Records."

"Why?"

"Shortest ever reconciliation. He'd only been back with his girlfriend a few hours, having convinced her he was never going back inside, when they got the knock on the door."

We both laughed but stopped quickly. Really, at the heart of the case, none of this was very funny. And although we'd relished discussing what punishments those minor players would have, we'd almost lost sight of the most important thing. A man had orchestrated the murder of his wife then sat back waiting for someone to fall for his callous pretence of innocence. When we spoke of the Mitchell case in future we would remember it was Karen Mitchell who was most important.

Chapter Twenty-Eight

It was the day of the wedding. Right up to the last moment I had been worried I would have to use my stick to help me walk up the aisle. Well, aisle was a bit of a stretch – it was just the space between rows of chairs at the register office. But still, I would have to make my way from one end of the room to the other. Jeremy had been wonderful, giving up his precious time to help me practise walking with just his arm to support me. And on the way out I would have Mick by my side.

The more I thought about it, I realised that in an odd sort of way John Mitchell had done me a favour. Six months ago I couldn't have imagined being able to ask Jeremy Parker to give me away. He was my boss and we'd never really spent any time together outside work. But everything we'd been through with the Mitchell case had drawn all the Nothing But Truth staff closer together. This was especially true for me, Susie and Jeremy and I was sure that going forward we would all be better people for the experience we'd had.

That thought struck me often these days but I always batted it away with the more realistic interpretation that we'd all learnt a lot from the case. It was nothing to do with John Mitchell himself. I couldn't yet bring myself to add the words "God rest his soul" or "rest in peace" when I thought of him. After all, he'd never spared a thought for his wife and the terrible fate he'd organised for her. And the fate he'd planned for me.

I was ready now. I would take my stick with me just in case. Mick had already gone on ahead and I was waiting for Jeremy to pick me up. Mick and I hadn't worried about the not seeing the bride on the day thing. We were both far too practical to waste time bothering about superstition and we never would have been able to agree which of us should move out the

night before anyway. I laughed to myself when I thought about how stubborn we both still

were. We probably could have tossed a coin but that method of making decisions had caused

enough rows in the past.

No, Mick had got ready at home with me helping him with the finishing touches. I'd turned

down Susie's offer to come and help with my hair and make-up. My short pixie haircut took

all of two minutes to style and I never wore more than a touch of mascara and lipstick.

The buzzer sounded and I let Jeremy in. He looked at me as proudly as any father of the

bride. A quick hug took the place of any words and minutes later we were in the stylish car

he'd insisted on hiring for the day.

I had expected to feel more emotional about the fact that my parents were missing this day. It

seemed as if they had been in my mind more often than ever lately. But whenever thoughts of

them threatened to cast a cloud over the occasion I firmly put those thoughts in a box and

closed the lid. I was sure they would have understood. Today was all about putting the bad

things that had happened to me away and looking towards the future.

Apart from my job at Nothing But Truth, everything would change after today. I'd discussed

it with Mick and agreed that even though we'd emptied the spare room, that space would

always remind me of the children that never were. That was no way to live. I understood

those parents who kept a dead child's room untouched like a shrine, but in my case the

children had never even existed. I'd convinced Mick and my counsellor that I had come to

terms with it and now I was working on convincing myself.

The journey to the register office was over in a flash and I could see all my friends standing outside, waiting to greet me before hurrying into the room where the ceremony would take place. All my friends, I thought. They were really just my work colleagues but I thought of them as my friends and almost my family. Susie, my unofficial matron of honour, was waiting with my bouquet. In no time at all I found myself on Jeremy's arm, waiting to walk into the main room.

"Are you sure?" he asked me, taking his father of the bride role perhaps a step too far.

"I've never been more sure of anything in my life, come on."

We walked slowly up the aisle formed by the gap between two sets of chairs. Mick glanced round at me just as I reached the front. His best man, a work colleague, proving we had a lot in common, patted his pocket to make sure he had the rings.

It was all over in a flash and then we were signing the register and posing for photos. We'd taken over one of the restaurants on the high street near the Nothing But Truth offices and everyone set off, leaving the newlyweds to follow.

"Happy, Mrs Bannister?"

"I am. How about you, Mr Bannister?"

We kissed. Properly this time instead of the chaste kiss in front of everyone during the ceremony.

"I know it sounds daft," I said, "But with all the bad luck I've had in the past few months I fully expected someone to stand up and object to the wedding."

"Yes, me too. And the registrar left an awfully long gap after she'd asked the question." Mick laughed, squeezing my hand. "Now, what did we agree? We're not going to let these past months spoil the years ahead, remember?"

I smiled. He knew me well enough to have worked out it would take me a long while to completely get over what had happened. And I hadn't told even him the whole truth about what happened on that balcony.

"Come on," I said. "Let's go and join our guests. And on the way you can tell me where we're going on honeymoon." Even though he knew how much I hated surprises, Mick had insisted on organising the short break we'd agreed as a compromise. I hadn't really wanted to go away. I wanted to get on with finding somewhere else to live. But Mick had insisted. He couldn't remember when he'd last had a holiday and he wanted me to himself for a while.

"Not telling. Not until we get to the airport and you see it on the departures board."

"Airport?" My pulse started to race. "But..."

"Sorry, I couldn't resist. Of course I haven't booked flights. I know your phobia list off by heart by now. No, we're driving, but it's a long drive."

There was no logic to my travel phobias. If there was it would have been long drives that frightened me, having lost my parents to a car accident. I didn't know a single person who even knew anyone who'd been in a plane crash, yet I couldn't bear the thought of flying.

The celebration meal was a great success. Jeremy stood to say a few words and everyone was relieved when he simply thanked me and Mick for allowing him to be part of this special day.

It was time to leave and do the traditional throwing of the bouquet. I knew that Jeremy's new PA had a huge crush on him. Time for a bit of matchmaking, perhaps. I aimed the small posy of flowers directly at her and as she caught it she fixed Jeremy with a stare he couldn't possibly mistake. By the time we were getting in the car, Jeremy was buying his admirer a drink at the bar.

We made a quick stop at our apartment to change and pick up the luggage. I hadn't had a clue what to pack so I had two huge trolley cases standing by, one with lightweight clothing, the other with jumpers and jackets. I looked at them with a defeated look on my face, telling myself it was just a few days, I would survive. Then I noticed Mick chuckling softly in the doorway.

"What? I can't help it if I hate travelling and being away from home."

"I know. And I've been cruel, keeping it from you where we're going, so you couldn't even worry yourself sick about a specific destination."

"Exactly."

"So I'm sure you'll be happy when I tell you I haven't booked anything. We're not going anywhere."

It took a few seconds for his words to filter through my misery but then I flew at him, my arms around his neck. "You mean it? We're staying at home? Oh, yes!"

Half an hour later we were in our comfiest clothes in front of the TV. Mick told me later how close he'd come to buying a bottle of champagne to celebrate with. But at the time he decided he wouldn't bother to mention it. I thought at that moment I was probably the happiest I'd ever been in my life.

We cracked open a bottle of red wine – as far from fizzy champagne as could be – and drank to our future together. When we caught ourselves dozing on the sofa we decided it would be more fitting for a wedding night if we adjourned to the bedroom. At last I felt relaxed and able to forget all that had gone before. I stopped short of thinking of this as a fresh start. Those had never gone well for me. No, this was simply me and my new husband starting out as we meant to go on. Okay we'd lived together for a couple of years anyway, but this was different. The commitment we'd made to each other today made that difference. We were a team and nothing would get in the way of our happiness.

****

Shortly after Meredith switched off the bedroom light a white Mercedes pulled into a parking space about a hundred metres up the road from the apartment block. Paula Reed turned off the engine and sat quietly for a few minutes, her eyes surveying the road. It was almost midnight and there was little traffic about. On the other side of the road an old man passed by, walking an ancient yorkshire terrier. He glanced at the car but by the look of the lenses in his glasses he couldn't see much. The car always drew admiring glances – it was a shame it would have to go soon. Paula felt as if chunks of her life had slowly been taken away from her, as if some all powerful being was playing a game of Jenga with all the things Paula valued.

First she'd lost her position at the clinic. She was told that if she didn't step down there would be an investigation that would be likely to lead to her being struck off. Although it was a terrible blow to her career, Paula had been able to deal with it because it coincided with her blossoming relationship with Daniel James. He'd been happy to agree that Paula should move to part-time hours including her role at Nothing But Truth. Then just as she was finding her feet there she was asked to leave. Well, she knew who to blame for both these humiliating experiences. Meredith James. Or, what was her new name? Meredith Bannister. Sounded like an old maid from an Agatha Christie novel.

After her meeting with Jeremy Parker when he'd pretty much told her, though not in so many words, that he was withdrawing his offer in order to keep Meredith happy, Paula had been boiling with rage. It was all she could do to get out of the building without letting her calm facade slip. She'd roared away in the Merc and headed for the nearest motorway, flooring the accelerator and driving recklessly fast until she felt the anger begin to recede. She had the speeding fine letter to prove the crazy speed she'd reached. It was so far above the limit she had to go to court and would probably lose her licence immediately. Thanks for that, Meredith, she thought.

With her psychology training, Paula should have been able to recognise how she always projected her mistakes and poor decisions onto Meredith. Paula had stepped into Michelle Ashe's shoes at Nothing But Truth knowing full well that Meredith worked there, no matter that she might have denied it. It was as if she was forcing herself into Meredith's domain so that she could once again use her as a scapegoat for everything that was wrong in her own life.

Paula knew Meredith had fulfilled that role back when they first met too. It may have been simply the connection that existed because Meredith was married to Paula's old flame. But that couldn't explain just how badly Paula had treated her. She should have either been objective and treated Meredith like any other patient, or declared a conflict of interest and asked another consultant to take her on. Paula had no crisis of conscience over what had gone on at the clinic. Perhaps she'd been a little over enthusiastic when trying to coax Meredith to talk about her imaginary children, but she'd done the same with other patients who had no personal connection whatsoever.

Paula shook her head. What was happening to her? She was starting to question her actions when she knew, absolutely knew, she had done things for the best of reasons. Her research could have been brilliant if she'd been allowed to continue. Whatever, things were coming to a head and they were starting to affect her relationship with Daniel. They'd barely been married when she was given her marching orders by Jeremy Parker. She had struggled to come up with an explanation for Daniel as to why she'd left Nothing But Truth and that had caused their first argument.

But the thing that was really going to challenge their fledgling marriage was the court appearance for speeding. What had possessed her to do it? She'd never understand why she reacted that way. She'd never done anything so stupid and dangerous before. She could easily have killed herself or someone else. And that was the problem. Daniel was always going on about dangerous driving and people who put others at risk by speeding or drink driving. One day she'd got sick of hearing him ranting.

"Why are you so obsessed by it, though?" she asked.

"I'm not sure you're going to like the answer, as I'm banned from mentioning my first wife."

"What's she got to do with it?"

"The day after Meredith and I got married her parents were killed in a car accident. They were wiped out by someone doing twice the speed limit."

That had shut Paula up for once. She couldn't understand why her husband would still be concerned about his ex-in-law's deaths. His dramatic comment that he was banned from mentioning Meredith was a bit over the top. But since they'd been reunited and rushed into marrying it was true that Paula had refused to discuss Daniel's life with his first wife.

Now Paula was tying herself in knots wondering if Daniel would ever be able to forgive what she had done. Would their unborn child be enough to keep them together once he found out she had committed what he considered an unforgivable offence? She had been given some breathing space when Daniel announced he had to go away for a few days for work. She'd hidden the summons letter and spent a couple of days brooding about how she should deal with the whole situation. Unfortunately she concluded there was nothing else for it but to come clean and throw herself on his mercy and when he returned tomorrow she planned to do just that.

But the way Paula's mind worked meant she couldn't rest even when she'd made that decision. The thought that kept going around in her head was that she wouldn't have been out in the car, speeding, if she hadn't been humiliated by Jeremy Parker. And that wouldn't have happened except for Meredith running to Jeremy and telling tales. Therefore, according to Paula's logic, the speeding summons was Meredith's fault.

Paula knew that today had been Meredith and Mick Bannister's wedding day. She was still in touch with a few people from Nothing But Truth and stalked their Facebook pages occasionally so she'd seen lots of posts and photos from the wedding. Someone had let slip that there was an exotic honeymoon planned at a destination that was being kept secret from Meredith. There had been lots of discussion about where it might be and speculation about long haul flights from Manchester Airport straight after the ceremony.

That's what had planted the seed of an idea in Paula's brain. She wanted some sort of revenge against Meredith but she would never have attacked her physically. The thought of her empty home gave Paula another target. She would damage the place Meredith felt at her safest. Let her come home from her honeymoon to find the place destroyed. The effects of that would last a long time especially with someone who was already vulnerable. The more she'd thought about it the more justified she felt. She'd warned Meredith years ago that if she caused her problems Paula would find a way to punish her.

Chapter Twenty-Nine

The piercing shriek of the smoke alarm worked its way into my dream. Seconds later I was wide awake, listening to the sound coming from the apartment's hallway. I shook Mick awake and we both hurriedly found shoes and dressing gowns. Mick went to open the bedroom door but flinched as his hand touched the metal handle. Red hot.

"Phone 999. Make sure the fire service are on their way," he said, before going to the en-suite and reaching an armful of towels. He placed them along the foot of the door. I was speaking to the emergency operator who told me there was already help on the way.

"All we can do is sit tight and wait," Mick said, taking my hand and trying to comfort me. Then I made a feeble attempt at humour.

"At least there's no balcony off this room's window," We both thought back to those other occasions when I had nearly lost my life. And when John Mitchell had lost his.

It was only minutes, but felt a lot longer, before we heard the sirens announcing the fire engine was close by. From the sound of it there was more than one. It seemed the whole building was affected.

Half an hour later we were both in an ambulance on the way to be checked out at the hospital. Neither of us had a scratch and we didn't feel as if we'd been affected by smoke but we had to do as we were told. After several hours we were both given the all clear and allowed to leave, but the fire fighters were stopping anyone entering our building. Still dressed in our night clothes, it was time to think of someone who wouldn't mind giving us a temporary home for a few days.

Jeremy Parker was the obvious choice. He rattled about a house that was far too big for one person and when I rang him he was more than pleased to help.

"You can stay as long as you like," he said. "I'll come and pick you up and we can do a bit of clothes shopping on the way."

We attracted a few stares wandering round Marks and Spencer's at Handforth Dean in our dressing gowns but we quickly chose a couple of outfits each and, after paying, got changed in the fitting rooms.

"It makes you think," Mick said when we stopped for a quick lunch in the cafe. "I deal with victims of crime all the time but I've never really thought about practicalities like this. You don't – until it happens to you."

"Crime?" Jeremy asked.

"Oh, yes. I had a call from the fire investigation team leader. It's definitely arson."

"Who would want to set fire to a building with dozens of people sleeping in it?" I asked. "Did everyone get out okay?"

"Yes. A few are being kept in hospital. Older people mainly. But they got everyone out."

"Thank God."

"I've been thinking about it," Mick went on. "For that bedroom door handle to be so hot, the rest of the apartment must have been ablaze. We've probably lost everything apart from what was in our bedroom."

I was devastated but knew it could have been a lot worse.

"Come on," Jeremy said. "Let's get going. I'm looking forward to having company for a change."

"The other thing my mate at the fire investigators told me," Mick said. "Was it might be more than just a couple of days before we can go back. Looks like the building's now unsafe. It could be months."

Jeremy did his best to look as if he didn't mind but I saw through it.

"Don't worry," I said. "We'll find somewhere to rent in the next week or so. We would have been moving out of the apartment anyway. This has just forced our hand a bit."

Mick squeezed my hand. He knew I was putting a brave face on the situation. After all we'd been through in the last few months, he could tell I was still trying to make other people feel better.

"I might nip into the station later," Mick said. "I know I'm on leave but they'll be setting up an investigation along with the fire service. I'd like to see where they're up to."

****

Paula Reed was sitting in the corner of her shower cubicle, her hands wrapped around her knees, cool water beating against her burnt shoulders. For a highly educated, supposedly intelligent woman, it turned out she knew very little about setting fires using petrol. When she'd emptied out the plastic container of fuel in the hallway of Meredith's apartment block, then stood back to throw a match into the fume filled space, she hadn't expected the first rush off flames to lick her own upper body.

She had known to drop to the floor and roll to put out the flames, and fortunately she'd rolled away from the petrol-soaked section of carpet. She'd staggered down the stairs and out of the building, reaching her car before the wailing of the alarms started. All thoughts of how terrible speeding was were wiped from her head as she drove to her own home. She ran up to the bathroom and peeled off her ruined clothes, knowing she had to cool her damaged skin as soon as possible.

Now she felt as if she would never be able to move from this position. She could feel her skin blistering despite the cold water but she was determined not to seek medical help. She knew enough from her early medical training to deal with these burns. They only covered a small proportion of the surface area of her body so she knew they wouldn't be life threatening. There might be some scarring though – how would she explain that to Daniel? And since she'd dropped to the floor to put out the flames she'd been suffering from slight abdominal pains. Was the baby okay?

Gradually she started to come to her senses and organise her priorities. She finally got out of the shower and inspected the damaged skin on her upper arms. It wasn't as bad as she'd feared. No worse than a severe case of sunburn. Next on the list was disposing of the clothes she'd been wearing. They went into a black bin bag. She dressed in a track suit and phoned 111. The medical service advisor told her to go to her local hospital if the pains became worse. Paula didn't plan to wait. She loaded the bin bag into her car and drove to the hospital with the windows open wide to try and get rid of the smell of burning.

Depositing the bin bag in one of the large waste bins on the way into the hospital, Paula booked in and waited her turn to be seen by one of the emergency doctors. A few hours later she was leaving the ultrasound department, reassured about the baby and clutching a scan picture. All the time she'd been in the hospital she'd been overhearing snippets of conversation about the serious fire at an apartment block. Nobody had died, apparently which was a relief. In her single-minded pursuit of vengeance against Meredith she hadn't stopped to think about the other people who might have been affected.

As she walked down the corridor on the way to the main entrance Paula stopped abruptly. Just going out of the door was a couple who looked familiar. But it couldn't be them – they were away on their honeymoon. Then it dawned on her. Meredith and Mick had been in their apartment when she'd set the fire. It was sheer luck that she hadn't killed them both.

****

I had been for a lie down in Jeremy's guest room and ended up sleeping for several hours. Yawning, I brushed my hair and opened the bedroom door, planning to go downstairs and join Jeremy, and Mick if he was back from the station, for a drink. At the top of the stairs I paused as I heard voices.

"I don't know how to tell her this, Jeremy. After all she's been through, I'm worried it might be the final straw."

I coughed so they'd know I was approaching, then joined the two men.

"What might be the final straw?" I asked with a smile that belied the lines of concern on my brow. Mick wasn't the only one worried about how I'd react to more bad news.

Mick sighed. He had no choice but to tell me. "The fire investigation. They have CCTV from a house further up the road, in the minutes just after the smoke alarms started going off. It shows a woman running to a white car and driving off."

"Okay. And why are you worried that's going to upset me so much?"

"They have the car number plate. It's a Merecedes registered to Mrs Paula James."

I felt the room spin as if I'd been drinking tequila shots for hours. Mick caught me before I hit the floor.

****

Paula James stood in the dock waiting to hear the judge pass sentence. Her solicitor had eventually convinced her to plead guilty, in the face of the damning CCTV evidence, so the sentence would be shorter than if she had insisted on pleading not guilty and going to a jury trial. Still, she was certain it would be custodial because of the reckless way she had endangered lives.

Paula's poker face hid a maelstrom of emotion, mostly focussed on the fact that Daniel had washed his hands of her. She shouldn't have been surprised – he had a track record of leaving wives when they were at their lowest ebb. He'd visited her once while she was on remand and that was only to tell her to her face the fact that they were finished. He planned to apply for sole custody of their child when it was born. The cruel irony of the situation wasn't wasted on Paula. She had tormented Meredith with stories of her "children" and how happy they were with Daniel. Now that fictional world was about to become reality, but with her child rather than Meredith's.

There was a lot of paper shuffling going on at the front of the court. Her solicitor had submitted a last minute plea for leniency on the grounds of her pregnancy. Paula cast another glance around the courtroom, hoping against hope that Daniel might have changed his mind and come to see her, even if it was only to see her disgraced. Was that who she thought it was on the back row? It was. Paula's humiliation was complete. Meredith had come to watch her being sent down.

Chapter Thirty

I felt as though I'd spent half my life at this hospital in the past six months. But at least today

we were here for a good reason. That's what everyone kept saying. That's what Mick must

have said at least half a dozen times on the way. But I couldn't shake off the feeling of fear.

What if? I kept asking myself. What if there's nothing there?

I'd been close to cancelling the appointment a dozen times but Mick had managed to talk me

round. He'd even managed to convince me that, even if my fears came true, we could deal

with it. Now we were here I just wanted to get it over with but it was already half an hour

past our appointment time and I could feel my blood pressure rising steadily.

"Meredith Bannister?" A nurse had emerged from the ultrasound scan room and was waiting

for me. Mick took me by the hand and led me towards the room as I tried hard to ignore my

full bladder. The instructions to drink so much water in advance of the scan were all very

well but they didn't take into account how long you had to wait when they were running

behind on appointments.

I was settled on the examination table, the radiographer squeezing gel onto my belly. It was

the moment of truth. I could remember those other times now thanks to my counselling. The

times when I'd been here, convinced I was pregnant, only for the scan to show nothing at all.

If that happened now I didn't know how I'd survive it. There was an unbearable wait of a few

minutes before the radiographer turned the screen so we could see it. The unmistakable

outline, similar to ones I'd seen in other women's scan pictures, was there before me and we

could hear the strong heartbeat through the speakers.

"Hi, baby," Mick whispered and I thought I saw a tear at the corner of his eye. But I must have been mistaken. Mick never showed his feelings. I meanwhile had tears streaming down my face. I knew I'd said the words plenty of times before but this was my fresh start.

The End

Printed in Great Britain
by Amazon

76917896R00180